# THE ART OF EFFECTIVE DREAMING

## ENCHANTED AUSTRALIA BOOK 3

## GILLIAN POLACK

*To the wonderful folk people who continue to enrich my life,
but especially to Folk Dance Canberra.*

# PROLOGUE

FAY'S SATURDAY AFTERNOON WAS MADE UP OF TWO CAR chases, one romantic idyll, a bag of flour, two litres of milk, sliced cheese on toast on an exotic island in the middle of the Caribbean, a loaf of bread, a lettuce, six tomatoes, a distant dream of flying into a silent night, and a tired argument with the girl who checked out the groceries. This girl was far too awake for her own good and wore a label saying "Hi, I'm..." Fay wanted to dream about that strange lack of name, but no-one should be that alert, so she simply paid for her goods and walked home.

Her slow stroll home included another car chase, not noticing the red lights and almost getting run over, a careful mental exercise where she pictured her dream hero, then at least six scenarios where she could be carried off by him. A block from home she decided that she was a modern woman and modern women don't get carried off by anyone. He could carry her groceries, though. They were too heavy. They grounded her and she hated them for it.

She left her bags and her dreams on the kitchen floor and grabbed a piece of paper. Fay scribbled madly until she had cleared her mind.

1

# CHAPTER ONE

*EVERYDAY LIFE IS DULL. NO, THAT'S WRONG. EVERYDAY LIFE is drearily, drably, impossibly dull.*

*You know, it's made up of all those flat details realist novelists love to write about, and that sicken me to read. I try not to think about those bits of life. Enough to have to go to the toilet without having to write about it in agonising detail. Sure, I brush my teeth, but why recall it as something important? Why dignify it with reams of prose then claim to be doing something literary? Something boring, I call it. Something drab.*

*School was dreary, except for English. University was fun... while it lasted. And I spent those years feeling guilty at studying my fantasies. Why didn't I do something useful like Law? Then I could have been paid a great deal more to be bored than I am being paid now. Even Catch-up Economics wasn't enough to make up for a missed legal career.*

*See, life's not only boring, it's full of wrong decisions. I was a wrong decision, for a start. My parents should have had a boy. Or I should have been an orphan. I dreamed of that, years ago. One of those times I was sitting in my room, thinking, "Isn't family supposed to be friendlier?" Too many TV shows. Too many pretend-happy families.*

*So of course I dreamed that I had been adopted and that*

3

someone, some day would discover me and whisk me to a romantic lifestyle. Shared rooms. Secret laughter and jokes. A little world that was my family. Only one thing went wrong. My life's a mess. And all because, when I was nine, I looked like my brother and sister.

You can't really blame me for trying to escape my world, can you? Actually, I've never worked out why everyone else doesn't seem to want to. Maybe they dream less. Or maybe my dreams are only noticeable to me.

Maybe, maybe, maybe. I don't believe in these maybes. I think that I just dream better than other people. What's the current jargon? More efficiently and effectively.

The art of effective dreaming.

Sometimes my dreams are so life-like they're a flicker away from reality. The other day I could just about see what's-his-name giving me the green cloak. I was so astonished I stepped back awkwardly and tumbled. I can't even remember why the green cloak was so important, or even which what's-his-name it was. For the flicker of reality, he was shorter than my average hero, and that's all I could tell. His context wisped away with the dream.

One day a hero will break through to my world, and I'll be less lonely. Less bored.

One day. One day I'll be able to throw away my Public Service approved footrest (for Public Servants with short legs who use keyboards a lot) and be with someone. I don't know what I'll do when this all happens. I'm not much of a doer. I like watching events, and talking them out. I'm not desperately into fast action and play. Sad, that.

I have a lovely little cove in my fantasy land, with a quiet cave. They are mine. When the world gets too much for me, I stand by the seashore and watch the waves. The cry of the seagulls keeps me company, and the gentle hush of the ocean. Sometimes I paddle, but I never swim. I don't dare go past the ledge that drops down suddenly, some metres out. The pull is stronger there. The sea is dangerous outside the protected *headland of my quiet, golden cove. There are a few bushes and plants and some shells, but I've never identified them. I've played with pebbles, and even the occasional shell. Mostly I sit there and find my peace.*

*Sometimes I sit there at night, and watch the stars. A few times I've slept in the cave. That's when I really needed the peace. I use the cave when even going to sleep in the real world is too much.*

*Little things mean a lot in the cove, and none of them are dreary. They are all charged with huge significance, and it's not a pretentious type of meaning that needs words and signs and signifiers and people telling you that something you have known all your life means something quite different. Meaning comes straight from the heart, in my little cove. It bypasses the brain entirely.*

*I don't even need a brain there, or to be competent at anything. I just am. I don't even have to like myself. I just have to be.*

———

Fay was listening to the speaker.

To be more precise, Fay was attempting to listen to the speaker. The chair was deep and comfortable, and the table was at just the right height to tempt her into crossing her arms and falling straight to sleep. She was doodling to help herself stay awake. She started doodling structures that reflected the economics the guy was droning on about. They were pretty puerile structures, she reflected.

In fact, he was really a very boring speaker. The most interesting thing about him was that his voice rasped and was in dissonance with his face. "In dissonance with his face" she wrote under a doodle, to emphasise the thought. He had a friendly, slightly droopy face that looked a little sly on the odd occasion. Odd, she thought. That's the word. She'd always thought that only fox-faced men could look sly. You know, the smooth, sleek, reddish-dark men, who are slightly intense and know exactly what they are doing.

Alberc was one of them. Foxy. Not female foxy, but male. Cunning and bright-eyed, and out to get certain results. These days he was a bit faded from his younger red-black self, having grown in age and prosperity. Alberc Bas had the paunch that a mayor must, and owned the big white house next to the market square.

Fay's doodles stopped reflecting the outer world and started reflecting the inner, as she lost touch with the speaker entirely. She sketched one of the animal figures on the second floor of the house, standing out in white relief from the white plaster stucco that faced the main street. Her hand wobbled, and the graceful figure turned into a gargoyle, so she drew crenellations around it and it slowly became the castle.

This was the first time she had drawn the castle, though it had been a part of her world for a long time. It was spoken of in the village, the doings of great interest to everyone. Whenever Fay wanted a good gossip she invented tales about the castle staff, who were inherited retainers, or related to the villagers, or a mixture of both. Some of them were the younger siblings of farmers. In fact, until the gargoyle appeared by mistake, the building had been a gracious manor house in her mind, almost Edwardian in character. She had used its grounds for tea parties and picnics. Now it turned out to be unashamedly older and more important, though perhaps in need of some money spent on the battlements. A castle. Fortified and slightly crumbling. *Like my mind*, Fay thought.

The town was more recent than the castle, for it was no walled town, and had no protective covering of its own. This surprised Fay. That made the castle older, perhaps ancient. She looked at her sketch of the west wall in pleased wonder. It was so nice when invention carried you into new knowledge.

She frowned at the gargoyle, her mind taking a sudden turn. *It might be that the castle is absolutely dead ancient*, she thought, *In fact, it probably is, but that doesn't take away from the sad fact that I cannot draw the stucco falcon and hare on the merchant's house. Sorry, on the mayor's house. I need drawing lessons. Betty got them – it isn't fair.* Her mind dwelled on the inequities of childhood.

A rustle distracted her, and she saw that the speaker had finished, and everyone else was shuffling out of the room. Her papers piled randomly, with the gargoyle on the top. Fay left also. She packed her desk up slowly, whispering "clean desk policy" as if they were a mantra to dispel the mood of the working day.

Visiting economists were useful because the day finished much faster. It finished much faster because Fay dreamed all the way through their talks. Even when she had to take notes and report on it, as she would in the morning, she somehow stayed conscious for just enough of it to do so. Her heart was reaching out to her fantasy land, however, and she could not wait to be on her way home.

The way home and to work, and taking a shower, and cooking, and ironing - these were the best times for dreaming. The best time of all, however, was just before sleep, because then, if she was lucky, a real dream would take up where her day-dream left off, and paint her little world in bright, bright colours. Her day-dreams, strangely enough, were in black and white, like her sketches. All the colour came from that mystical moment between sleeping and waking. The green cloak came then, and the importance of putting it on.

During the day, it hovered near. It was at night that Fay remembered its significance. But she could only visualise it in her mind's eye during the day. Deep down inside her was a half-expressed wish - and unexpressed fear - that one day she would remember the imperatives of the night. That her dreams would become reality. One day.

Until then, she kept on dreaming, happy, scatty, and thinking her life a great bore. Sometimes, she even believed she only dreamed to while away the time.

So why did she take the west wall of the castle home with her, and ponder it all through the half hour walk? Why did she sit down after dinner, with fresh charcoal and paper and sketch until her hands were black and her face smudged? And why was the result of the sketch a falcon, poised over a fuzzy and somewhat obscure animal? And why, when she went to bed, did she immediately imagine herself knocking at the door of the merchant's house and asking to see Belle?

# CHAPTER TWO

*The trees they do grow high,*
*And the leaves they are so green;*
*But the day is past and gone, sweetheart,*
*That you and I have seen.*
*"It's a cold winter's night,*
*And I must abide alone:*
*He is young but a daily growing.*

*"O Father, Father dear,*
*Great wrong to me you've done,*
*For you've married me to a boy who is too young,*
*For I am twice twelve and he is but fourteen"*
*He is young but a daily growing.*

*"O Daughter, Daughter dear,*
*If better be and fit*
*We will send him to the Court awhile to point his*
*    pretty wit"*

*To let the lovely ladies know they may not touch and*
*    taste*
*I will bind a bunch of ribbons red*
*About his pretty waist*

9

*At the age of fourteen,*
*He was a married man,*
*And at the age of fifteen,*
*The father of a son,*
*And at the age of sixteen,*
*His grave it was a green,*
*And that did put an end to his growing. (Traditional)*

---

THE DOOR NEEDED OILING, FAY NOTICED. IT ALWAYS needed oiling. It didn't matter how important Alberc grew, and how he made his daughters dress up and show themselves off, he never could remember to have the door oiled.

Or maybe it was Bellezour's fault. Since the death of her mother five years earlier, she had been responsible for the running of the house. Fay could well imagine it was Belle's fault. Hinges never got on her nerves. Belle had admitted, time and again, that she was never upset by old houses and their noises. It felt homey, she claimed, her long eyes crinkled with amusement, and ghosts could be friends as much as any other being could. Sometimes Fay doubted her friend's sense, although it was a huge advantage to Fay herself to be accepted by the leading family in the village.

*Town, not village*, she corrected herself, silently. They never call it a village. Not with a common, and a square, with a church and a castle. *People were so touchy*, she grinned, as she patiently waited for a servant to answer the door. It was a slow household at the best of times.

Would Belle mind if she went straight in? Fay doubted it, so she carefully lifted the latch and pushed. It was a heavy door. Was it made of oak? Fay wasn't much good at identifying wood. It was heavy, anyway, and the most wonderful reddish colour, and carved with whimsical figures. That was Belle's mother's doing. She had been very fond of whimsical figures, apparently. Fay had never known her. It was soft to the touch, but then, wood always was. Or was it? Fay was in a mood for doubting today. She would start doubting her own name if she wasn't careful. Fay set the door gently closed and walked into the cool hallway. She listened.

There was the sound of argument upstairs. It was very unlike Belle to lift her voice (a soft and restless creature, Bellezour Anma), but it was certainly her voice. Fay was tempted to leave,. The ignoble side of her nature got the better of her.

She walked up the stairs, slowly, clutching the banister. The clutching was a reminder that while she was in the house, in fact while she was in this world at all, she should give herself wholly to being there. It did not matter that she had devised the scene beforehand: they were real people. The banister was a real banister. That was one of her reminders. Like being surprised at Belle's distress.

As she reached the top of the stairs, a door slammed. Fay walked towards Belle's room, oddly hesitant. A gentle sobbing was now the only noise. Fay knocked.

A tear-stained Bellezour Anma opened the door, her face flushed and unhappy. She sniffed and gave a weak smile. "I'm glad you came," she said, enveloping Fay in a warm hug. "I was just wishing I had a shoulder to cry on."

Fay refrained from saying that it looked as if Belle had been doing the crying quite thoroughly without the assistance of a stray shoulder. She gently disentangled herself from her friend and sat down, looking quizzical.

Bellezour laughed a little embarrassed laugh, and also sat down. There was an awkward silence for a moment. Fay was not going to break it. She was here in her capacity as observer of romance, not a participant, and she would *not* give way. This was, in a way, her quiet revenge for the house turning into the castle wall, during that lecture.

Finally, "I'm getting married," Bellezour announced.

Fay couldn't help herself. "You aren't," she said, her voice full of all the warmth suitable to such a pronouncement. It was her mother's training coming out, she reflected. There are some announcements you always react to in a certain way. "Who to?" She posed the obligatory question. Then she started regretting her enthusiasm, and let some doubt creep in. "But why are you crying then? Doesn't your father approve?"

This set off a whole new stream of tears. When the storm had finally abated, Bellezour explained, but not very coherently. It was an arranged marriage, and father and daughter had just had a head-splitting argument over it. "He's too young," Belle explained, "I'm twice twelve," (Fay had to stop and do some arithmetic here - never her strong point.) "And he is but fourteen."

"He is young, but he's daily growing," finished Fay, sardonically.

"Whatever made you say that?" Belle asked.

"Why?"

"Well, it seems rather unlike you. You have spent two years scolding me for poetic language and for not being concrete and pragmatic. Besides, it sounds familiar."

"I have?" Fay considered it and apologised. Even the words were hers - 'concrete' and 'pragmatic' were definitely not a part of Bellezour Anma's vocabulary. "Oh, it's just part of a song," she finished, lamely.

"Get that out of your head right now!" Bellezour

12

said. "We have had this discussion before. I am not part of any song. And I do *not* want to marry a fourteen year old, however handsome and well-connected, and I have no choice in the matter, and all you can tell me is that he'll get older. Well, I'll get older too, and I'll be old and grey and our children will be as brothers and sisters to my husband. I'll be nothing but a wizened old lady." She burst into tears again.

Fay suddenly felt remorseful for her neglect. Even imaginary friends needed help. So she spent a slow hour reassuring the weeping damsel, and, by the time Bellezour was calm and philosophical about her fate, Fay was fast asleep with dreams erratic and strange.

---

When she woke in the morning, she felt as if she had cried all night, or had indeed seen a friend through a crisis. Her head was heavy and the sheets clean and tempting. Still she dragged herself out of bed and went to work, conveniently forgetting breakfast.

It did not help her mood any that all her colleagues took one look at her bloodshot eyes and dour face and assumed she was suffering a hangover. After the fourth person had, quite independently of the other three, teased her in what he felt was a gentle and subtle manner (*sledgehammer subtle*, Fay thought) she was angry and awake and altogether alive.

---

*Munching carrots and drinking tea, that's all my evenings consist of at the moment. Munching carrots and drinking tea. Not very exciting.*

*There is not a thing of interest on TV, and I'm too lazy to get out my flute, and I'm too bored even to draw. If I were a drinker, I would drink myself into smithereens. What's a* smithereen? And how do you drink yourself into it? All I know about them is that they are small and that there are lots of them. How do I know they are small? What if I drink myself into a single, giant smithereen?

The novelty of my lovely new home has worn off and I no longer feel tempted to do things to it. Technically speaking, I know it's mine (well, the bits the bank doesn't own) but personally speaking it doesn't feel homey yet. I've had all my friends over to dinner and half my family to stay and I still look around wondering how on earth I can lay claim to it and make it mine.

I don't quite belong here, I suppose, the way I don't quite belong at work. I'm at home in bed - I feel quite real when I sleep. And when I'm singing in the shower. Only I start wishing the shower were a waterfall and I was bathing in a romantic gorge. Somehow all my excruciating modesty gets put to the side in my dreams. Oh, how nice is a dream world, where I am not traumatised by all my hang-ups and limitations. Where I don't stop playing in an orchestra because people might (God forbid) actually hear me.

How much of my fading away is my own doing? Is the world so unbearable? Or am I just terrified of it? Serves the world right if I'm terrified. It just doesn't know what it's missing. The richness of my dreams, hidden forever under a veil of security. Scribbles are the only real communication I have with the world, and only I get to see them. This is as it should be. Like my solitary flute playing. The inner universe is my audience, not the outer world. The inner universe and the schoolbook I scribble in.

Oh, but I'm full of cute sayings tonight.

An empty, tidy house does wonders for the ideas, rattling about like stray peas. What was it a friend once said about another friend? That the thoughts in her head were like two peas inside her skull, rattling around in the empty space. Some friend. But that's me in my house, with the big euca-

*lypts standing between this empty brainbox and a big boring world.*

*Am I a neurotic? A manic depressive? Who knows? The words sound good. All I know is it's early to bed tonight. I want to find out what's happening to Belle. I really had no idea she'd be so terribly upset by her marriage. As her father told her, it means power and a secure position, and she was old to be unmarried. Yet all she could do was cry. Is that why I'm not married? Fear of an uneven match? Rubbish. I'm not married because I'm not prepared to sacrifice my dream world to anyone. You hear that, world? My dreams of knights in shining armour do me just fine!*

———

"What on earth are you doing?" Fay asked.

"I'm sewing," answered Bellezour Anma.

That was obvious, but Fay knew that Belle, for all her apparent frail femininity, hated sewing. She did beautiful work, but often admitted that she detested every stitch of it. So why now? Was she determined to prove her martyrdom or something?

Fay asked the question. Belle's frown lifted and she laughed. She didn't answer the question properly. Instead she said, "For my husband. He needs this," and she waved her work in the air. Then she asked a question of her own. It surprised Fay, this query, so much that her jaw dropped and she took on her famous dumb dog look. At least, she assumed it was her famous dumb dog look. She certainly felt like a dumb dog. Her mouth gaped for a moment before she shut it with a snap, and tried, feebly, to answer.

"Your wedding?" was all the reply she could manage, in a numbed, wailing voice, "Your wedding?" her voice rose on the third syllable, "But I came today to ask you when you had planned to have it. I didn't know you were already married."

"In the spring," Belle said, calmly biting off a thread.

"But, but why are you still here?" spluttered Fay.

"Here?" asked Belle, in confusion.

"In your father's house," prompted Fay, biblically. Belle looked around in confusion. Then she stopped herself and laughed.

"Fay, how could you walk right through the castle grounds, through the courtyard and up the turret stairs and not know where you are?"

It seemed she had forgiven the lapse over the wedding. Fay sighed in relief. Then Bellezour's words registered. Fay whirled around and out the door, almost tripping in her haste. It was as well she had not tripped, for there was no wooden landing outside the door, but a stone ledge and below that ledge, a well of spiral stairs, leading round and down into dizzying darkness.

"This is my favourite room," came Belle's voice. "No-one likes the stairs except me, and I can see the whole town from up here."

Fay gulped and turned around, back to the security of the room. "Let me see the view," she asked, her voice cautious.

Sure enough, the turret window faced the town. Looking out, Fay drew deep breaths to steady her nerves. This scene, she thought, must be from her unconscious mind, (*Subconscious mind? Do I even know what I'm thinking about*, she wondered?) just like the castle wall that had appeared on paper the other day. All Fay had intended to do was visit Belle and talk about her plans for the wedding. Fay had intended to recommend colours and clothes, and generally help Belle face a changing future. And suddenly it was all in the past and Belle was *in* that future. So was Fay.

She was not going to destroy the fragile reality of

the dream by shifting back three months. Doggedly she looked out the window. Still dogged – no escaping that today, Fay fretted.

She knew the town. After all, Fay reassured herself, she created it. But she had never seen it from on high. That was maybe where this scene came from: a secret desire to see what the village looked like, laid out like a map. Sorry, town. It didn't make nearly as much sense to her as it should have, sitting there in the distance, like a model. She could identify the common and the pond. That was all.

Fay turned to the green and gold room and asked Bellezour to show her where everything was. Belle had a funny look in her eye - a little determined and curious - but she didn't ask any obvious questions, such as where Fay had been these last months, and why she had been so stunned to see the tower stairs. She looked into her friend's face solemnly, then smiled gently. Until she saw that smile, Fay had not realised how upset Belle had been at her negligence. It was like a spring flower showing how drab and plain the winter had been. Now she knew she was forgiven, but was not entirely certain what for. She had a feeling, somehow, that it was not for missing the wedding.

"Look," Belle pointed, "there's the green."

"Well, yes, I worked *that* one out," muttered Fay, ungratefully.

Bellezour chuckled at the sour tone. "To the right of the green you can see the shops. See, the large one is the inn, where the bench is."

"The bench?" queried Fay, "You have the sight of an eagle."

Belle laughed again. "Oh, I can't see the bench, stupid. But I can see the row of old men sitting on it. Just as I can see the morris dancers on the green."

Fay could just make out the streaks of brown and

grey that must be these gentlemen. She couldn't see the morris dancers at all.

"Then Persa's house and Enlai's and Flor's must be over there," she said, pointing to a row of buildings to the south of the green. While most of the shops had thatched roofs, some of the houses had jaunty red tiles instead, witness to the local pottery industry. Not pantiles, though. She had come across curved pantiles on a roof during a visit to the UK and they fascinated her, but they made no appearance in her town. Maybe another town, another day, another dream. A special pantile dream. What a strange thought: pantile dreaming where thoughts were curved and slotted into one another in neat protection.

"And there's the church," said Belle, pointing to the north of the green.

"Now why couldn't I spot that?" asked Fay.

"Stupid, I guess," answered her friend.

With her eyes, Fay followed the path leading from the church, past the pond, and to the gallows tree. It was at the very edge of the green, and was surrounded by a picket fence to keep the cows out. The whole scene was far enough away to resemble a miniature. Just past the giant tree was a street, leading to the church and the shops. That, at last, was the way it had seemed on the ground. From up here it was just a strip of white-ish grey, creating a blank space between the houses.

She knew that the ornamented two-story place was Alberc's. The white stucco was visible, and the elaborate shape. By now she had her bearings and could see just past this mayoral residence (how grand the words sounded and how small the place looked from a distance) to the red-brick triangle of the market square. It seemed terribly tiny for a market square. On the far side of the square was the Assembly Hall - the town's pride and joy. It was a new wooden building. No wattle and daub, no brick. The paint shone in the sunlight as if it were polished.

Fay didn't even try to sort out the maze of houses round the public buildings. She knew where her friends lived - that was enough. She gave a huge sigh and decided that she felt sleepy. Time for bed.

"No," cried Bellezour Anma. Her voice was unusually sharp and commanding. "Don't fade on me."

Fay rubbed her eyes. "But I'm tired," she murmured, "I've had enough dreaming."

"I don't care," said Belle, defiantly, "You wanted to know what I am doing, so you can spare the time to help me with it."

"Oh," said Fay, and obligingly sat down. She sat down on a pile of cushions, and slid over them in her sleepiness. As she hit the floor, Belle's laugh rang out and Fay became uncomfortably aware of the room again. "Okay" she said, trying to retain her reasonableness, "What are you doing?"

"My husband is young, so we are sending him to court to get an education. These are his clothes."

"Oh," said Fay, again, intelligently, and helped her friend sew ribbon until the colours all merged in a kaleidoscope, and she was definitely and indubitably asleep. *More effective than counting sheep*, thought Fay, as she woke up the next morning, relaxed and contented in her own bed. Though it would have been nice to imagine the wedding.

———

*It's strange, to wake up so happy and to end so unhappy. I guess things were too nice and sweet early on, because by morning tea time I was all restless. Couldn't sit still. Found photocopying to do, and filing, and everything else petty and small and full of movement. Couldn't stay still. It was as if a wrongness deep inside impelled me to move, move, move and never to think. Couldn't sit still, even a moment. All my real work suspended while time passed, passed, passed so slowly.*

*It wasn't until I left work that I realised what was happening.*

*I was scared. My world has done something without me.*

*No, not true. As I sit here with my cup of tea, I know it's not true. I'm just worried my world might be doing things without me. Not worried, petrified. So my subconscious was hard at work without my tender guidance, and made me miss the wedding. I see enough weddings in real life, and I reckon it would have been a little sad, anyway, to see a twenty-four year old friend marry a teenaged boy. I'm scared of the wedding, in a way. That's why I skipped to when Belle was going to be alone again, almost single, the way I created her. That makes sense. It brings it back to ordinariness again. A manageable world.*

*But what if my world did get away from me? What if it was Bellezour who reached out last night and kept me awake a bit longer, and what if it wasn't me? Does that mean that it could become just as deadly dull as reality?*

*I won't see Belle tonight. No chances. I'll take no chances. I'll make up a quaint and funny imagining, something totally irrelevant and rather silly. I'll tame the town I saw from the tower, and bring it back into perspective. Then maybe I can think safely about visiting old friends or getting involved in emotions or people again.*

*I'll use a few of the people who sat outside the pub, I think. I don't know them - I don't know their names. It will be an easy imagining to do: like back in the days when I was a kid. And it won't hurt me. It will be safe.*

*And I may not wake up happy, but tomorrow I'll be able to cope with everyday life again. Please God, let me be able to cope with everyday life again.*

# CHAPTER THREE

FAY WANDERED DOWN TO THE POND, CAREFULLY averting her gaze from the castle whenever the streets twisted to give her a glimpse. She felt a bit aggrieved, because it really felt as if the streets were twisting on purpose, just to upset her. She ploughed doggedly on, delicately hopping over open drains, walking around animals or children as if they were lumps of stone or brick.

They meant as much to her as stone or brick. Fay preferred adults or inanimate objects. The first you could talk to and the second you could use. She hadn't liked childhood, she reasoned, so why should she like children? It was completely an invention that all women loved children. Completely.

Eventually she skirted around the gallows tree. Her eyes hugged the ground as she went round it and she tried not to smell the rotting sweetness of the decayed meat. Obviously there was a crime problem in the town.

Fay decided that if ever she created a new town, she wouldn't fall prey to romanticisation. There would be no gallows tree, or stocks or any form of punishment. There would be no crime and no punishment. With the thought, the scene wavered and grew almost transparent. Like a watercolour against the light.

Fay picked up a stick and whacked it against each upright of the fence around the tree. She went round and round the gallows tree, bashing with the stick until the world felt solid again. By that time she had quite a little crowd of children staring at her and pointing. She made a face and a threatening gesture and then sighed in relief when they drifted away.

Eventually she reached the pond where two men were fishing. Fay wondered who had the rights to fish the pond, since it was on common property. It seemed unlikely that the whole town could do so the way they had with their cows and sheep until recently. Alberc Bas had made the common land accessible on a rotation system only when he became mayor. It was no use to anyone bare and overused, or so he claimed.

Maybe the pond was on rotation too. Maybe it moved spots on a regular basis, or got swished around in its bed from time to time to meet Alberc's ideas of town rule. *A rotating pond wouldn't move spots or swish around*, Fay suddenly thought. It would have a little whirlpool at its heart. A ghost of a smile appeared on her face.

Anyway, there were two tattered old men fishing there with lines that looked very tangled. Fay wondered what special ability it took to get lines so tangled in a calm pond. Maybe that miniature whirlpool really existed? Fay shrugged her shoulders and took off her shoes so that she could slide down to the water's edge.

Fay's toes touched the water with a faint thrill of forbidden pleasure. For some reason she always remembered the camping trip she had been on as a child where she was not allowed to sit on the bank and let her feet drift. Fay defied her parents even when she dreamed. As her feet softened and became waterlogged by the water, Fay relaxed. The tattered old men stood there, scarecrow silent; good company. *A pleasant way to spend an afternoon*, Fay thought. Village noises seemed distant and even the mooing of a cow on the common sounded as if it came from the other side of the world.

Just when Fay was almost asleep, the whole scene woke up. Fay lifted her chin and looked around, wanting to know what all the movement and noise was about.

There were her two scarecrows gesticulating at each other wildly. Old and angry men, arms flying about, tempers raging. Before Fay's fascinated gaze, another man joined them. He was younger, greying rather than greyed. He was very drunk and it showed in his voice and his movements.

"Wassa marrer?" he asked. The two fisherman explained first together then one at a time, interrupting each other and confusing the third party.

Fay leaned back and laughed. All three looked at her.

"What're you cackling about?" the tallest asked, his voice high with age and aggression.

"You were both arguing over the fish. If you can't work out who caught it, why don't you share it?" Fay said practically. All three men looked at her suspiciously.

"Bloody fool," one said and all three turned away. It looked so orchestrated, that Fay burst into helpless laughter again, silent this time. She did not want aged wrath to descend upon her. As she silently giggled, her feet plashing the water, the scene played itself out a few yards away.

The drunk offered to arbitrate and the other two accepted his authority with apparent equanimity. The fish was placed on the ground and the tipsy one stared at it for many minutes, deep in thought. Then "I have a solution," he declared, in sonorous tones.

He picked up the fish and walked away. When the others chased him, he shouted over his shoulder, "If I take it, it's the perfect solution." Fay wondered if he was as drunk as he had seemed, because he certainly ran fast.

Relaxed and amused, Fay swung her feet out of the water. They were white and sodden and she looked at them in quiet delight. She waved them around for a minute, twisting and twirling her ankles until most of the water was gone. Then she put her shoes back on. Fay regarded her feet then, shod and sober, with a certain seriousness.

She then walked south, towards Persa Doucor's house. It was a long time since she had seen Persa. Persa was not a serious person and perfectly fitted Fay's silly mood. Small and round and bouncy, Persa was always getting caught up in some excitement or other, generally of her own making. This time she bowled Fay over in brown-haired enthusiasm.

"Fay, save me!" she shrieked. How such a high-pitched squeal could come from such a round face was always a puzzlement to Fay.

"What from?" she asked, sensibly.

In answer, Persa dragged her inside the house and plonked her down on the living room chair. "I just had to get inside without Enlai seeing me," she explained.

"That's why you shrieked?" Fay asked.

"Yes, I mean, no. I mean, I was hiding behind you."

"But he could surely hear you."

"Yes, but he wouldn't dare follow when I was with you."

"Follow?" Fay queried, her face wrinkling in bewilderment. "Persa, what mischief have you been up to now?"

"No mischief," said Persa, her face as sober as it could be, which always made her look unlikely and angelic. It was a look Fay distrusted, and with reason. "It's just that he was making eyes at me."

"Persa, he's known you all your life. Why should he make eyes at you now?"

"I don't know," replied the girl, "All I know is he teases me and looks at me just so, and then spends half his time with Flor."

"Well," Fay interjected reasonably, "he's been interested in Flor for a long time."

"Then why is he making eyes at me?" Persa demanded. "He should just marry Flor and be done with. That's why I'm avoiding him."

*Some avoidance,* Fay thought cynically.

"I'm saving myself up for the soldiers. If I can marry a soldier, I'll get to go to court."

Soldiers? This was new. Fay plunged in, trying to make sense of it. "What soldiers? Where? And why on earth would a soldier get you to court? And why do you want to go to court anyway?"

Persa giggled. Her giggle was low-pitched and feminine. "The soldiers from court, silly! They'll go back there one day. It's part of the new agreement. The prince will be here soon to govern until his lordship comes of age."

"Tough on Belle." Fay commented.

"Oh," said Persa ingenuously, "I forgot you were friends. You should call her the lady Bellezour now. I do."

"You," said Fay, "I don't believe you remember to call anyone anything polite for more than three minutes at a stretch."

Persa squealed in horror and started attacking Fay with her mother's beautifully embroidered furnishings. Fay defended herself manfully until a voice shouting,

"Excuse me!" made them both stop in horrified awareness of their maidenly dignity. It was Enlai, looking very amused.

"Enlai Devers, what do you mean walking in here without so much as a by-your-leave and interrupting the quiet discussion between friends."

"Yes, I saw how quiet it was," Enlai commented, "In fact, I looked four times and said "Excuse me" so often my throat is hoarse."

"Liar," accused Persa.

"I never lie," commented Enlai off-handedly.

"Liar," answered Fay, and proceeded to back her accusation up. "What about the time when you told me you'd won a fortune in the lottery, and wanted some money to hide--"

"Okay, okay, so my throat isn't hoarse," Enlai interrupted quickly, throwing a horrified look at Persa. "But I did knock and very loudly too. I wanted to, to--"

"Now listen for his excuses," commented Persa, drolly. "The truth is he just wanted to know what we were up to! He can't bear to see me accosting someone on the street without knowing why."

"I give up," said Enlai. "What were you up to?"

"None of your business," said Persa, pertly.

"Actually," Fay explained, determined to see some order to this sudden conversation, "I was visiting Persa."

"Were you?" Persa's eyes were wide open at this.

Enlai laughed at them both. "And Persa was so enthusiastic to see you that she squeaked 'Save me' and dragged you indoors."

"Why she squealed 'Save me' is none of your concern," said Fay, sternly. Persa giggled. "But I was visiting Persa, and now that you have interrupted my visit in such a rude and untimely manner..."

"Go for it!" barracked Persa, softly.

"I'll be on my way," finished Fay. "I know when I'm not wanted."

"I suppose I'd better leave, too," said Enlai, "otherwise Persa will get me to clean up the mess you two idiots have made."

As Persa showed them out the door, full of dignity and propriety, she had the cheek to whisper in Fay's ear, "Now he's making eyes at you." From Enlai's attentive manner when he insisted on walking her safely past the gallows, Fay could only agree.

———

*God, nightmares can be awful. And nightmares created by stinking humid weather are the very worst. Partly this is because you don't expect them. You go to bed all cheerful and zippy, and then you toss and turn for an eternity. I was trying to get out of a dreadful situation. I don't remember what it was, but it made my heart beat fast and I wanted to hide my face in my hands. I kept thinking all through my nightmare, "Where is the green cloak? I need the green cloak!" It was as if the cloak had the ability to solve my problems. A sort of seven league cloak, perhaps, transporting instantly away from all the carnage. It wasn't actually carnage, but it threatened to be, which was worse. It was blackmail and terrorism, and a terrible lack of logic.*

*I remember it. We all piled on this bus, my friends and I, and of course I caught it after running down tree-lined streets for miles and miles because the person I was going with was late and the bus couldn't wait even though we had tickets and there wouldn't be another. And then it took us to a Wild West entertainment park, where everyone took on cowboy roles. Except that something had gone wrong and no-one was allowed out of the park until they had killed another person. So all my friends were hunting each other and acting as if they were dropouts from Lord of the Flies, and I was* going around saying, "Don't believe it, you don't have to kill anyone."

And, like one does in dreams, I tried to magic my way out, and change the beginning and the middle and the ending. Only I kept coming back, standing outside the saloon trying to stop everyone from killing each other. All I could do, just before I woke up, was teleport from place to place, telling myself that it was only a dream and therefore I had to be able to find a solution. It's only in real life we never find solutions. And I wanted the green cloak for just a fleeting instant, and that instant brought it back as a sort of reality to me.

I know a bit more about its significance now. It means safety. I wish I knew why, how, when or where. But if I'd have had the cloak in the dream, then my friends wouldn't have had to go out so enthusiastically to kill each other. And I wouldn't have been left in the remnants of a nightmare, like a bad headache colouring my day depressing.

What colour is depressing? It is a purple-black, bruise colour. Or is it red and angry? No, it's not red, because anger dispels depression. Depression is not enough adrenalin, I reckon, and not working to face up to whatever is wrong. I'm never depressed except after nightmares. Mind you, I'm not very often angry either. There's not a lot to get mad about. Anger implies some sort of close contact with the world, tactile reach, close caring.

Somehow, I don't **care** about things. I watch the dying millions on the 6:30 news and feel that it ought to concern me but it doesn't, not really. I hear of famine and war and plague and disaster, and somehow think, no, that's nothing to do with me. I see the homeless and think, no, not me; I see the jobless and think, no, not me. I'm heartless, perhaps. Or am I so bored that I'm alienated by everything? Who the hell knows? I must be a dreadfully dull person on the outside. The inside is different.

Inside I have friends. I'm going to visit Belle tonight, I think, and find out what's happening. I mean I know the plot, but I don't know what it means to her until I see her. And she may be lonely there in her big castle, now her husband is at court.

I've decided he's at court, because otherwise she'll have me helping sew clothes again. That was awful. Hated it. I think the bunches of ribbon were worst. It didn't make it a scrap better that I lifted the plot from a song and that the song included bunches of ribbons. They were a bore to sew. Well, not a bore, but terribly fiddly. Ah well, it was in good cause. At least all the court ladies will know that he's married and not a bright young thing to be toyed with... Belle hopes. Bellezour Anma, full of hopes and ideals.

I never thought about it before, but what will happen to her when her young husband dies? The song doesn't say, and I invented Belle so long ago that she's almost real, and I don't know what she'll say or do. It is a little scary that I have to live through the scene before I know, almost as if the scene is independent of me.

Well, it isn't. I'm sticking to known plots and songs and things from now on. The fewer cute new developments in my world the better. So there, nightmare. You're not going to invade my dream-world. So there.

Beside, they don't have guns in my imagining. Ha, fooled you, nightmare. And I'll put on a fan or something and the humidity won't affect me, not one jot. So there.

———

"I am a man upon the land,
I am a silkie on the sea,
And when I'm far and far frae land,
My home it is in Sule Skerrie." (Traditional)

———

Fay was suffering from shock. She was on the receiving end of too many surprises these days, but she was an addict and could not stop dreaming. Instead of being at the castle, or in the castle, or even near the castle, she was down by the sea. And she wasn't in her sweet little cove either, nor could she seem to get there. That would have been fine, because her cove was the safest place in the universe.

Whenever she closed her eyes and tried to imagine whatever she tried to imagine, the result was the same. No cove. Nothing she tried worked. Everything she tried failed miserably. Instead of the town or the castle or the cove, Fay was by the sea. She didn't recognise the spot. She was listening to the hushing sound of the ocean, her hair being whipped by the salt-laden breeze. Every time she thought of a place she knew, her temple throbbed with a dull pain, but nothing happened: she remained by the sea. Finally Fay gave up and sat down on one of the jutting rocks by the stony shore. It was pleasant there, if a bit cold.

She had been here before, she remembered, a long, long time ago. Just down south a little, there was a lonely house on the shore, nestled into a sheltered nook. South-east of the house were the rocks where the seals came. Fay remembered it well because she had created a particularly vivid imagining there once upon a time.

"Once upon a time" was the appropriate phrase. She had dreamed a fairy tale based on a folk-song. She had created a selkie who married a woman. The seal men and women had fascinated her then. The thought of being able to run away to sea for safety and to explore the land for adventure had been liberating.

The woman had lived in the house. She had fine light brown hair that glowed in the sunlight. This woman (Fay remembered the hair but not the name) would daily negotiate the wind-pulled shrubs and head inland a little before she reached the seal rocks. There she would wait, year in, year out, and hope that one day her seal-husband would come back. Fay almost purred in contentment, remembering the sad, romantic tale. The woman's loneliness of the past somehow fitted in with the cold seashore of the present.

She decided that if she couldn't get to her cove, at least there were friends who were still visitable. Fay had befriended the selkie's son and had used his laughter for light entertainment in her teens. That was before she met Persa and Belle. It was odd and peculiarly Fayish, she reflected, that Belle's house predated Belle herself. Imagination was a strange creature.

In her teens, it was far more important to know someone male, anyone male. Even a not-quite-human male. So they swum, and built castles, and generally acted like eighteen going on five.

This was why Fay kept men out of her dreams so often now. For all she told herself over and over that she led a romantic dream life, in practice her dreams were safe ones, where she was surrounded with friends, and with safe environments. Especially where men were concerned. Safety was better. Really it was.

She walked down the rough path to the cottage, over anthills and around deep knots of grass. When she came to the cottage though, there was no-one there. This was not a problem, for there was a fire burning in the grate. Someone had done repairs to the place, since she had been there last. Quite extensive repairs, by the look of things. The whole roof had been redone in smart blue pantiles. No more thatch. Pantiles. This was turning into a pantile dream after all. Fay chuckled softly. It amused Fay to see her vague thoughts realised so quickly, and then it saddened her a bit.

Blue pantiles. That meant the seal lady must be dead, for she had sworn by thatch.

Fay looked critically at the outside of the cottage from the distance of the path, before she went on down to the seal rocks. Yes, it looked smart, she admitted, and even snug, but not quite... serious. The tattered old thatch she was used to was much more sombre, and in keeping with the bleak shore. No. It was too jaunty.

Fay shrugged the jauntiness to one side, and started to walk to the shore. The roof might look zippy and young, but she was getting very tired. It was late afternoon, and the sun gleamed red on the glossy feathers of the birds. She briefly gained a streak of energy and raced up to them. Of course they winged away, in a most satisfactory flurry.

All the grass had been carefully cut near the path. *Ah well, it was safe from snakes then*, Fay thought, and shuddered, for she had not associated snakes with the clumpy bushes and tall grass before.

Then she turned around, despite her wish to reach the shore. The seal rocks beckoned her mind, but she was cold and headachy and tired. *Tired and cold*, she thought, and wondered where her feet were taking her. She remembered the dying fire in the cottage and let her feet plod her toward it. All she had energy for when she was back in the cottage was to refresh the fire. She sat down in the big chair, and watched the flames slowly reach into the fuel, until it was hot and comforting. Then she slept.

When she woke, it was to a clatter of dishes and a crick in her neck. She put her hand to her head and felt a dull throb. *Serve me right for sleeping sitting up*, she thought. *Sleeping sitting up?*

She jolted upright in horror, her head almost splitting in agony. She was still in the cottage. Fay shut her eyes and wished to go home. She thought of her nice cool bed linen, and the quiet of her room. She could feel it, her fingers stroking the cool sheets. Then someone dropped something and the clatter sent the sheets far away. And here she was, stuck in a blasted cottage by a blasted godforsaken shore, with no idea why she came here or why the hell she could not return home.

She winced in agony, for her head felt as if all the rocks the seals slept on had been hurled at her temples and at the back of her neck. She cried. The tears were not angry tears, but rain from the eyes of the forsaken. Slowly, slowly, they trickled down her cheeks, and slowly, slowly, she put her hands to her head. When she supported her head firmly, the flood came. She wept as if the universe had ended, as if all she loved were gone. At that moment, she felt, indeed, that it had. Paradoxically, she didn't miss her family, only her cool, cool bed, and her imaginary friends. Alone. Fay felt terribly, terribly alone.

"Hush, then," a deep voice murmured. "I didn't know you were awake, or I'd've been more quiet."

Fay didn't look up; she didn't want to. Her sobbing continued, in the same desperate way as before. Gently, feather-light, a hand touched her neck, stroking it.

"You're as knotted up as an old tree," the voice commented, amused. "You must have the mother of a headache."

Firm hands pushed her forward in the chair, and kneaded slowly at her shoulders, stroking up into the hairline. After a few strokes, it stopped.

"This is not helping you much," the voice said, sagely. "You must lie down on the floor."

Uncharacteristically, Fay obeyed. Somehow, in between getting out of the comfortable chair and lying down in front of the glowing fire, the tears ceased. One last sob dragged itself from her reluctant throat, and

Fay lay on the floor, her head in her arms, eyes tightly shut.

The warm hands slowly massaged her neck and her back. No attempt was made to divest her of clothes, and Fay only let the thought that there was a person behind those comforting hands flicker very faintly through her mind before dismissing it entirely. After a while the hands slowed down, and stopped. They rested lightly on her neck for a moment. Then Fay slept again.

———

*I feel grotty. Grotty. Grotty. Grotty. It's a horrible word and it exactly expresses my life today.*

*No more headache, but ooh, my tummy. I have cramps and nausea and I can hardly hold this pen. I'm at work, too. That's the only redeeming feature. Three hundred and fifty-two of us have mild food poisoning. The sad result of eating contaminated food at a lunchtime event.*

*Never eat massaman curry, that's all I can say. I thought it was something to do with an aching dream I had a few nights back, but no, I didn't share the nightmare with three hundred and fifty-one other people. I have food poisoning, pure and simple. One of the lucky souls who did not eat the food (she had a very unhealthy lunch of Twisties and cake and is 100% fine) gave me a herbal tea bag. She says it should help cleanse the system. Something's got to cleanse the system.*

*I'm working, but very slowly. I've written a letter and made lots of phone calls to industry and sent a fax and an-alysed a paper. But it was uphill all the way. Now it's lunchtime and I wish I was home. I could go to bed and sleep it off. No, better than that, I could go to bed and take my ill-ness to my imaginary world and get Belle to take care of me.*

Or my seal friend. His hands were a huge comfort on that nightmare night. At least I assume it was him.

Fay, don't be daft. This is the result of feeling so very un-well - you start imagining things. You were in his home, by his fire, and he did not shake you and ask you who you were, or anything drastic. Therefore it must have been him.

Maybe he had a cold. That would account for his voice sounding so deep. Or maybe the headache meant that I was not hearing properly. I don't know.

All I know is that the scene is haunting me. I know it was the product of a headache and that I was lucky enough to have slept it out, but it nags my mind.

And God, I feel sick. I think I'm going to give up and go home. Don't care that it gives a bad impression. Look at this wobbly writing and at the even more wobbly brain. Take my advice, never get food poisoning.

————

I feel better. Not perfect, but better. Now I'm all sniffly and sneezy, though. Two days in bed I've had, for food poisoning, and all I can do is act as if I have a bad cold. And it's ruining my make-up.

I'm all dolled up tonight for a reception. And I've got an escort. Swish, heh? I'm dressed in a short, short black lace dress and I'm wearing the brightest of sandals and the brightest of opals. Blue and red and green and glinty. I'm not sure what colour glinty is, but I'm sure it is bright. Terribly, frightfully, excruciatingly elegant.

Mind you, receptions themselves are nothing to write home about. Pretty much a dime a dozen in this city. All those embassies, you see, and such a small population. They positively ooze bonhomie, Canberra's embassy staff. Or at least, they do once a year. This is that once. It's some national day or other. I don't even know where I'm going. The truth is

*I'm escorting Fred who has to go and who hates to. I'm the barrier between him and boredom. That's a laugh. Me!*

*Not much chance for dreaming tonight. Come to think of it, not much chance of dreaming for days now. It was almost impossible to call up my imaginary world when I was almost dying of nausea and cramps and diarrhoea. I slept. I dreamed mostly of my childhood. The other two were dolled up to the nines in satin and silk, and I was stuck wearing polyester. It wasn't that bad. I just remember it as being that bad – big difference.*

*Cinderella. Maybe that's why I'm wearing lace now. Anti-Cinderella.*

*Maybe it's also why I accepted Fred's last-minute plea, even though he admitted he'd already asked three other women, including his sister. I don't want to be left out of normal socialising. Yes, that's it. I want to be normal. I guess the nightmare the other night put the fear of God into me about my dreamworld. I was scared I'd die there like the girl in that book. I can't remember the book, though.*

*I only wish there were a way to instantly cure a cold. Going out with the sniffles makes a poor contrast with my elegant lace dress. From the sublime to the gorblimey, with the lace, of course, being the sublime. And the glinty stuff.*

*Maybe when I get back in a few hours I'll do some dreaming again. Or maybe I won't. Maybe I'm too sickly to dream, and ought to practice being convalescent instead. That makes me sound mid-Victorian when really my dress is mid-sixties. Oh, life wasn't meant to be sneezy!*

---

"Belle? Belle?" rose Fay's voice, querulously. "Bellezour? Where are you?" She wandered in and out of empty corridors and felt exceedingly lost. Occasionally someone would pass her and she'd wonder, a bit aimlessly, if she had the courage to ask them where Belle was. No, Fay decided eventually. She had no courage at all. Not a jot. Today was not a day of courage.

She wafted her snuffed-up self down the endless darkness until, finally, she found a door. That door led to a courtyard. It was a big square filled with bustle and bleating. There was grass, some animals, and lots of people. She caught a glimpse of Belle amongst the crowd, and tried to deftly wend her way to where Belle had been.

After she had tripped over three sheep, upset a coop of chickens and stepped on a farmer's foot, Fay gave up and sat down, cross-legged, in the middle of the court. Tears streamed out of her bleary eyes. She had a cold and it was all too, too much. It had been too much before she had even got here. And she didn't even know why she had come. She didn't know *anything*. She was not even proud of being so sorry for herself.

It was at this point that Belle came across her. Belle-the-authoritative. The sound of Belle ordering a path and the feel of being gently dragged out of the throng made Fay blink, and her tears dried up. When Belle had her friend ensconced in a chair, and a hot drink steaming in her hands, she asked, calmly and firmly, "Now then, Fay, what's wrong? This isn't at all like you."

Fay snuffled and whispered into her cup, "I'm sick."

"You've been sick before without crying oceans over a bunch of sheep."

"I didn't," said Fay, indignantly.

"That's better," said Belle, approvingly. "Though, you know, the reason I brought you in was so that you wouldn't make the wool soggy. It would not be a good tribute if it was soggy. Don't you agree?" Bellezour smiled her sweetest smile.

Fay only succeeded in looking bewildered. "Tribute?"

"It's that time of the decade," Belle explained, glibly.

"Not only are we stuck with rampant soldiers in our midst, we have to pay the Crown its dues."

"Rampant soldiers?" queried Fay.

"It's really not your day, is it?" Fay shook her head, mutely. "Well, drink up - it will help."

"But it doesn't taste of anything," Fay complained.

"You've a cold," accused Bellezour. Fay nodded mutely. "You've got a cold and you feel sorry for yourself. What a state of affairs." Belle curled up in silent laughter.

"You're not very sympathetic," accused Fay.

"Should I be?" Belle's laughing eyes pierced Fay's gloom.

"I suppose not," she answered. "Since I've not been very supportive of you recently."

"And you think I'm a figment of your imagination," added Belle.

"Do not."

"Do."

"Do not."

"Do. Anyway, what's next for me in whatever story you're making up now?"

"Oh," said Fay airily, being (to tell the truth) some-what rattled at her character's independence. "You're pregnant."

The pause was a long one. A whisper came from Belle, "How did you know? I haven't told anyone. It must have been from his visit. He came to see me after he had been at Court a month. He was wearing my red ribbons around his waist.

"He spent a lot of time playing with his friends in the small courtyard. I looked over the wall when I heard them laughing. It was play, though they are not quite children anymore and they took it so very seri-ously. Small courtiers, all of them, and not a one over sixteen years. All the games courtiers play, chess and challenges, and trials of the heart. He was the best-looking of them all, but so young, so young…"

Fay felt very guilty at the look of Belle's face. "I'm sorry," she said, and hugged her friend warmly. "I should have been more considerate."

"Don't tell me," said Belle, sarcastically, "the next story you make up for me will be happy." Fay nodded, vigorously. "You'll marry me to a noble knight, my own age." Belle spoke as if she half-believed in Fay's omnipotence.

Fay dispelled illusion with a half-laugh, "I can't even seem to marry myself off. Whenever I dream of a handsome knight, I wake out of the dream before I get married."

"Maybe you're scared," suggested Belle, seriously.

"Maybe I'm terrified," retorted Fay, cheerfully, "but that's the real world. I can't even get married in a dream."

"Well," said Belle, practically, "What can you do in a dream? If I'm in a dream of yours can you make my husband my own age?"

"No," said Fay, soberly, "Once I've started a story I can't seem to get out of it until it has run its course. All I can do is never dream you again."

"Don't do that," smiled Bellezour, "I might not survive."

"No, I wouldn't do that, not to you," and Fay was deadly serious. "Belle, things are going to be worse for you before they get better. I'm sorry. I really didn't mean to hurt you. It was all so much fun when I started, and it was such a charming, sad, little folksong. But I promise, when the story is over, I'll come to you and I'll say 'Belle, what do you want to next with your life?' and we'll plan it together."

There was another silence.

Fay broke it, "Hey, your horrible concoction has worked. My head is clear."

"It's not a horrible concoction," said Belle, indignantly, "and just for that comment, you can come and help me."

"Doing what?" asked Fay, suspiciously.

"Counting sheep, measuring linen, stacking pottery - the tribute has to be ready tonight. His Highness has promised to take it himself, before he resumes his role."

"Resumes his role?" asked Fay, suspicious to the end. The words were *not* Belle's.

Belle took the high ground. "He is governing this fair land in my lord's absence," said she, haughtily.

"My, how pretentious you sound," commented Fay.

At that Belle dragged her out and kept her very busy for a long while.

Fay reflected, during the interminable counting of various items and the wild hunts for the missing elements of the tribute, that at last all her stories (well, most of them) were dovetailing nicely. The same information was reaching her from all sides. The prince, for one thing, appeared by hearsay wherever she went. There was only one small problem - why that information? Sure, it was a logical consequence of what she had caused to happen, but...

Ah well, logical minds are their own rewards, sighed she, as she measured out twenty ells of fine damask.

Eventually Belle rescued her. The excuse she used was dinner, but, in fact, Belle was as sick of the tribute process as Fay. The result was that she talked about everything except damask, pots, sheep, tiles and anything else that might have been assembled in the courtyard. Fay, now that she was less bleary-eyed, was tempted to giggle over the lack of enthusiastic loyalty shown by Belle to her king. Belle was politely scathing about royalty, in fact, and Fay did remark, her eyes wide and innocent, that she had heard a lot about the prince, and why wasn't he invited to dinner? Belle was prevented from giving an appropriate retort by the stifled chuckle of one of the servants.

She turned her temper aside with visible care (making Fay wonder why Belle was so sensitive on the subject of princes) and asked, absolutely non sequitur, what was Fay's happiest image.

"The green cloak," Fay replied without hesitation, then wondered why she had said it. Belle asked her what green cloak and Fay turned the question by saying, "No, you didn't ask why, only what, and now it's your turn to answer. What's your happiest image?"

Bellezour was much more hesitant, "A dragonfly on the water at sunset," was her final decision, "I think."

"Nice to know you think," was Fay's polite response, "Now, what about your saddest."

Now it was Bellezour's turn to reply unhesitatingly, "A lonely child."

*Reflections of your own youth*, Fay thought.

Her own saddest image was much longer coming and when it arrived it was not an image at all. "When I was a child, "she began, slowly, "I read a book. It was a very old book, and very old-fashioned. In it, a lovely old aunt, or grandmother, had this drawer. Whenever the children came to visit, she would let them choose an item, and she would tell them a story about it - her first ball, her naughty cousin, and so forth."

"Why is that so sad?" asked Belle, "I think it is sweet."

"Oh, it's not that the old lady is sad. It's just that when I was in Guides - a sort of society for girls - I went to visit an old lady who had obviously read that book. She had drawers and drawers full of items that obviously meant a great deal to her. But there were no relatives to tell the stories to."

"She told you this?" Belle queried.

"Yes," said Fay, a lump suddenly making her voice froggy, "but she wouldn't tell me any of the stories, even though we had both read the book. She said she had saved them for her grandchildren, and the tales would die with her. And when she died, I had to clean out the drawers and everything there was rubbish. There were scraps of felt and streamer, and tissue; odds and ends of material and ribbon; a page from a book - nothing was whole, and no-one had any way of knowing what it meant any more."

"All the meaning it had in the world was in the old lady's mind," breathed Belle. "And why does it scare you so, Fay?"

"I'm like that old lady? When I die, all that anyone will know of this whole world are the bits and pieces I've drawn when I'm bored, or the odd scraps I've written in my notepad. The other day I drew that plaster picture from outside your old house. Who will know that Bellezour Anma lived inside a house, just from seeing a pencil sketch of a falcon and a hare?"

"And you are afraid that I will disappear when you die," whispered Belle.

"That most of all," Fay replied. "Because I have no proof that you live outside my mind, and you're the only person in this whole world I have ever been able to talk to freely."

"Yet you don't really believe I exist."

"When I'm here with you, I believe. But I make up the stories on my way home from work. And I live them in those odd moments before I sleep. Belief and knowing are different."

"What would it take to convince you of my reality, of the reality of this world around you?"

Belle's eyes were hypnotic, but Fay could only answer miserably, "I don't know, truly, I don't know."

Just before she faded away, Belle asked wistfully, "Come again tomorrow?"

"I'll try," promised Fay, "I'll try."

Odd that she hadn't noticed it before. Belle knew how she got there.

"I'll try," she promised again, this time mumbling into her bedclothes.

———

*Work is neat today. There's no reason or logic behind it, but it is. I'm doing exactly the same dull old stuff as always; it's just that, somehow, I'm enjoying it. Better be careful – I might get addicted to it. Addicted to work – how unFayish.*

*So far today, I've sent out an urgent minute to the Minister's office trying the chase up a decision that should have been made two weeks ago. I've put a bomb under an economist (one of my favourite activities – I love making the lives of economists miserable) and I've done all my filing and all my typing and cleared out my desk a hundred percent.*

*One hundred percent is an awful lot of clearing for a messy Fay. There is a giant pile of papers on the floor, waiting patiently to be recycled. I have a theory that once they are recycled they come back again, get written on or printed on, and the whole process starts again. There's a paper plot – a permanent invasion of my desk by a mere seven pages worth of paper molecules. What does a paper molecule look like, I wonder? Is it latticed and rainbow coloured? Or is it flat white and brick like?*

*I know why I'm cheerful, too. It's the sudden and magic disappearance of a cold. Going to bed early was such a good idea. The night's sleep seems to have done wonders.*

*I suppose this means I should do something super-exciting tonight. I could watch TV (shock, horror) or go to a movie (oh, unheard of!) or spend the evening on the phone (now, who to ring?) or, or... I could go to bed early and keep my promise to Belle, and visit her. Put down coldly on paper like that, it looks a bit stupid. I mean, imagine going to bed to keep a promise to an invention of your own. An idea that's almost ludicrous.*

*Well, I may do it nonetheless. It's more exciting than the alternatives.*

———

"Well, I'm here!" announced Fay with a flourish.

Belle looked up at her, consideringly, "It only took you three days."

Fay deflated immediately. "I was so sure I had it right this time."

"Don't worry," said Belle, "I'm used to you. Anyway, I'm being nice to you today."

"Why," asked Fay.

"I want you to do me a favour."

All sorts of strange thoughts passed through Fay's wayward mind. She wondered if Belle wanted her to describe the world she lived in, or to explain how she got to and fro, or to make up a story she (Belle) could see happen. All of Fay's thoughts concerned the odd awareness Belle seemed to display of who Fay was.

Unfortunately for Fay's theories, Belle wanted nothing of the sort. "I've got a touch of morning sickness and I don't want to have to explain it to the world, so I'm pretending I've got a cold and I'm staying in bed." Belle grinned conspiratorially – she certainly didn't look as if she was suffering from morning sickness. "And Persa's been a pest and 'borrowed' my embroidery."

"Why on earth?" ask Fay, bewildered. To borrow a half-finished cushion cover was not her idea of a sensible act.

"Who knows? Persa's a law unto herself. Anyway,

now I've got a bit of time on my own and no-one's bothering me to tell them to do this or that or the other – Gods, I'm sick of being in charge of this tumble-down household – I want to do something calming."

"Counting to five hundred is more calming than embroidery," suggested Fay, helpfully. "And talking to me is more soothing than almost anything."

Belle threw a cushion at her. It was a strange propensity her friends in this world had, reflected Fay, that they always threw cushions. Fay backed off, laughing, " Okay – I'll see you when I have tamed the dread Persa Doucor."

Fay chuckled her way out of the castle and along the streets. She was so amused that she walked by instinct, which meant, of course, that she went right through the square without noticing. Berating herself good humouredly for her stupidity, she turned to retrace her steps and walked into someone. "Oh, I'm so sorry," she said to the young man. He was merry looking, although not handsome, with a snub nose and pale blue eyes. His hair seemed very untidy, a glossy shock of brown straw. Fay's good humour even reached to this unplanned stranger, and she smiled.

"It's nice to see you looking cheerful for a change," he commented.

It wasn't the comment that surprised her, but his tone of voice. It was as if he was referring to her, personally.

"But you've never met me before," stated Fay, firmly and logically, "Anyway, I'm always happy," she lied. After all, if she was visiting Persa, she should get in some practice at lying: she might need it.

The man grinned. "Either you have a twin or you're a born liar," he said.

"It's just not my day for people being nice to me," Fay sighed, "because I have not got a twin. At least, I

45

don't think I do." This was an intriguing possibility, but she dismissed it. "When did you see me sad?"

"When you played Sleeping Beauty on my favourite chair," was the dry comment.

Fay stood tall in sheer astonishment. She looked into his face very searchingly. "Either you've changed a lot or something is very peculiar," she said.

"Why?"

"Well, I was visiting a friend. I thought it was him," she grinned, a bit abashed, "I don't normally let absolute strangers massage me without at least worrying about it drastically, and thanking them profusely. Anyway, I can thank you now, retrospectively."

"You can," although he accepted the apology gracefully, he looked at her peculiarly.

"That house was empty for fifty years," he explained, "We had to fix the roof entirely and do some rather dramatic things to the west wall. Who do you know who lived there? And how did you do your disappearing act? It intrigued me."

"Oh, did it?" asked Fay, a bit acerbically. "I expect you think I just sort of faded away."

"Well, something of the sort," laughed the man.

"Do you have a name?" Fay demanded, determined to shake off the lurking worry of that fifty-year emptiness. Her imaginings were supposed to be timeless and for a friend to have faded fifty years ago...

"Sometimes," came the swift response, "And you?"

"All the time," answered Fay, haughtily, "and it's Fay."

"That's a very short name," said the man, and tried it out, experimentally, "Fay, Faee."

"So what do I call you," Fay asked. "My mother would answer, 'Anything as long as it's not late for dinner', so if you don't give me a name I might try that."

"Oh, anything but," pleaded the young man. "I'm Biaus Gilbert."

"Are you one of the soldiers?" Fay asked. "Belle mentioned them, and Persa is already quite silly about them."

"Yes," he answered quite dryly, "I've seen her silliness with some of the men. And yes, I suppose you could call me a soldier."

Then the penny dropped, "Biaus Gilbert – that means Handsome Gilbert." The man laughed and nodded completely unashamed of his name, "Is the Biaus bit your name, or an honorific?"

He said, "An honorific."

"But it can't be," wailed Fay. Gilbert stood still in amused astonishment, obviously his name normally produced a different reaction. "Gilbert is a real name, and I never invented it or stole it or borrowed it from *anywhere*."

"Why should you have to steal my name?" the gentleman obviously dealt exceptionally well with surreal conversations, because the tone was still amused curiosity.

"Because... because... Well, just because," Fay said, lamely. She wasn't going to tell this determined gentleman that she couldn't work out how he had got into her safe little world. She was distressed and disturbed, but also a little excited. They spoke the same language, and he had been nice about the headache incident. She had been allowed to escape from it almost unembarrassed. No, there was no way she could tell him that he must be an invention, and that she could not tell how she had invented him, or where from. To get out of it, she hastily recalled her errand. "Oh blow, I forgot," she exclaimed, a little hurriedly, "Belle's embroidery."

"Now what has Belle's embroidery got to do with my name, whoever Belle might be."

"You know, Bellezour Anma, up at the castle?" the man nodded, "Well, I promised her I would get it, because she's in bed with a cold and Persa's got it."

"The cold?" Gilbert teased.

"Don't be mean," Fay instructed, and held out her hand. "It's been nice meeting you properly."

"It has, hasn't it," and Gilbert's eyes twinkled. "I think I'll walk you to Persa's house and on to the castle. You never know, you might run into a strange man and do yourself some damage."

Fay felt very untrusting of him at that moment, and a bit futile, with her hand held out and not taken, so she swallowed whatever nonsense she might have been tempted into saying, put her hand firmly by her side, nodded, and started walking.

Gilbert kept up a lively conversation on anything and everything until they reached Persa's house: Persa wasn't in, but her mother hunted the embroidery up. It was all very quick and quiet. Fay was a bit surprised, because Persa's mother was usually as chatty as her daughter (an inherited trait? Or did they just compete?). Perhaps Gilbert was a sobering influence. She looked surreptitiously at his humorous face, and doubted it.

She couldn't find out if the quietness meant there was something wrong in the household, not with a stranger present, so she asked Mère Doucor to give her love to Persa, and the couple left. As they walked down the steps, Enlai hailed them from next door.

Or rather, he hailed Gilbert, "So you've found her," he said, his tone a bit relieved.

"Found her?" Gilbert sounded confused, to Fay's surprise. He had not struck her as someone easily confused. "Excuse me a moment," said the gentleman at her side, who then crossed the patch of grass to where Enlai stood, arms crossed, leaning on the porch.

They talked very quickly, with eyes flashing towards Fay now and again. Fay was understandably bewildered. She felt like Number One on a Most Wanted list. At the end of it, Gilbert laughed. That was reassuring. He didn't explain anything, however. In fact, he was far less merry for the walk back to the castle, and more of a stranger.

Just before they reached the castle gate, he absented himself with a polite farewell.

Until she reached Belle's chamber, Fay puzzled and worried and tore the whole incident into its commonest parts in her mind. In the end, she decided to accept it as a positive, because Gilbert's manner had been more polite, but still friendly after he spoke to Enlai. Whatever she was or was not did not seem important, next to that.

One thing, however, still fretted the back of her mind. Where did the young man come from? Why was he here? No individual answering to his description should exist in her little world. What was worse, she liked him... and he seemed disturbingly real.

———

*Two days of normal existence. Will I ever survive it? How did I achieve it? What did I do? I presented a paper on behalf of the Department to a community organisation and they had a party in the evening. I caught the last flight home.*

*The party was entertaining. There was a lot of food, and a great number of very sober dignitaries. We sat on school chairs outside, on a very balmy evening. We listened politely to at least fifty percent of the dignitaries make more or less tactful speeches. I'm very accustomed to hearing dignitaries make more or less tactful speeches. But the concert that followed!*

———

*So much for that diary entry. It was a fizzle. I started laughing about that concert and just could not write any more. Not a word. I was so taken with one little child in a choir being off-key and singing stoutly straight into the microphone that I chuckled right off to sleep. No need for dreaming when life is that merry. And that child so bravely off-key. And so sincere. So very sincere.*

*It reminded me a bit about my own tone deafness. It went when I learned the flute. But if I had the courage of that child maybe I could have... Stop laughing, Fay.*

*And now, right now, I just want to think about dreaming. The party got me thinking about it from a new angle. Someone else's dream, someone else's life reaching out to me. It made real life seem like my imaginings, for just a little.*

*I felt alive, and a part of the world. None of this stuff about Gilbert appearing from nowhere. Gee, but he was nice though. He speaks my language. Strange, that. Very rare, even in my imaginary world.*

*Except he isn't quite the sort of man I would design, if I were doing a romantic-type dream. Next time I'm going for big romance. Very traditional. I'm going to meet my Knight in Shining Armour, my Fairy Tale Prince. Muscles and a good singing voice. No snub-nose wonder for me.*

*Why am I in such a hurry to get some romance into my dream life? I didn't care a jot for romance the other day. I'm scared that I'll lose the world I step in just before sleep. I'm scared I'll lose it to the real world. I would dearly love to retain whatever it is in me that keeps me separate, even if it means getting bored to tears every single working day. But I still want that romance. Now.*

———

*It's all very well talking glibly about what I want and what I don't want, but I never seem to feel quite well.*

*My darling mother blames it on my quiet life. She says I need to get out a bit more, meet some men. My brother suggests aerobics. All these suggestions have been repeated twice a week, every week, season in and season out, through the friendly medium of the omnipresent telephone. They have driven my other-world far, far away. Sometimes I want to unplug that telephone. And sometimes I want to throw that telephone at the nearest wall. Since I can't unplug my family.*

*I am hag-ridden and have a chip on my shoulder. My hair is torn out and strewn over the floor and my nails are bitten to the quick. Sack cloth and ashes are my garb. I am not melodramatic. This is pragmatic Fay speaking.*

*Oh, I'm so sick of well-meant advice by relatives: I don't want to go to aerobics; I am not hanging out for a lawyer; and despite all my unhappiness in my present job (so Dad is right – but don't let him know that) I am not hunting for a promotion. I am neither a dilly fluffy female, nor a career woman. I am myself. Vague and dreamy at the best of times – but still myself.*

*Why is everyone so unhappy with me being me? Is it a crime to want to lead a quiet life? Is it a sin not to be ambitious? Is it a catastrophic error not to go out dancing, dressed to kill?*

*Woe is me! My whole family can run my life better than I can. I know, because they tell me so. Incessantly. Well, that was why I left home. Only they've decided to take it up again. For two years they (sort-of, most of the time) left me alone. Now there seems to be a conspiracy. My family is out to get me! No, seriously, when even uncle rings up (uncle never rings, and especially not me) then they must be jointly worried.*

*When I look in my mirror I can't see anything particularly peculiar. I'm not coming out in blue or green stripes. My hair (despite my attempts to pull it out by the roots) is the* same as always, and my eyes haven't changed colour. Now that would be an interesting phenomenon – I want tiger-striped eyes, please.

Why is my superlatively supportive family so worried now, then? I went to the doctor and received my certificate of normalcy. They disbelieved the doctor.

I don't want to go to a psychologist. My mind is as normal as it has ever been (which is to say, not) and I don't feel any more like discussing it than I used to. And though I have always been teased for being a dreamer, it's never caused Uncle Bill to ring me up before. That was the real shocker. Sure, I like him – but as a counsellor?

What is getting into my family? The only one who is still sane is Granny and I can't ask her what beetles have crept into the other's brains, now can I?

Life is tough.

# CHAPTER FOUR

THE COVE WAS THE QUIETEST PLACE ON EARTH. No
telephone. No family.

Only the hush-hush-hushing of the waves and the
cry of the gulls. Only the scribble on the sand drawn by
the feet of birds, and the ripples and sweeps etched by
the ebbing tide. Only the moss and lichen and old
hanging stones of the quiet cave.

Fay sat inside the still cave, away from the summer's
heat for a few minutes. Inside the cave was almost
complete silence. A fragrant mossy nest, like sitting on
a tombstone in winter. Quietude, as well as quiet. Fay
reassured herself that death would be like this – calm,
and pleasant loneliness. No telephones. No family. No
outside world.

After a little, she emerged from the cold into the
blinding sunlight. Fay spread her arms wide to welcome in the warmth of the afternoon. Gradually, her
whole body became somnolent with the heat. She
opened her eyes and squinted at the glittering sea. It
was a choice between swimming and the cool cave.
Fighting the tide reminded her too much of her family.
Why bring them with her into this safe place? Fay

blinked a few times and returned to the quietude she sought.

After the bright sunlight, the cave was too dark. She shut her eyes and counted to a hundred. It was too much effort to re-open the eyes. Two hundred she reached, then three. Finally, relaxed and attuned to the dark silence, she opened her eyes and stepped right in.

There was a dark figure moving in the corner. Fay screamed.

"No," it said, in a deep and familiar voice, "Best not come in here."

"What are you doing here?" Fay cried tearfully. "This is my cove and no-one else can come here."

The man became very still at that. Blending in with the cave. "So you are the witch," he said, placidly.

"I'm no witch," Fay defended, "But, Gilbert, I come here to be alone – you can't be here. Nobody comes here."

"Maybe I'm 'nobody'," he laughed.

"Can't be," said Fay, "Otherwise your name would be Ulysses and I'd know exactly who you were."

"This conversation isn't making any sense," exclaimed the man, and he dragged Fay into the bright sunlight. "It's Fay!" he exclaimed.

"Well, who did you think I was, the Man of la Mancha? The Wicked Witch of the West? Humpty Dumpty?" she asked.

"The Wicked Witch would have been a good bet, according to what I've heard."

"What have you heard?"

"Do you know what happens to people who come here?" Gilbert was tentative.

"Nobody comes here, but me. It's my place. I don't let them," Fay replied, simply.

"Sometimes people come," Gilbert replied grimly, "and they go back changed."

"How changed?" Fay asked, curiously.

That's what I'm here to find out, since--" Gilbert cut himself off abruptly.

"Since what?"

"None of your business," said Gilbert, with his cheekiest smile, his good temper mysteriously restored. "You've answered all my questions and there isn't much mystery left. Which is a relief."

"For you," Fay pointed out, "But not for me. Now I have nowhere safe to go."

"What do you mean?" Gilbert was puzzled.

"This is, I mean was, my special, private place. And now it isn't."

"It can be, you know. I'll make sure no-one ever comes here," Gilbert said, gently.

Fay did not question this statement. It did not, however, cheer her up. "But it was special because no-one had ever been here. Don't you see? Now that I've seen you here, it's different."

"Well, let's make it positively different."

"How?" This was not a question, but Fay's defiant statement of the impossible.

"Since I've ruined your place, I'll atone. I promise that whenever you desperately need help, and you come here, help will be forthcoming."

"How?" This time Fay's question was genuine curiosity.

Gilbert shook his head, the shock of hair flying everywhere. "That's my business," he laughed, "oh Wicked Witch of the West."

"Do you even know anything about the Wicked Witch of the West?" Fay asked.

"Of course I don't," said Gilbert, "or any of the others you mentioned. Tell me about them." His voice was inviting and friendly.

And so Fay sat on the bright sand with Gilbert until

the sun had gone and the moonlight shone gentle on the waves, telling him of Ulysses, and Circe, and the Cyclops and the wanderer's return home to Penelope. She told Gilbert about the Trojan War and the Wizard of Oz, about Lewis Carroll and of the strange, heroic Man of La Mancha. Odd bedfellows they seemed, these characters, but Gilbert was fascinated.

"If you're the Wicked Witch, then I'm Don Quixote," he claimed, when the tales were finished and he lay at Fay's feet, content.

"How come I get the baddie?" Fay asked.

"Well, which would you rather be, bad or stupid?" came the teasing response.

"Well, which do you think I am, greedy or idealistic?"

"A fair question," grinned Gilbert. "I'll have to reserve my position on that."

"Oh, you," Fay snorted, disgusted.

———

Fay decided she couldn't keep quiet. Her odd experience was, to be sure, not something to be shouted to the skies, but still she had to talk it out with someone.

Her family, under the circumstances, was out. In fact, so were most people.

November was not a confiding time of year, Fay admitted to herself, ruefully. So she did the obvious. Fay hurried to her best friend.

———

*Strange, to feel lonely because I've seen Belle, but that's what has happened. She didn't really want to see me, I think.*

*Well, it felt that way. She tweaked her baby and cuddled her baby and fussed over her baby. She said utterly silly things to him and altogether seemed to ignore me and my problems. 'Oh,' she said, 'um and 'aha' and 'is that so', but it felt as if she was humouring me.*

*Fay, be honest with yourself. You cuddled and tweaked the baby and said how beautiful he was, but were you paying any more attention to him than Belle was paying to you?*

*Of course not. The baby was just an accessory to the story, and I'm real. I hadn't even decided what was to become of him.*

*When I went to sleep last night I had almost decided he would die young – maybe at two or three – but that was because Bellezour couldn't care less about my cove being invaded. I felt so bad at thinking I should kill off an infant because I was in a state of pique. Very bad indeed. Serves me right; I should never have had such a thought.*

*And when I tried to find out more about Gilbert, she said that he was a knight. Great lot of use, that statement. I mean, it's pretty obvious that he's a knight. The sword and dagger, for one thing. Dead giveaways. Your local carpenter doesn't carry a whacking great sword everywhere, now does he?*

*Although Gilbert does wear them as if they are not so important. They just sort of hang there. But even out of armour he has a look of battle-preparedness. So I realised he was a knight. I am not that stupid. And I need someone to talk to.*

*Oh Belle, why wouldn't you listen? And why wouldn't you help me?*

*Tonight, I reckon, I need real consolation. If I can't find it through my family and my best friend is no use (and Persa and Enlai and Flor would be terrifically useful for this sort of thing I don't think) then I'm going to fade into a real, old fashioned romance. All rose coloured and glassy. Maybe I don't mean that the way it came out. Rose-coloured and perfumed. No glasses. I have perfect vision. Something about me is perfect, at least.*

*Let's see. Ingredients for romance: castle. No, skip the castle. Belle's has been getting on my nerves. Persa's a ro-*

mantic (sometimes). Where would she set it? Knowing Persa it would be somewhere way out of reach of her parent's destabilising (read normalising) influence.

So, a forest in the woods. Now why doesn't that make sense? Oops, I meant to write 'a cottage in the woods'. Really, it isn't my day. Or my week. Or even my year. I need to go back to childhood and start again. Or I need a romance.

A very English red-tiled, no, a thatched cottage with white wattle-and-daub walls and a vegetable garden and a spinning wheel and a couple of fine-haired goats (sheep are just too dumb) and a nice roaring fire. No, no fire. Too much Gilbert, with a fire. Well, a couple of fruit trees then, and mountains of preserves and pickles all ready for the harsh forest winter.

It's late autumn and the weather is about to change. I've had my once-yearly visit to that hallowed shrine of the local village (ten miles away) and sold my embroidery (see, in this dream I am going to be talented: not myself at all). Why does embroidery appear in my dreams all the time? Maybe I should start collecting it in real life. Or maybe I should just get over it.

Better put a harp in the room as well. All isolated witches (sorry, wise women – I'm too young to be a witch) play harps. And now I am completely and beautifully alone.

A nice stormy night passed and I gave succor to forest creatures. Ah, how charming. A bit too sweet? No, there is a bit of Disney in this one – a snuggly squirrel with splintered leg, I think. Not a biting squirrel, but a nice polite one who has never even heard of rabies. Good.

And when I hunt around to see what else has been hurt by the storm (as well as my vegetable garden, when the wind has kindly harvested all my late lettuces) I come across a knight slain nigh his shield, With a down, derry, derry, derry down down. Oops, wrong image again. Your mind is not its usual self, is it Fay? Well, then, a wounded knight. Horse bolted etc.

*Once I have established what the guy looks like, I'll be all ready for a brand-new dream in an entirely new world. This is not a world where I know anyone. I have been brought up by a wise woman (defunct), and I am mysteriously an or-phan, as all the nicest fairy tales would have it. I have long black hair, not short fuzzy-coloured hair. Well, my hair isn't really the colour of fuzz. It is just that I am in a bit of a mood. I need this romance: it will give me a new mood.*

*The knight can have short hair. Isn't that big of me? No it isn't, because I've changed my mind. I think he'll be a sort of Prince Valiant. Hair just long enough to tie back with a thing when he needs to get it out of the way. Black and wiry – the sort of hair that always looks tidy. In fact, altogether, he's the sort of person who always looks beautifully neat even after storm-tossed branches have ungently removed him from his crazed horse and broken his leg (and, like the squirrel, he is not rabid – oops again, let's not go there).*

*Now I've got a good start to the romance. And he can have a rich tenor voice – and that's the lot.*

*This is the umpteenth time I have created him, and he'd better work. I need that romance tonight. Before I wanted it because imaginings are **au fond** romantic, but now, for some reason, now is different. I need it.*

*So I'll eat dinner and clean the house just to get me in the cottage-y mood, then I'll curl up and dream a bit before I sleep. Nice to have a new dream for a change, even if it's an old-new dream.*

———

*I have a young sister*
*Far over the sea;*
*Three are the things*
*That she sent to me.*

*She sent me a cherry*

59

*Without any stone,*
*She sent me a dove*
*Without even a bone.*
*She said, love your sweetheart without longing.*

*How can a cherry*
*Be without a stone?*
*And how can a dove*
*Be without a bone?*
*And how can I love my sweetheart without longing?*

*When the cherry was in bloom,*
*It had not yet a stone;*
*When the dove was in egg,*
*It had not even a bone.*
*When the maiden hath her sweetheart, there can be*
    *no longing. (Traditional)*

———

Fay's dreaming that night was unexpected in an expected way.

She shied away from the romantic interlude at the last minute, deciding that she only wanted it as revenge on Gilbert. And that revenge was not enough, given her mood. It would not even have been fun to do, since her heart wasn't into falling in love with a stranger in the woods. Not tonight, anyhow. Maybe tomorrow.

Fay decided to investigate Enlai's peculiarities instead. What on earth had he been telling Gilbert, and why?

She remembered the gestures he had made in her direction, and the sharp nod of Gilbert's head in response. *There was something big there*, she thought. *Something that needed sorting.* Something unplanned that needed fixing back into the world she knew and had created.

This investigation didn't exactly get very far, but it made a pleasant evening nonetheless. An evening that behaved – how nice of it. She found Enlai at home for a change. He looked sober, but brightened up when he saw Fay enter.

"I didn't hear the knock on the door," he exclaimed, "What a pleasant surprise."

"Nice of you to be so pleased to see me," commented Fay, wryly, and promptly sat down. Enlai grinned abashedly and admitted that his friends were not speaking to him right now, and that his girlfriend had dropped him entirely.

"So Persa was right, and the two of you are not getting on," Fay commented.

"I get on as well with Persa as I ever did," Enlai said, "Which is to say we squabble all the time."

"You know I didn't mean Persa," sourly answered Fay. She didn't like the nasty tone, so she changed the topic a little. "Are you still making eyes at Persa?" she queried. "She claimed you were, not so long ago."

"Oh that," scoffed Enlai, "That was work."

"Buttering up Persa is work?" asked Fay, her eyes pretend-innocent.

"Oh, you know what I mean," answered Enlai, and that was all she could get out of him.

Desertion by his friends couldn't be complete, for Persa turned up in a short while, cheeky and full of good humour. Enlai and Fay were by this time in the middle of a much-needed deep and meaningful chat about nothing in particular, and had just finished a plate of buttered crumpets.

Enlai frowned when he opened the door, and frowned more deeply when Persa asked, blithely,

"What, none for me? And I gave you a full hour of Fay to yourself, too. Trust me never to be generous again."

She looked across at Fay, "He asked me *specially* if he could see you and under the circumstances, I said I would arrange it the next time you came round. Well, I wasn't home the last time, and Mère is not really up to plotting these days, so delaying coming over was the best I could do," and she cast a baleful glare in Enlai's direction, "And you did not even begin to appreciate my sacrifice AT ALL, which I think is decidedly culpable, since Fay is *my* friend and all you want to see her for is--"

Enlai shushed her. "I only want to get to know you better, Fay," he pleaded. "Truly, there is no ulterior motive."

"Ach," sniffed Persa, "Don't believe him. But I won't give your game away, Enlai, now everyone's deserted you, except me."

"Oh, do be discreet!" cried Enlai, in annoyance. "First you say you'll keep it a secret even from Fay, and now you're about to spill it to the whole world."

"Was not," retorted Persa, inelegantly.

"Was too." Fay entered the argument with her accepted share of the refrain.

Both her friends turned to stare, open-mouthed. Then all three laughed and, obscurely, the conversation turned to riddles. Or maybe not so obscurely.

Riddle games were a favourite with all the younger adults in the village (er, *town*, amended Fay, as she wondered how to get more information out of either friend), especially the old, difficult rhyming riddles. They totally mystified Fay, however. Mostly she left it that way on purpose. It was nice, she told herself, to have one area of total incompetence in a purely artificial world. Saved her from cockiness.

But today she was planning a little quiet revenge.

She knew the riddle Enlai would ask and had decided, just before entering the world, that Persa would not be able to guess it. Persa was to have rescued her if Enlai proved difficult, which he had on occasion. Besides, she was always pleased to see Persa, while she was sometimes not at all pleased to see Enlai. These reactions to her creations were a mystery to Fay and she had given up on it ages ago.

The riddle was lifted from an old folksong, as was Fay's wont. Enlai decided to introduce his riddle with style. He stood up again – having sat down during the squabble with Persa, in order, Fay assumed, to assert his relaxed state in his own home – and he went over to the windowsill, artfully leaning on it. His pose made Fay want to giggle, and incited Persa to say, "Oh, get on with it, otherwise I'll ask first today."

"What kind of bird has no bones? What kind of cherry has no stone? What kind of lover has no yearning?" He asked it, his voice still and distant. His eyes were firmly fixed on the scene outside, as if the riddle game had no meaning. This was Enlai's usual habit during riddling. It was as if he wanted to distance himself from Persa's fury. And today, the sound and the fury were not long coming.

"What kind of riddle is *that*?" she asked, scornfully. "Firstly it's three questions, which is illegal. Secondly, it doesn't rhyme, which is illogical."

"And thirdly, it is easy enough to answer, which is irrational," completed Fay. For the second time in an hour she was faced with the ungracefully dropped jaws of friends. The submerged giggle of moments before emerged joyously, as an infectious chuckle.

Not so infectious that Enlai didn't ask, his face wreathed with a most reluctant smile, "Well, what is the answer then?"

"Answers," said Fay, "Persa's right. It's three questions, not one."

"All right then, answers," amended Enlai, irritably, "And I'm still waiting to hear them."

Fay impudently walked over to the window and posed herself on the opposite side to Enlai, artfully staring into the distance.

"Go for it, Fay," barracked Persa, her one-girl fan club.

Fay spoke in a manner that she hoped was as dreamily distant as Enlai's own. She was too busy trying to suppress her laughter, however, and her voice came out breathless and a little croaky. Enlai was still not amused. "When a bird is in the egg, it has no bone. When a cherry is in flower, it has no stone. And when a maiden has her lover, then there can be no longing."

The wind was the only voice that whispered through the room. Fay smiled sweetly into the stunned silence. Revenge was a most wonderful thing. As she made her departure, the word 'revenge' resonated in her mind. But as she found herself in a warm bed shortly after, it was the last answer she had given that stuck in her mind.

"When a maiden has her lover, then there can be no longing."

---

*I get awfully tangled sometimes, but at least it means I'm in control. It is not "I think therefore I am", it is "I am tangled therefore I am in control." That is me, Fay. My motto.*

*I was looking through some university textbooks to throw them out and discovered that my whole riddle scene was based on the wrong riddle.*

*I had been thinking about that European balalaika song, where a boy asks a girl the questions and she calls him an* idiot and answers him. I wanted to call Enlai an idiot and have now missed my big opportunity. Because the riddle I used isn't that at all. I can't for the life of me remember the questions in the riddle scene in the song, so I guess I replaced them in my mind with one I did remember.

It proves that Enlai and Persa are figments of my imagination, if we make the same mistakes. What a relief!

Anyway, for the record (just to make sure I don't get confused again – the source turned out to be in those lecture notes – so I am deconfusing, which is a shame) the riddle sequence comes from an old poem that begins (although not in my impossible modern English) "I have a young sister, far o'er the sea, and three be the things that she gave unto me." So all that is clear.

I can go to work tomorrow with a mind as pure as driven snow. It means going to work. I should not even get into such thoughts so early in the morning. I should just pick myself up and go. This whole last hour I've done nothing but put off going to work. Perish the thought.

Well, virtue is its own reward and all that. And besides, I have a certain amount of boring paper to shuffle around my desk before I get to go home. Sooner I get there, sooner I get back. And tonight I have a dinner guest. Shh, don't tell anyone, but it's Fred.

I'd better cook something halfway decent, I suppose. None of my usual rubbish. Pity. I have always wanted to serve instant noodles at a dinner party.

He's not coming till eight, so I have lots of time. I'll pick up some fresh bread and salad veggies on the way home from work. Summer is such an advantage. You can feed someone delicious food with next to no work.

Should I try to find out the real words of the riddle? No, I'm too lazy. Besides, it's probably boring. And there are a lot more songs and things rattling through my brain, ready to dream about – why add to the number?

*Ave        Caesar,        we-who-are-about-to-go-to-work salute you.*

---

*I don't like babysitting*
*During the Bon festival*
*The snow is falling*
*And the baby is crying*

*Even if the Bon comes*
*I can't be happy*
*I can see lights of my parent's house*
*Twinkling in the distance*

*I want to go home at once*
*To my parents*
*I can see the lights of my parents' house*
*Twinkling in the distance (Traditional, Japan)*

---

Old English sayings were going through one of those annoying stages where, whatever one did, they haunted, Fay pondered. She had done the unexpected and turned up at the green without a plot in sight. Not a thought to rattle about in that great brain space, much less a whole sequence of them. It was time, she thought, to take life as it came... in a controlled way.

Practically speaking, this meant wandering around the town common, seeing what there was to see. There was not a great deal to see, and nothing to hear. The snow was too thick. It blanketed everything past twenty yards: visibility was gracefully low.

For the occasion, the anti-fur Fay, who spent her waking life telling people that killing animals for luxury clothing was immoral, had a beautiful white (fur) coat, that snuggled around her in satisfying warmth. It was heavy, and soft, and the snow seemed to slide off. For a moment, Fay imagined whimsical snowflakes settling on her hood, shouting "Yippee!", waving their hands, and taking off down the slope of her back and arms.

She was almost convinced that she was a human slippery-slide for uncontrollable (and cheeky) snowflakes, when the sombre mood of the day caught up with her in the form of the gallows tree and an old English poem. Old English was quite obviously invading her week. In this case, not for the better.

The rascal who had stolen the fish that time when she was paddling her feet in the pond had played one too many tricks. He was hanging from the gallows tree. The cold blanketed scent and the body dangled. Not pleasant. Not what Fay had expected to see. After first identifying the corpse, Fay did not let her gaze focus. This prince who was governing in Bellezour's husband's stead was obviously harsh. The dangling body made her feel very sick. Fay found it impossible to turn away, however, and she was forced to find some words to break the horrid spell the corpse had placed on her. More ancient English found its way to her brain.

"Foweles in the frith," she chanted, as if it were a life-saving formula, "Foweles in the frith, the fisses in the flod and I mon waxe wod. Mulch sorw I walk with, for best of bone and blod." She didn't know about pronunciation. It was enough that it was words, and that they were there to hand.

It half-worked. She was able to move back a step. To help disassociate further from the grisly sight, Fay tried calling up the meaning of the words. This took her mind back to those university textbooks she had not looked at in years. "Birds in the forest, fishes in the sea, and I must unhappy be. I walk in sorrow for all mankind." A bit on the Christian side, but then, someone had tried to convert her in the shopping centre the day before, so a bit of Christianity seemed not inappropriate.

A spell to break a spell. Something she couldn't quite believe in to distance herself from something she couldn't help detesting.

Fay gave a huge sigh of release and turned her back on the tree and its fence of palings. She walked right into Gilbert. "What are you doing here?" she asked, crossly, her beautiful, sorrowful mood entirely broken. This was not the kind of surprise she had expected either.

"I saw you from a distance and decided to find out where you had been all these months."

"None of your business," answered Fay, irritably.

"On the contrary, it is my business," Gilbert answered smoothly.

"Why?" asked Fay, and then quickly added, "No, don't tell me. I'm not at all sure I want to hear the answer."

Gilbert took her arm and drew her inexorably to the inn. Fay allowed herself to be taken surprisingly meekly, her bad temper disappearing as quickly as it had come.

"What did *he* do?" she asked, gesticulating back at the tree.

"It's rude to point with your thumb," Gilbert commented, sagely.

"I know," and Fay grinned, "It's also rude to bump into women in the dark and drag them off to strange destinations, so we're even."

"I'd hardly call the inn a strange destination," came the mild answer, as Gilbert opened the door and ushered her inside. When they were settled in a very quiet corner of the warm room, furs dumped on a neighbouring table and a glass of wine in front of each of them, Gilbert explained the body. "The Prince caught the man poaching," he said briefly.

"I thought the Prince had the reputation of being a fair man." Any chance to complain about killing people. Especially for minor crimes. God, she hated punitive societies! Just as much as she hated fur coats. Fay looked across at the one she had been wearing and wondered at herself briefly.

Gilbert grinned, "Well, the poaching was an excuse. He had done, er, other things, which are better not discussed."

Gilbert seemed a bit embarrassed and Fay pressed for an explanation. Gilbert was very diffident, and Fay had to pin him down with unaccustomed force. Even for such a slippery personality, Gilbert seemed somewhat shy of discussing the matter in detail. Finally, Curious Fay extracted a reply. "Sorcery," was the reluctant admission. "The King's men have been on the watch for months now, because of, well, evil happenings. Which I will not tell you about, so stop bothering me." The strength of this last sentence struck Fay because everything else Gilbert had said had been quiet, as if he was scared of being overheard.

"Sorcery," Fay wondered.

Gilbert lowered his voice again, "There is still a great deal of evil around, so I expect more hangings this next year."

"On spurious pretexts," asked Fay, nastily. She believed in the rule of justice and did not believe in sorcery. She did believe in poaching. And it should not be a hanging offence. She glared at Gilbert.

"If necessary," Gilbert said, stiffly.

Fay found it hard to associate the drunken rogue who had run off with a fish with such evil as Gilbert obviously had in mind. She didn't believe he was being stiff about anything minor either. But to her sorcery was the stuff of dreams and novels, and had nothing to do with hanging people, though. A confusion.

She sighed – her second of the day. This sigh was in exasperation and a little bit in distrust. It disturbed her that Gilbert could so easily accept the Prince's decision. But he was so reluctant to discuss it that she was loath to press the matter further. She couldn't resist one final impudent question, however, "So why did you tell me? Why didn't you lie glibly?" then she added, as an afterthought, because she was really uncomfortable about the whole thing, "You're very good at lying glibly, you know."

To her surprise, Gilbert did not laugh. Instead, he looked at her seriously. "I thought you had to know," he said, soberly, "under the circumstances."

Under what circumstances? Fay was desperately curious, but could get no more information from the knight. This serious and silent and even sad side of him was entirely new, as was the irrational belief in sorcery.

Fay began to be intrigued by the man all over again as they sat and talked, and talked, and talked. It was all deep and meaningful (even if certain words did not emerge from the morass of thoughts – sorcery was silent, and so was poaching and so were words like gallows and punishment), and was only disturbed when Persa plonked down to join them. She made a mocking bow to Gilbert from her seated position as if to say she would have curtseyed only it was too cold and she was too lazy.

Persa launched straight into her subject matter.

Fay wondered at it. Even Persa was almost serious today. What had got into her little world? Maybe Fay had come with the underlying expectation of a lot of misery. That would certainly provide an explanation for the unaccustomed sobriety.

Persa wanted Fay's help. Fay started to focus on what her friend was saying. Help was something that she could focus on. Deep and meaningful talk came from a different part of the brain to frivol however, so focussing took a bit of work.

"It's a crime what Alberc is doing," she said, indignantly, "Just because Belle isn't there to baby-sit the children of his houseguests does not at all excuse what he is doing, and what he did during the mid-winter festival."

Fay admitted to confusion, and even Gilbert admitted ignorance, although he looked intrigued. For a moment Persa looked a little frightened, as if Gilbert's interest were to be avoided or she had just taken a dangerous step, but her normal assertiveness quickly bounced back and she told her little tale with the maximum of drama and colour.

It appeared that Alberc had encouraged a great many people to visit since Belle had left. He was shoring up his position as a most important local man, especially since Belle's move to the castle had not resulted in the expected kudos. When Fay asked, naively, 'why not', Persa exclaimed that she should know, since it was her fault. Since the two had become friends, Bellezour had taken to thinking for herself and become independent. The Lord Mayor did not get a look-in at the castle or in castle affairs.

"It's like what's happened to you," inserted Fay, slyly, "Since knowing me you have become cheeky and mischievous and no respecter of persons."

"Hear, hear," said Gilbert feelingly.

Persa blushed (Fay was most astounded at this – had not known Persa was capable of the thing) but asserted boldly, "No, I've always been like this. Only now I play

71

on a bigger stage." Her audience laughed, and Persa went on with her scarce-touched tale.

With his eldest out of the house and into the nobility, Alberc's sense of dignity and self-worth had risen. Not that it was low to begin with. But now he had decided not to let his younger children do the menial work he had expected of his wife and of Belle as a matter of course. So he "called in a few favours", because only his wife and Belle had been able to eliminate the stinginess from his magnificent soul.

Even those two had only been able to make him unmiserly on some fronts. There remained a core of it deep within. A core the town had not known about. Generous in everything except money, was the town's verdict on their mayor. Only now his generosity was being called in as favours. Some women helped with housework, some men did standard upkeep. No-one had been asked to do much and no-one was really worried about it. Indeed, it had been the cause of many pleasantries in the town and the town easily forgave that which kept it amused.

"Oh, that explains why you weren't slaughtered ages ago," commented Fay. Persa turned up her nose haughtily and continued with her tale.

Despite herself, Fay turned dreamy. She tried to upbraid herself – a dream within a dream was not a good thing – but it was no use. Too much warmth and mulled wine. Sweet, dreamy Fay took over and banished to a far, far distant place the practical, important young lady Persa had sought.

Gilbert on the other hand, began to look wider and wider awake. He did not look precisely angry, but would be if it were within him to be so. He was full of unleashed activity. With effort, Fay dragged herself back to the tale, and away from Gilbert's intense concentration. This was very difficult, somehow, for

Gilbert's face seemed so much more alive than Persa's story.

The tale was a sad one, and Fay soon felt guilty over her teasing and not paying attention. Alberc had taken in a young girl – just a child – to do all the daily duties. She was the daughter of farmers who had lost all their money in the drought, three years before, and owed their survival to the mayor. Now he had taken her, in grand feudal style, as a servant, almost as a serf.

Persa had visited the mayor. The mayor's house was open to certain key dignitaries and he had several overnight visitors, as had become his custom. So she had decided she was a dignitary and had gone visiting without an invitation. Fay found it fascinating that Persa thought this kind of behaviour a positive trait. She couldn't imagine herself walking into Alberc's house on a festival just to see what was going on.

It was traditional for live-in servants to be allowed to go home at Midwinter, for it was a family time. Bellezour Anma did not visit her father, however, since castle duties were pressing, and so her father refused to allow the child to visit her parents. What he lacked in compassion, he made up for in pettiness.

Persa had discovered the child in the attic, rocking a lavish cradle in which the son of a guest was housed. The attic was plainly furnished, with the cradle being the only artisan-crafted item in sight, and the cradle furnishings being more luxurious than anything else in the room. The room was quite obviously serving as the whole living quarters for the young girl.

She was rocking the cradle back and forth, back and forth, back and forth, back and forth. Her eyes were focused on the twinkling lights of the town beneath. The cradle rocked back and forth, back and forth. Tears leaked from her eyes and she was singing the baby to sleep with an old, old lament. When Persa asked what was wrong, and took her on her knee (for the two were friends) young Fontaus burst into tears.

It was Midwinter and she was not home. It was Midwinter and she had nothing to wear to celebrate. It was Midwinter and there was no feast. It was Midwinter and all she could do was rock the cradle back and forth, back and forth, back and forth. All she could do was rock the cradle back and forth, and stare at the lights below. She looked at the light of her parent's house, flickering in the distance.

"What can I do?" asked Fay, gently, "Do you want me to talk to Belle about it?"

"No need," said Gilbert, briskly, "This is my affair." He left the two women to the dregs of the mulled ale and Fay with her astonishment. She joked to herself that she should nurse the astonishment along with the mulled ale as she rose to follow Gilbert. Persa stopped her.

"He can do better by himself," she said.

"Why?" asked Fay, blankly. "I don't understand. Was I just an excuse?"

Persa nodded, a tear glinting in her eyes. "Can't we just sit here until he comes back," she pleaded. "Buy me some ale for Midwinter."

"I've got no money," stated Fay, glumly.

Suddenly a merry laugh rang out, and Persa was herself. "No money," she scolded, "How typical. How very typical." Persa bought them both drinks and supper, and they sat in the warm inn. One thing suddenly occurred to Fay as she poked at the food in front of her.

"Why is the inn open, if it's Midwinter?" she asked.

"Orders of the Prince," said Persa. "That's why I looked for you here. He said that a town this size should have somewhere where people can go if they need to get out. Belle is away, so he said the inn would do. He's paying well, so my cousin doesn't mind."

Her cousin, of course. That was the real reason Persa knew Fay was at the inn. Persa would make a very good head of a secret service, Fay reflected. She investigated everything and she knew everyone. Or was related to everyone. Sometimes she even knew the people she was related to.

Belle and presumably the Prince were therefore away this Midwinter. And Belle's father had taken to power very strongly indeed. She wondered what Gilbert would do to restore him to sanity. Something drastic, she hoped, and grinned, even though she knew she would never have the courage to ask that question. Not with the look on Gilbert's face as he walked out the door.

*I've discovered Gilbert's strange side tonight,* Fay thought disconsolately. *There's a part of him that's firmly hidden behind steel doors – permanently under lock and key.* She wasn't sure she liked it. Mind you, today there were many things she was not sure she could like.

She hid all this from Persa though, and matched her drink for drink. Especially since Persa was paying and, Fay decided, for no good reason, really, that Persa owed her, big time.

When Gilbert came back, all three made merry along with the innkeeper. Despite the prince's best wishes, the inn emptied after midnight, and the four had a roistering Midwinter.

And Fay woke warm in her own bed, as usual. Only this time it was to the warmth of the Australian summer, and she immediately longed for the aching cold of her imaginary world. Mulled ale was, perhaps, addictive.

# CHAPTER FIVE

*WAS IT A DATE? OR WAS IT A VISIT TO THE DAM? OR A DAM date?*

*It was a nice dam. I can't think when I was there last. I spent ages sitting on the banks and looking at mossy rocks. It was almost as good as dreaming. Almost.*

*Except that I didn't know what I was doing there with Fred. Fred. Of all people. Why did I go down to the woods with Fred? I went down to the woods today and I did not go alone. I went with Fred. It sounds so funny. He even looks a little like a teddy bear sometimes. Just a little. But really, it wasn't teddy bears. And not more exciting activities either. Just the woods and Fred.*

*Well, we did pick berries. But Fred's a wimp. We stopped at the first sign of blood. His blood, anyway. Blackberries can be a bloody business. I fell in a hole and damaged myself quite badly, but I didn't make nearly the fuss Fred made about a tiny tear from a blackberry thorn. Next year we should maybe think of blueberries. That is, if there is a next year. Fred and I ate our twenty berries and sat by the bank, half-dreaming.*

*Can half-dreaming with Fred add up to real dreaming with Gilbert?*

*Why haven't I dreamed in so long? More to the point,*

why haven't I even needed to dream? I haven't even missed it; well, not much. I like the thought of having a fantasy world, but I don't feel the need to be in it. That's maybe what it is.

Things have been busy, I guess, and, dare I say it, possibly happy. I am not quite sure about the happiness bit. I am not unhappy, anyway. That is a big improvement. And I am not too bored, either.

Finally I've been given some responsibility at work, and, though it's frustrating, it's also challenging. The new boss expects more from me and although most of the 'more' is irrational (like his personality), I seem to spend a great deal of my free time thinking it out. Which is a good thing. Thinking is always good, isn't it?

Even at home, I sit in front of the TV and think about how to deal with things and plan my day to fit everything in. I don't want to have to take papers home, so I take my thoughts home. Totally irrational, but there it is.

My boss's irrationality is catching, I do believe. Should I go to a doctor and get it diagnosed?

Anyway, suddenly it is autumn and I get this giant yearning. What are they doing in that world of mine? Things were starting to take on a life of their own last time I was there. Which was a fair whack of a while ago, now I think about it.

It started when Belle moved to the castle. I mean, the fantasy world developing some of its own appurtenances. Nice word, appurtenances.

Anyway, Persa has more to her – still silly, but there's a brain behind the silliness. I bet she was as surprised by this as I am. She had a reputation as the town twerp, and now she is growing out of it. I like her more now.

Enlai does things with no explanation whatsoever (except he still seems to think he is special, in an 'I need more' kind of a way). He likes secrets. But then, he always did. I designed him as a little secretive, perhaps. So he may not be really changing. Not the way the others are.

*Flor has faded from view. I need to work that one out. Why did she fade from view? Does she not like me? Does she have private problems? We were such good friends for a while there. Not as close and me and Belle, but we still had some pleasant times.*

*My seal friend has been dead fifty years. No, I don't want to think about that one. I just don't. That is no-go area. Destruction zone.*

*And Gilbert has appeared, all by himself, out of nowhere. One day I guess I will sort that. Or maybe I will leave it a mystery. Maybe he came in because I needed a mystery. Though it is a mystery why I should have a mystery that looks like a snub-nosed soldier (sounds like a variety of wombat)! Maybe Gilbert really lives down a very deep hole and that is why I didn't see him till recently. It is beyond me. But then, lots of things are beyond me, so this is not surprising.*

*My friends are changing and so is my friendship circle. Maybe it's the Prince. I'll just have to meet him one day. No, I won't. I do not want to meet him. Not ever.*

*I guess I'm scared. Don't be stupid, Fay. How can you be scared of an invention in your own imagination? I dunno, but I am. Partly it's Gilbert's fault. Illogic upon illogic here – you're blaming one imaginary figure for you being scared of another one and doing it in the third person in order to distance yourself from it.*

*But it's true. Ever since Gilbert said that thing about sorcerers and hinted that I might be considered to be one, I've been a bit, well, a bit concerned. Even, let me admit it, a bit scared of Gilbert. He's an immensely nice man, but that sudden shaking off of silliness as if it were a cloak, as if authority were natural to him, it worried me. I've never known anyone like that, ever.*

*How could I possibly have imagined it? I know I did, but still. Those locked rooms in his mind were not my imagination. Not. Not. Not.*

*Two months ago I dreamed a horrid little dream, prob-*

*ably based upon whatever mood I was in that day, then I forget about it, nicely and simply. A natural thing to do, with something as petty as day dreaming. And then today it comes rushing back as if I dreamed it last night, or read it in a novel, or as if someone was calling me. Yes, that's what it feels like. A distant beckoning. I like that phrase 'a distant beckoning': it sounds poetic.*

*All it means is that I was too tired to go to work today, and slipped into that slightly unreal state you sometimes get from pain relievers (headaches, my friend, are headaches and must be cured if they cannot be endured). Even as I worked, my eyes would half-close and, in an instant, away from the slope of the desk, and from the papers scattered in the slope, in a mere instant I saw an array of things.*

*Most of the dreams fled the moment I started awake, properly. I was positive I had fallen asleep, and looked to see if:*

*a) anyone had noticed, and*
*b) I had been asleep long.*

*To my surprise not even a minute had passed (very proud of my deductive processes here).*

*All I am left with now is the memory of someone letting a bright, warm-coloured bird out of its cage. It was a very important image. The bird was reluctant and had no wish to go. Maybe the world was too big and too unpredictable a place. I don't know.*

*But I remember my heart lifting with the bird's as it left the cage and flew into the sky. And my heart sang with the man's (though I don't know how I know he was male, for all I remember is the hand on the cage door) as the bird found freedom. Security may be a green cloak, but happiness is that man's hand on the open cage door.*

*I wish I had something to link these images to. I feel dislocated, I think, when stray images float in my mind, laden* with meaning. I am a Miro painting and what I really want is to be a human being. Frankly, I'm not sure I know how to be a human being. I am not certain I know how to be a Miro painting, either. But I can live with not knowing how to be a painting. I am not sure I can live with not knowing how to be human.

Maybe midnight is not a good time to start. But then again, maybe it's as good a time as any.

How to be a human being? Lesson One – stop dreaming.

No, I can't do that. Or rather, I can't do it intentionally. These last two months were okay because it came naturally, but dreaming is important to me as an 'in case'. I need my emergency people. I need my friends. There is no-one in my real world as rich, as complex or as caring as Belle, nor as funny and embarrassing as Persa, or as must-know-everything and confused as Enlai. Gilbert I don't know about. I like him a lot, I think, and I'm scared of him, too. How did he get there? He's a little bit of reality haunting my dream. I'm not a big one for reality.

Is that why lesson two – go out more – never really eventuates? I get one or two dates, but the sort of male that is interested in me is the sort who misreads me badly. What they read me as, I don't know, but it has nothing to do with who I am.

Apart from being a dreamer, who am I? Am I anyone, if not a dreamer?

Fay, child, this is altogether too difficult and theoretical for this time of night. Maybe you should go and dream, and in dreaming find out how to be human.

But what if it's dreaming that sets me up as distant from reality? I've certainly been more in touch this past little while, without any dreams whatsoever. But now a wistful yearning has come over me. I feel like Keats gone wrong. The nightingale ought to be singing me Lethe-wards, but somehow I come too late, and all that surrounds me is dusk.

Oh, what a strange mood I am in today (tonight, rather).

*I think I'm overtired and my brain is o'erwrought. Too much pseudo-poetry. I wonder if the caged bird is from poetry? I can't remember. I guess it doesn't matter. Maybe I'd better put my o'erwrought brain to bed. Sleep might dispel daydreams and bring back some common sense. That is to say, if I ever had any.*

———

Fay had a strange dream that night. She had gone to bed, half intending to visit the fantasy world. Instead she had drifted into what could only have been a nightmare. It had all the sharpness of reality, and all the pain.

She was floating above her little world. Her floating self wafted from the castle down the route her eyes had followed when she visited Belle. She drifted over the common, and past the gallows tree. Fay saw a decaying body hanging from the tree. For one instant, a foul stench reached her, then it was gone.

The dream lost all scent. With that loss a little of that twisted reality wisped away. Fay floated above the common and almost enjoyed it. As she passed over the corpse she felt a chill wind and a stabbing in her left temple. Fay drifted past the tree, still high above it but descending as she floated. The cold bit more deeply and she swivelled, unable to take her eyes off the gruesome thing creaking in the wind. It glowed death-green before the whole scene flickered and disappeared.

She was back in her bed, cold as ice. Fay's vision was blurred with pain. And in the very back of her mind's eye she saw Enlai's face, warped in laughter.

# CHAPTER SIX

NOTHING. NOTHING. NOTHING. NOTHING. NOTHING.

If I say it often enough, it might go away. I might be able to get rid of that strange thing that has developed at work. I might get back to the safety of my dream-world. It's midwinter and I haven't dreamed properly since summer. I've been too ill, physically and emotionally.

Old and tattered, that's me. That's not the trouble. I can cope with illness. I can deal perfectly well with being bed-ridden. What I can't deal with is Enlai's eyes looking out from my boss's face, peeking and prying into my everyday world. It makes me feel sick inside. That's why I haven't dreamed for months. How could I dream, when the dream faces me at work?

I'm scared of what I'll find. Enlai Devers is imaginary. There is no link between one world and another - save in my mind. Enlai Devers is imaginary. I had a nightmare about my dream-world just that once. Everything else is not real. Not even the nightmare is real. Enlai Devers is imaginary.

There is nothing. Nothing. Nothing. Nothing.

And I am going to get better. I am going to get so well I won't collapse in bed after work with nervous headaches, and I'll have dreams and not nightmares, and I'll remember what *that blasted green coat was for and who opened that damn-fool cage and let the bird out.*

*And I'll feel happy inside. I've almost forgotten what it's like to feel happy inside. Most extraordinary. I would have said I was a bored person, not an unhappy one. Fay dear, be courageous. What me? Brave? How? Why?*

*Enlai Devers is imaginary.*

*Okay – I will. Be courageous. Tonight I'll dream Belle again. She cured a cold once in a dream, maybe she can cure an Enlai nightmare. Or the fact that I am being haunted in a different way by another man.*

*What is it with the men in my life? Even the men in my dream life? Belle will know. No, I won't ask her yet. I'll just visit her. I'll get back into this dreaming-thing slowly, you know. It's like having a drug – you've got to accustom yourself.*

———

Enlai. That's who Fay decided to see in the end. Enlai-Devers-the-imaginary. She wanted to get to the bottom of his strange attitudes, but not to the bottom of his connection with her boss. Nor the feeling that he was behind that dream. She didn't want to look into his eyes.

It was always 'that' dream in her mind. She firmly disassociated it with anything else to do with her little world. Because of this she found herself denying the sense of reality that had crept into the world, the fact that she could touch things and hear things and feel things rather than just picture them in her mind's eye. Because if the world was real, then that dream was real.

She dismissed all thoughts. All thoughts. Well, all conscious thoughts.

This was not a day for deep delvings. It was to be Fay-the-detective at work. Before she went to bed, in fact, throughout the early part of the evening, she tried to work out what sort of detective she wanted to be. Fay at first had giant visages of herself as an opium-smoking violin player, or as a trench-coated begunned and behatted American. Neither, somehow, fitted the inner image of herself. She tried to make her profile look like Basil Rathbone's or to look tough and seedy. No go. Miss Marple? But what does Miss Marple look like? Fay could not for the life of her remember. Wizened and intelligent? Shrivelled and curious? Fat and prying? None of them fitted. Maybe she was elegant and petite and dainty. Nope. Not that either.

But Fay was determined she would have a costume. She would not be disguised, but she would be appropriately in character. Only... only the appropriate character eluded her, somehow. A TV detective? Impossible. Fay grinned at her own snobbishness as she heard herself think that she would not descend so low.

Then she had a brainwave. She would dress as a particular type of person, the sort everyone expected to ask questions. A real, everyday life detective – a person who adores finding out about things and retailing them to others. Slowly she pieced together the sort of person she was thinking about. A robust, rotund, larger-than-life lady with a big smile, gaudy clothes and a secret heart. For a moment Fay was tempted to introduce this woman into her world as a new character. She would be very satisfying, came the thought. Alas, this thought was swiftly followed by the feeling that, although Fay wanted to ape this woman's clothes, she had no wish to meet her.

The large lady was given no name, and so was barred from the gates of heaven.

The last thing Fay did before bed was the dishes (getting a bit slack on the housework, was our Fay) and she used that peaceful time to put together a motley outfit in her mind. Washing dishes was very good for that sort of thinking.

Ugg boots. Dark skirt with bands of bright colours. A patchwork (lurid) jacket and sheepskin (tattered) coat. Four scarves, two of which were knitted (badly), one of which was long enough to trail along the ground (and slightly muddy). A beanie with Collingwood colours (boo, hiss). Perfect outfit for a perfectly inquisitive investigator. And very appropriate that she had no taste in football teams. Fay wondered why the sudden passion about football. All these emotions were stirring and they didn't even belong to her. Enlai-the-imaginary again?

And she went to sleep. Placidly, peacefully, like a child, Fay went to sleep. She had spent so much time preparing her scenario and waiting to see Enlai Devers and find out what made his mercurial character tick that she had tired herself out.

Fay laughed at herself the next morning, but treasured the thought of her glamorous investigatory outfit. When she did get back to her dream world (one of these days, she promised) the great detective would strike. Fay imagined herself as a cobra gently swaying back and forth, tongue viciously flickering. Her imagination was in good order. But not quite good enough.

Six months was the delay before she went back to her little world. Six months without dreaming. At the end of that time, Fay looked back and marvelled. How could she have survived so very long? To her total intrigue, it seemed like a kind of upside down miracle, as if the real world were asserting itself.

She had a sweet-sour relationship with Fred in that time. It was a bit problematic at first (and currently, but Fay would not go so far as to admit that) because she kept comparing Fred with Gilbert. Fred was much better looking and was, after all, almost her boyfriend, while Gilbert was merely a clownish dream acquaintance who joked easily, gave a good massage and occasionally surprised her with a show of authority. Gilbert kept intruding. Fred's slightly pigeon-toed pace wasn't as neat as Gilbert's tidy footsteps. Fred's perfect hair wasn't tousled enough.

This is what drove Fay away from the real world again, in late, bitter winter. Work was unpredictable and less dull, but her heart was not in it. Home was solitary, again. And the dream world had asserted itself, even in the midst of a developing relationship. It annoyed and irritated her.

When she went shopping, Enlai's face would look back, half a shadow in a shop window. When she went walking, his languorous pose would flicker in the corner of her eye, threatening as a dragon wing. But when she went to hold Fred's hand she would find herself drawing back, because Fred's hand was smaller and cooler than Gilbert's.

She refused to take the irritation out on Gilbert, despite the fact that it was his unwarranted emotional intrusion into her mind that was breaking up a perfectly good relationship with – admittedly somewhat wimpish – Fred. So Fay justified to herself in a fit of melodrama. Gilbert haunted her, and she had to blame someone. Enlai kept on appearing in windows and in the shadows of others' eyes, and Fay had to do something acute.

Talking to Mr. Eyes-in-Windows seemed like a good idea, as did putting on her investigatory outfit and getting to the bottom of things. This time she would simply knock on his door and ask some questions. Questions from friend to friend. And if he didn't answer, she would strangle him with one of those scarves. A friendly strangulation to match the friendly haunting he had been giving her. She was very pleased with her logic, and even more pleased when she found herself outside Enlai's door.

She knocked, but no-one answered. She turned round and looked down the street. She saw the flicker of a shadow turn the corner and she ran to chase it. Panting, she just missed it as it turned another corner. It was Enlai, but he was moving far too quickly to catch up. So no simple questions and answers this time. *He must be imaginary*, she thought, *like dragons*, and kept walking. Well, he was behaving like a dragon-shadow, at any rate.

She saw a group of dancers, and stopped to admire their sheer vigour. No sticks in this group, just ker-chiefs and bells. *It isn't bells on her fingers and bells on her toes*, thought Fay, *It's bells round their ankles*. Flor was there, but was too focussed on the dance to notice Fay. Either that or she was studiously ignoring her. Flor looked fragile in amongst the hefty men, but it was Fay who felt fragile watching. They had exchanged the ker-chiefs for sticks. The thump hurt her brain. She gave it all up as a bad job and let herself fall asleep.

————

There was one good side effect of her visit to the dream-world: Enlai appearing in the faces of others and in mirrors and in windows didn't bother her as much as it had. She was growing accustomed to his face. His face in windows, his eyes behind the eyes of others. If he was watching her, it was not crucial. It was a part of the background to her life. No more real than skiing snowflakes.

She put on her detective costume another time, however, to banish the need for it. Not that she really meant to dream. Not really. She wasn't even in bed. What she did was walk to a winter party, rugged up in a bright skirt, moon boots (sheepskin she just did not possess), a (tattered) sheepskin coat, four scarves and a beanie. An utterly foul outfit, she thought, satisfied.

———

*Well, it's a nice night for a walk. The moon is big and thunderous. Not that it looks threatening, but in autumn it often betokens a storm. It ought to betoken a storm, anyway, if I somewhat associate it with autumn rains. The heavy blowy sort that leave you fidgety and the world oh-so-clean. A cheese-gold moon, low in the sky, and so big you could eat your dinner from it.*

*God, I'm tired. Not sleeping tired, or even sitting down tired, but tired in the soul. I guess it's a sort of self-victimisation that makes me want to see Enlai tonight.*

*I guess I'm going to dream, although I'm still half-reluctant to do so. There are heaps of reasons why I would rather think of dreaming than actually do it. I don't want to run into Gilbert while I'm still seeing Fred, for one thing. It would make my dream-world less than sparkling.*

*Why do I keep thinking about Gilbert, I guess is the big sixty-four dollar question. Well, I do, and I don't want to spoil the only incipient serious relationship I have had in ages because I can't get my dream life under control. And I hardly know him, anyway, I just covet him. So there.*

*It sounds as if I'm scolding someone, when I don't really feel that strongly about it, only a little reluctant. I don't want to see Belle, because she's about to be absolutely miserable and it's all my fault. I guess I didn't think of her as a real person when I made up that particular narrative, and now it has to run its course whether I like it or not. I've caused her so very much unhappiness already. I'm not nice. Not nice at all.*

*And Enlai? I thought I wanted to sort him out, until this very second. He is my friend in one of my dream-worlds. My most important dream-world. I don't know how, but he has somehow changed. He's different in the dream-world and he's here, somehow, in the real world. Not fully here. Not walking along the street. Not buying me coffee. Just an echo and I kind of ignored it. And now I see him again and, this instant, my feet firmly clumping on the pavement, I find I can't ignore it any more.*

*The trouble now is quite simple. I thought I saw him in the eyes of my boss, peering out. And I saw his face reflected in shop windows, but when I turned around no-one was there. The first gave me quite a shock, but a minor one. After all, I have to get dreams from somewhere.*

*Only. Only. The longer I think about it, and those shop windows, the more it worries me. Something is wrong, and I can't quite see it.*

*Ah well, it's not as if I can't start a new world from scratch tomorrow, if I wanted to. Dragons. I haven't had a dragon-ish world for so long. Red deserts and vast horizons.*

# CHAPTER SEVEN

HARSH COPPER SAND. THE SUN A RUST-RED GLARE. THE sky cruel-bright. The shadow of a dragon on the sand, flitting and shifting as it flew away from her.

Fay looked down at the Martian soil and into her own shadow. It was the only cool place on the landscape, now that the dragon-dark had flitted away. And in her shadow her eyes found a little green, gently soothing the darkness.

Fay moved. She stepped away from the faint grass of her shadow and, swishing her feet over the top of the sand, she plunged uphill a few paces. Looking back at where she had been, Fay saw the emerald tinge spread, slowly, but visibly. It held her unwilling gaze. It was not grass: it was a sight-magnet. And there, in her new shadow, more grass started growing.

This was not what she had planned! Fay panicked and ran back downhill, where the ground became firmer as the sand solidified. Under her feet the slippery copper visibly coalesced into good dark soil. Sometimes she found herself staggering through sand, and sometimes she ran lightly over the grass that had grown from her shade. There seemed no logic in it. Just change. This couldn't be happening. Her shadow was small: there was no grass. There could not be grass.

It was dragons, she convinced herself. Dragons. Only dragons. Dragons in a searing landscape. Their world was desert. Dragons. Dragons. Dragons.

The word echoed in the still air as she ran away from what she couldn't understand. But what she couldn't understand followed her and caught up. Where the desert had been silent, she heard a magpie calling, then a thrush, and after that the chittering of a flock of starlings.

Suddenly, as suddenly as the last dragon-shadow had vanished in the heat, a thought flitted through her mind. A real dream. This was a real dream. A bit nightmarish. Uncontrollable. But a dream. *But how could it be,* Fay argued. *I'm walking to a party. This world is a construct. The reality is the street at night. There is a big moon overhead, not a sun. I'm not asleep and this is not real. So where were the lampposts and the pavement? Why am I running? And why is the grass growing?*

Fay careered to a halt, laughing. Why *did* grass grow, anyway? Not because it hated dragons, she suspected. Not even grass could hate dragons, she reasoned. Her mind, she feared, had fled along with the sand.

Fay took stock of the sky with its suspiciously woolly clouds floating pleasantly, then looked back at the ground. Yes, it was all pasture. A knobbly pasture, at that. Nothing smooth or slippery about it. No sand. No dragon-shadows. Her own shadow had somehow transformed one world into another.

And Fay had just the tiniest suspicion that she knew which one. Her subconscious had obviously said "See Enlai", and it obviously didn't matter *how* much her conscious mind said "See dragons", her subconscious insisted on dragging her the closest it could to Enlai.

Who didn't exist. She had to remember to remind herself that he didn't exist.

Fay walked to the top of the hill, just to prove her theory. It was getting hotter. No it wasn't, it was just that she had done a lot of running and a lot of walking, and now she was plodding back up the stupid hill. Mind you, walking back up a sand dune might have been tougher. But the hill was still a hill, and the day was a warm one.

Over the hill she could see the pasture giving way to a sprinkling of houses, and to a more generous sprinkling of trees. A well-trod path led into very familiar territory after that, finally turning into streets and a town. Soon, Enlai's and Persa's houses would be visible. Fay nodded, having ascertained they were there; then she turned right round and walked back to her hill.

She was not going to see Enlai. This was pure pique. Fay admitted it openly. She refused to let her subconscious dictate to her. Why should she? Didn't she have a right to a conscious mind? And why shouldn't she sulk? Fay pouted her way right back to the top of the hill. It was a good pout. Worth framing.

She turned to look back at the town, hot and breathless with the exertion. Her moon boots and many scarves were not at all suited to walking vigorously in warm weather. Mind you, they would not have been suited to the desert, either. Why hadn't they transformed into something appropriate, like a big loose cottony thingy. Big loose cottony thingies would have been good for the desert. And then she could have seen those dragons. She was doubly piqued at only catching the shadows flitting away. Fay flipped the end of a scarf towards the town in disgust, and pivoted. She waltzed down the other side of the hill, back to where she had started this woeful exercise. She was still sulking, but her pout was less picture-perfect.

The pasture refused to become dragon country again, no matter how often she told it (grumpily) what it had to look like. It remained obstinately green and pleasant. "Bloody landscapes," she swore, "Always got a mind of their own. Never listen to their betters. Stop being picturesque," her voice rose higher and louder, "And start being dangerous." The pasture just stayed there, the way pasture will, milk-maid pretty.

Fay decided to give up on detective work and return home. There was a trick she had, when dreams were too vivid or when they turned into nightmares. First she would centre herself, getting back into her body. Then she would note where each body part was, reaching out with her mind into them. Finally, she would wrap her arms around herself for security, then she would open her eyes wide to view the outside world. It never failed.

It almost never failed. Fay sat down. In fact, she plonked down on the ground. The plonk matched the pout perfectly. That should have helped, too, since she was walking in real life. But she had no sensation of walking. The plonk felt like a plonk should—abrupt and untidy. In fact, she could feel the grass beneath her, warm and slightly damp. It was patently not going to resolve itself into pavement anytime soon.

*I'm not going to cry,* Fay decided, firmly. *After all, I survived last time the world misbehaved.* But the last time, she realised with a sinking feeling, she had excused everything. Things go out of control when you're not well. You get nightmares, for instance. She could understand the world not acting as it should when she was ill.

This time, however, there was nothing wrong except... she didn't have a song prepared. Maybe that was what she needed. A folksong. *Is there one about returning to ordinary life?* Fay wondered, but in vain. She didn't know how to apply folksongs to herself, anyway, only to her friends, and there was no song she knew that would create a Narnia-like door back to reality. Why hadn't C.S. Lewis written folksongs? Sad waste of a life.

Fay's right leg was developing a bad case of pins and needles. "How can you get pins and needles in a dream when you are walking in real life?" she puzzled aloud, feeling as if she should rename herself Alice. The magnitude of the wrongness her mind was working on made her angry, and she stamped her foot into the recalcitrant grass, hard, hard into the ground, driving the pins and needles back where they belonged. Not that she was very sure where pins and needles belonged when they weren't plaguing her right leg.

Then she decided that, if she were in Wonderland, then she would use Wonderland logic. Fay walked to a spreading oak nearby and curled up under it. She wondered, fleetingly, where she would wake up, and then fell slowly into slumber. In her dream she turned round and walked home, never reaching her friend's house. In her dream she unlocked the front door and walked straight through to the bedroom. In her dream she divested herself of her detective clothing. And in her dream she fell asleep.

When she woke up, she was in her own bed, and the phone was ringing.

---

*You know, I ought to have been upset by it all. But I'm not. It was such a strange evening that I'm not sure I can sort it out, but I'm not upset. In fact, I'm quite pleased.*

*It's all Fred's fault (says I to myself with a funny kind of half-pleased grin)— he worried about me when I didn't turn up last night.*

*True! And no-one ever worries about me. I'm just Fay.*

*No-one even notices me, mostly. Well, Fred noticed me and he rang me and I almost like the fact that I piled my clothes ready then fell asleep. It was strange to dream going out and not getting there. And I have my thoughts tangled today. It is being noticed that did it. It's nice to be noticed.*

*Maybe I should write my dreams down; turn them into a novel. Dreams that real should sell! Then I could leave the Public Service (now there's a dream worth having), and forget everything I have ever known about economics, and become a normal human being. Well, maybe just a near-normal human being. Mustn't tempt Fate by wishing for something too outlandish.*

———

Fay had the strange dream again that night. She had gone to bed, intending to visit the fantasy world, quite merry. Instead she had drifted into the nightmare. It had all the sharpness of reality, and all the pain. It was not the same nightmare as the last time. It was sufficiently close, however, to make her ill-wish the very thought of nightmares. This one was just too unpleasant.

She floated above her little world. Fay moved gently from the castle down the route her eyes had followed from the castle room. She drifted over the common and past the gallows tree. She saw a decaying body hanging from the tree. For one instant a foul stench reached her, then it was gone. The dream was suddenly leached of all scent, and for a moment its cruel reality was gentled.

As she passed over the corpse she felt a chill wind. A stiletto stabbed at her left temple. Fay drifted past the tree, still high above it but floating inexorably downwards. The cold bit more deeply into her head. She swivelled, unable to take her eyes off the gruesome thing creaking in the wind. It glowed death-green for a moment before the whole scene flickered.

She thought, *I have been here before. I will be home soon.* This time, however, after the flickering, the scene firmed. Fay did not fade. In fact, she found herself standing in the middle of the common, cold and desolate.

Of the sensations she had while floating, only the stabbing was left, and it was strident as a migraine. Fay looked around and saw Gilbert walking past. She waved and shouted his name. He looked over at her and his face turned bleak. He turned his back on her and walked away, briskly.

Fay did not know what to do. She was as numb inside as out. She had never seen a face as emptied as Gilbert's in that moment. It was hard—she could not imagine him looking at her in such a way. As if she were wicked. Yet he had. He had looked at her with nothing in his eyes. Careful, lonely, unhappy nothing.

For a few moments she stood there, then she herself moved on, in the opposite direction to Gilbert. However hurt she might be, Fay decided that she still had her pride. And her head was throbbing as if she would die. Her body felt cold and stiff.

So internally focused was Fay that she walked into something on the path. Except it was not something—it was someone. It was a morris dancer, standing still, his stick uplifted as if he were in the middle of a dance. She wondered why the bells on his wrists and the bells on his legs did not jangle when she bumped into him. Then she stood back and wondered why he had not moved. It was as if her brain was in slow motion. Or as if the whole world were askew.

Finally Fay looked, letting her sight reach out past the icy cold that was numbing her mind. What she saw, she did not understand.

At first she thought she had made a mistake and that the dancer was a statue. It was so life-like, she marvelled. Every detail of cloth and cap was precise and a little displaced, again, as if the dancer had been caught mid-movement. Then she noticed it. At the morrisman's left temple was a mark. Her hand reached her own temple and she winced. The mark on him exactly matched where her head hurt.

Then she saw the look in his eyes. If she had been part-frozen both inside and outside, he had been fully frozen. But his eyes were fully alive, and suffering. His body was caught in frozen death, but inside his mind felt everything. She put her hands on his shoulders and willed his body back to life, but she could do nothing. It was not something she had invented in the world, so she could do nothing, nothing to solve it. She felt her own throbbing temple and wondered if she had escaped his fate, or if the parallel ice was coincidence.

Fay would have asked Gilbert, but the look on his face had scared her, deep down. She never wanted anyone to look at her like that again. Fay thought of asking Belle. Then she thought better of it.

I should leave, Fay resolved. This is not safe. This is sorcery.

And she forced herself to wake up, and put two hot water bottles in her bed despite the summer heat. She took two painkillers and two sleeping tablets, regardless of whether they mixed or not. And she returned to full sleep, escaping the agony of those eyes in the frozen face.

# CHAPTER EIGHT

FAY FORGOT BELLE. SHE FORGOT GILBERT. SHE FORGOT her preoccupation with Enlai. She was determined to forget everything about her little world.

If you had asked her, she would have said that her interest in Fred rooted her more and more firmly in ordinary reality, and that she had begun to wonder if reality was so very ordinary after all. But no-one asked. Still, the answer was there, just in case. Fay was very determined to forget.

Fay decided she was in love. That nightmares were just nightmares. That her life was happening in the real world. These decisions were a huge relief. She ran into love, her arms outspread. She was ready to embrace daily life. The headaches faded. She refused to think of Belle, or Persa, or Gilbert, or Enlai-who-didn't-exist. It was a conscious and careful refusal.

Like many women almost in love, she started noticing the world as if it had been sketched anew. Fay superimposed her burgeoning emotions and new-recovered health onto the outside world. More and more it seemed bright, sparkling; raindrops were grey-silver gems, dew-drops were placid crystals and tears were miracles of mournfulness.

She started to enjoy work, and to look forward to her spare time. And Fay attributed this to love. But it may have been the fact that she was healthier, and that her worn eyes could actually look at the world again. Attributing merriment to love, however, meant that her interest in the ordinary fed upon itself, and grew. There were spaces to be filled with activities and with friends. So she invited an old, old friend to stay over Christmas, a period that is not usually kind to singles.

Kath always had lots of plans for Fay. It was one side of their relationship. The other side was Fay listening to Kath's problems. This time, however, Kath's problems were in abeyance and she explained her plans to Fay with explicit abandon. "I'm worried about you," she said. "You're fey Fay all over again. Exactly like you were at university. It's not healthy.

"Fred is a godsend," she said. "You're not doing enough to push the relationship along. I think we can improve on things in that regard.

"I feel so bad for you," she said. "I feel sorrow at your sorrow. I want to see you get back into life. Find some happiness. You know."

Fay wasn't sure she knew, but she went along with Kath's plans.

Fay's years of drear dullness had distressed her. Kath explained this in excruciating and embarrassing detail. Kath sought to cheer her friend up. This was explained three times over. The explanations were followed with lots of plans and thoughts. Lots of activity. Fay found herself caught up in enjoyment. Kath was smug and Fay was surprised. Just like old times.

The romantic side of Kath's organising was patently obvious—she had Fay invite Fred along to Christmas lunch, along with two other singles. "A cast-out's Chrissie" she called it, and helped shop and cook. Kath glowed in satisfaction as she saw Fay spark up, put on some make-up and find a sexy dress from the depths of her wardrobe. They ate seafood and salad and creamy desserts on Christmas Day, eschewing traditional food because of the heat.

Kath basked in virtue-won-out when Fred agreed to a Boxing Day picnic, shared a late night pizza, went to a film with them, went to the Art Gallery, and generally shared the holiday period with the two women.

The Boxing Day picnic was riotous. Fred flirted openly with both women, and Fay found something inside her relax and respond. It was too long with no man even pretending admiration, she told herself. And it was very cute to watch Fred flirt. He was more a model of sobriety than a flirt in his normal self. She settled down into the holidays as if they were real 'time out" and there were solutions in the real world. Fred smiled and fed her chocolates at the cinema and she melted a little more. She was very happy.

And when Kath went back to her home, she rang Fay up. Her tone had a tinge of desperation. Apparently Fred had written to her, twice. He liked her. "But I wanted him to like *you*," said Kath.

"And what do you think of him?" asked Fay.

"Well, he's perfect for you," said Kath, despondently. "Not for me, for you."

Kath was surprised, but honest. "He's lovely," she replied, "but…"

"But?"

"No spark."

"Oh."

"And besides, he's not Christian."

"But he goes to Church."

"My dear, Anglican, not Pentecostal."

"Oh," said Fay. She commiserated as best she could. Her reactions were surprisingly mixed. There was a little bitterness that Fred could so easily reject her. And lead her astray. And that her emotions could do the same thing. There was a dollop of anger, although none at Kath.

But mostly, there was a bubbling laughter.

Fay envisaged those three days in the old year as if she were an outsider. She had been acting as if Fred were going to be hers (Fay, fortunately for her self-esteem had never allowed herself to think of the romance as anything but burgeoning, or, on a sad slow day, a distant possibility) and Kath had been blatantly flinging Fred in her direction. To complete the triangle, Fred had been chasing Kath—who did not want him. *Worst on Fred's ego*, Fay thought, and rather traumatic for poor Kath who had thought she was doing Fay the biggest of favours. But for herself? Fay laughed and laughed inside herself. She laughed and laughed and laughed.

That evening she sought out Gilbert to tell him the whole sorry story. Somehow it was a story she had to tell him. The laughter had dispelled the memory of her most recent dreams, and all she remembered was the man from her little cove, who liked listening to stories about Humpty Dumpty and the Wicked Witch of the West.

She acted on intuition and found him in her secret cove. He was seated cross-legged in the cave, the shadows deep behind him. There was a lassitude about him, as if he had undergone a deep illness or a sustained sorrow. When she greeted him he looked shocked, almost scared. Then he stood up. Gilbert walked up to Fay, his arms open wide.

"You're alive!" he said, and hugged her deeply.

She extracted herself from his muffling embrace. "Of course I am," she said, annoyed, "I didn't come here to be told that."

Gilbert chuckled and said ruefully, "Then I suppose I had better not ask where you have been for so long."

"Falling in love," said Fay, honestly, "and then out of it again."

Gilbert looked at her a long time, then calmly said, "Well, it doesn't seem to have hurt you."

"No, I wasn't really in love. At least, I don't really know. He was... well, he filled a big gap in my everyday life and I liked him."

"But?" prompted Gilbert.

"Why 'But?'" flared Fay. "Why do you assume I'd need to qualify anything?"

Gilbert chuckled again. "I don't know," he admitted, "If I said you didn't look hurt or betrayed, you would probably lose your temper at me again."

Fay looked at him suspiciously, then conceded the point. "Okay," she admitted, "But I'm not going to tell you what the 'but' referred to." Suddenly she wanted to keep her laughter at Fred's perfidy to herself. There were other things she suddenly realised she didn't want to talk about much, too. Fay had secrets. The thought of herself as secretive made her smile a little wry. But it didn't stop her from not telling all about Fred and Kath or mentioning her most recent visits.

It wasn't just the dragons. Somehow she was managing to keep the morris-man incident deep inside, where none of its elements could leak out and damage her. In fact, she told herself, it must have been a dream within a dream. It had been so surreal, and the look on Gilbert's face was unimaginable, seeing him so friendly beside her.

Gilbert laughed and invited her back to his cottage for the evening meal. Fay looked at the sun suspiciously, as if Gilbert had magically caused it to be evening simply to lure her to his cottage. Then she looked at the absurd innocence of Gilbert's face, laughed, and accepted the invitation.

When the two returned to the cove at dawn, Fay

gave the sun a private salute, as if it knew better than she the false limpidity of Gilbert's gaze. And she felt a little healing of the sort that not even Fred's chocolates could give.

It was very hard to slip away from her world this time, and she excused herself very gently and promised her lover that she would not leave it so long the next time. "Not quite, anyway," and kissed him even as she felt the bedclothes warm against her skin in the real world.

When she felt her bedclothes wrapping her safely and warmly, she vaguely thought that there were things they should have spoken of. She shrugged her shoulders and went to sleep.

———

*Two things haunt me.*

*One is that old song. It sounds derogatory when you say it like that—"Oh, that old song"—but I didn't mean it as derogatory. I meant it to pin down reality—strings of melody drifting through my brain. "Crazy in love, that's me." It seems mad, I suppose, objectively, to fall in love with a figment of your own imagination, but I've gone and done it and it's not at all mad. Life has a lovely inner glow.*

*I feel bitter about Fred. I didn't at the beginning, but I really feel horrid about it now. He used me. There's no two ways about it. He used me to cushion his own life and make it more comfortable, and then he used me as a yellow brick road to my good friend. I preferred Fred at the beginning, when he admitted he was just going out with me for the sake of company. It was honest.*

*Here I talk about honesty as if it were important. It certainly isn't with Gilbert. He's hiding all sorts of things, and I know he is—and I couldn't care less. I hide things from him, too. I guess the difference is that we know we have secrets.*

*We're not using each other. In fact, I'm pretty sure he loves me reluctantly. He as good as admitted it two nights ago.*

*Thank goodness he also believes in long conversations. I now know (for what it's worth) that he was sounding me out as a potential sorcerer. He is not quite sure what I am now (or if he has any ideas, he's hiding them) but is convinced that either I'm not evil or I'm so powerful that it really makes no difference. Me, I think he was just doing some ex post facto justification. We made love, and this had to somehow be fitted into his neat little patterns. How funny, that a man with such unruly hair puts everything into neat little patterns.*

*Two nights ago was magic. So magic that I had to see Belle and tell her. It has been too long. Too long for her as well as for me. I had forgotten in my cruel way (the side of me I like least) that Belle's husband was to die after the birth of the child. Sure enough, he had karked it. Put like that, it is not quite real—it is faintly humorous in a macabre kind of way. Is my sense of humour really that warped?*

*But the truth is not at all humorous. Belle could not love her husband (at least, I certainly hope she couldn't — it's not only the wrong-ness of the age gap to the liberated twenty-first century woman, it's also my guilt at planning the marriage) but she is dedicated, virtuous and would have fitted him into her life. She cared for him. There can be no doubt about that. It was a playful, gentle caring, with the ribbons she made for his waist and the way she watched him and protected him. "And at the age of sixteen, his grave it was green, and death had put an end to his growing." I lifted the plot straight from a song and thought it was a fine idea to try it out on Belle. Only the world of my dreams is much more real now.*

*That world glows for me. And as it glows for me, it dims for Bellezour Anma. Because she is alone. I left Belle to deal with the death of her husband alone while I flirted with reality.*

And so I saw her last night. 'Saw' is the operative word. I was agonised with guilt. I watched from the central arch of the big gate, as she went about her business. For a half hour, perhaps longer, I watched, then she went upstairs. Perhaps she went to consult with this Prince-person. And I left.

I couldn't seek out Gilbert to talk about it. It is my burden. I have somehow to come to grips with the fact that I have hurt her, through trying to play God. And in hurting Belle, I have hurt myself.

I need someone like myself, to lay out my life as neatly as I laid out Belle's, and to tell me, honestly, what was happening. When it comes down to it, I was as dishonest to Belle as Fred was to me, and about something far more fundamental. So who am I to demand straight dealing?

Who am I?

# CHAPTER NINE

FAY WANDERED UP LANEWAYS AND DOWN STREETS. IT WAS still chill winter, but there was a hint of warming in the air. Fay hoped the warming was not only in the air. She wanted it to be a bridge inside her, something to link whatever it was that seemed to be tearing her apart. So she was in the town, restlessly wandering, using the walking to drift through her own mind, to think, to identify problems, and the problems within the problems.

Belle must hate her. Fay hated herself, so how could Belle not hate her. And Fay could not accept Gilbert. She was in love, but now that she was in the town and not the safety of the cove, in her vagrant mind's eye she saw a look on his face when she pictured it. The look said he hated her soul, even as he loved her. For her, there was no gap in time between that look and his declaration of love. And he wasn't there to absorb her attention and make her forget. Gilbert's face was stone; then he had welcomed her into his heart. The two were irreconcilable. Like Fay having consciously hurt her closest friend.

It was not possible; it had happened. And it happened inside her memory, over and over and over again.

That dead morris dancer; the cruelty in the air the day she was lost in the town square: they were sorcery. A vicious word. A simple definition. Harsh magic that froze life, simply because it could. Sorcery.

Like Fay's songs which ruined lives, simply because they were fun to sing. Fay's glacial heart was thawing, and with the spring melt came all the hurt and damage from the frost bite.

She felt the results of the actions she had taken when she was imprisoned by those frozen emotions. Gilbert's love, Belle's friendship: they melted hard ice. Fay had to cure her hurts herself. And she admitted this, over and over and over again, as she walked restlessly up and down the streets of the town, backwards and forwards, edging through it to the centre in slow stages.

Over and over and over again she catalogued every wrong she had ever done to any friend in this fantasy world. In the real world, too. Every callous thought and every inconsiderate action was hauled up before her inner gaze and proffered to the passing houses. There was no atonement, just guilt laid upon guilt laid upon guilt. It was an Aztec orgy of self-mutilation.

The introspection finished when she reached the common. She edged past the gallows tree, avoiding touching even the picket fence. There was no body there now, although the tree creaked in expectation. Fay saw her own body hanging there, deep in the shadow of her mind's eye. Hanging in punishment for all she had done, for all she was. For her sorcery.

Fay scuttled across the common, towards the castle. She didn't look where the morris dancer had been. She did not dare.

And she came safely to the castle. She was let in

without question, and directed to the courtyard. The whole town was assembled. She had been stripping her soul in empty streets with no thought as to why those streets might be empty. The streets were vacant because there was a riot in the castle courtyard. Too much colour, too many people, and too much music, all in relentlessly happy common time.

Belle would be here, Fay realised. She would be playing lady bountiful. One did that, at a village festival. Or even at a town fair, Fay corrected herself. Not a good time for an apology. But Fay had to start somewhere. Should she start making it up to Belle? Or should she turn it over in her mind a bit longer, thinking it out, sorting it out?

Right now the question was marvellously theoretical. From where Fay was standing, Belle was not to be seen. There was the briefest glimpse of Gilbert, surrounded by soldiers, but Fay couldn't catch his eye. Couldn't? Or didn't want to? *Stop it*, she told herself. *You're acting like an adolescent.*

Persa's mother was chatting with friends, and Persa and Flor were standing together amicably. Enlai was leaning against a stone wall, watching. His favourite activity, watching. Preferably posed.

She would check with Persa, she decided. Persa knew where everyone was, and what everyone was doing. So Fay stopped edging and scuttling and trying not to exist, and slowly moved through the crowds towards Persa. The movement took on the feel of dancing, enhanced by the relentless drumbeat that controlled the music. As she came closer to her friend, Fay realised that it *was* a dance beat. It was very much common time. In fact, it was morris dancers.

Fay stopped short, knocking into a person who had been walking behind her. All she could see were the dancers. She had come to think of morris men and gallows as her personal totems of evil. But she had come so far, and the crowd had moved in behind: she couldn't turn and leave. And then Persa turned round a fraction and squinted at Fay. Persa waved her over. Fay had no choice but to join her friend and they watched the dancing in silence.

"I hate morris dancers," Persa said, in Fay's ear, where no-one could hear.

"So why are you watching?"

"I work here, remember?" was the scornful answer, "I am supposed to be helping everyone enjoy things."

"Then help *me* enjoy things," said Fay, "Let's go get something to drink."

"Good idea," said Flor, acknowledging Fay's existence for the first time in... how long? Since well before Belle's baby, at least. In fact, since Belle had become such a close friend. *How odd, that some people like their friends exclusive*, Fay thought. "I'll get us all a cup of whatever's going." Flor faded into the crowd.

"That was *not* what I meant," said Fay, peevishly. "Have you see Belle?"

Persa gestured with her thumb to a black-draped dais opposite. Belle was a white face trapped in a sea of black. "She had to come, because it's traditional, but I think it's cruel to make her."

"It isn't fair at all, is it?" agreed Fay. "I guess it's not a good time to speak to her."

"Today she's on duty," agreed Persa, "No time for us at all. I can sneak you into the private dinner tonight if you like — I know she'll want to see you."

"But she may be tired. I'll come back another time."

"That'd be better," said Persa approvingly, "She needs more people thinking about her needs and not the baby's or the Prince's or the town's or the soldiers', or the blasted morris men's." And Persa looked shocked at herself, "I didn't say that," she defended. "I didn't say anything about morris men. Just ignore it. It sort of slipped out."

Fay just nodded. If no-one was supposed to know, then Fay supposed no-one knew she had seen the morris dancer on the green, except Gilbert. She didn't know if this was good or bad.

The two friends stood there in silence, watching the white handkerchiefs clashing, with Belle's unrelieved black dais and clothes setting off the white-costumed dancers. The dance finished and the dancers took a break for a quick swig of beer from a keg. They were merry, in a grim way, obviously determined to enjoy the occasion and mourn their dead companion, no matter how difficult it was to do both at once.

Fay saw their set smiles as a continuation of her earlier flagellation. Despite the festival, it was a day for introspection.

She set herself to watch Belle and the dancers—if the morris dancers could do two things at once, then so could she, and she was perfectly placed for it. Trust Persa to get the best vantage point, even to watch something she hated.

Flor did not return with drinks. It had obviously been an excuse to get away. Fay shrugged her shoulders and kept watching as stick hit stick then swung round into figure eights as the dancers jigged a hey. The unrelenting clack was giving her a headache.

Out of the corner of her eye, she saw a lightning bolt. This lightning travelled slowly. A javelin of green light. It was tinged with red-gold and she could see clear through it to the castle behind. It flew down from one of the turrets and arced towards the courtyard. Heading for the dais. Heading straight for Belle.

"No!" Fay screamed, but the crowd was so noisy, the band so loud, that her shout was swallowed. Fay shouted again and moved her arms, feebly, as if they could deflect the bright spear.

When she looked she could see its intent, as if emotion radiated from it with the light, and as if the slowness of it was solely for her benefit. Or as if she was linked to it, in an horrific way. She made an empty fist, framing it, and moved her arm hard. To her surprise, the movement worked. Not much, but it worked. The light-spear jumped in its arc in an entirely unnatural fashion.

Instead of hitting Belle, it struck the raised sticks of two clashing morris men. The stocks immediately flickered and flamed brightly, and then so did the morris men. As the spear had moved slowly, the flames travelled quickly. It was all over in the count of five. Two charred corpses, with ashes where their sticks had been. And Belle watching from the dais, her pale face like a stunned rabbit caught in car's headlights.

Fay was overtaken by a huge lassitude, as if she had run a marathon. She faded. Intentionally. And this time, when she found herself at home, she convinced herself, intentionally, that the whole thing had been a nightmare.

The possibility of it being real was too much.

———

*I have been taken in hand, unexpectedly. Some old university friends have taken pity on me and dragged me caravanning in the mountains. I guess it's therapeutic.*

*There's something quite exhilarating about being soaked to the skin at 1800 metres. It has definitely stopped me imagining lurid things about Belle, and continuing to fall in love with my own creation. I keep having to remind myself that Gilbert must be my own creation, even if I don't remember creating him. He is like that green pasture. From my subconscious mind, or something. Desirable, but not real.*

Today I had a run-in that has changed the face of Australian politics. It's had its impact on me, too. A supposedly charming party leader was also climbing the mountain today. He was pontificating to the press at the top of Kosciusko and all the returning walkers warned us we might run across him and his herd of muscular cameramen.

Well, though it is late summer, there's still snow in the high ranges, and some nice thick icy slush went right across the tourist track. It was very tourist-aware snow, in fact, for it got icier and icier and harder and harder to trek. Feckless Fay chose to wear old and shapeless runners. Not only did my feet get damp, but, not to put too fine a point on it, I got stuck.

About two metres from the end of the ice patch, my shoes wouldn't grip. I made the giant error of looking down and discovering that there were hundreds of metres of rocky mountain below the snow, and, since I was above the treeline, not a stray shrub to break my fall.

What was worse, I blocked the path.

Across the snow from me was a behatted, dark-glassed and extremely glowering political leader. He stood there and frowned down on me, arms crossed. He was very big and his frown was very daunting.

The camera crew was charming and helped me out. My eyes were generously given a close-up of muscles. Those muscles didn't help the politician when he strode out onto the ice, slipped in the snow and tumbled down the mountain. They were too busy filming.

At least I have proof I am effectual in the real world, in a strange sort of way. Not the sort of proof I would have chosen if someone had given me the option.

———

Fay woke up with a sweating nightmare. Hot and cold at once. Everything ached damply. She could feel the beginnings of a migraine. Colours flashed before her eyes. Dutifully she went to the medicine cabinet and swallowed a varied handful of pills. Then she rang work.

So much for the restful effects of a mountain holiday.

After this she was supposed to go back to bed (doctor's orders) but found she couldn't. The nightmare had dissipated a little, even though being out of bed was agony. She wished for the warmth and strength of Gilbert's hands, then immediately regretted that wish. For the nightmare was closely linked to her world of dreams, and even wistfully wishing for Gilbert brought the wickedness of it back.

Dark night. Enlai's eyes. It had been Enlai's eyes again. Again and again and again. Accusing. Mocking. Threatening. Thieving. Amber eyes of a cat. Crueller than Fay had ever invented Enlai to be. It was as if he had thrust himself into her dreams and then deliberately shrugged off the veils of civilization.

Fay shivered, despite the heat. But the migraine had been caught too late and the tablets would not help unless she slept. Her eyes were glazed — her feet stumbled. The pain was too great. She returned to bed. But not to sleep. Not with agony crashing through her skull.

———

Pain automatically sent her to Belle. Her brain was not working: it was her common sense that took her to where she might find healing. Fay sat in Belle's bright tower room and waited. She sat as uncomfortably as possible, for she was determined to stay awake. The evil gaze that stole her sleeping dreams would not take her waking ones if she could help it.

Despite herself, her eyes drooped. She fell into a half-slumber, concentrating on the hard cushion beneath her, as if the focus on its uncomfortable embroidery (all knots and lumps) could keep her awake. It did. At least sufficiently awake to avoid those eyes and the nightmare.

The pain did not disappear. She sat there, hour after hour, trembling, focussing on the cushion, her eyes shut despite herself. In the background of her thought, Fay was dimly wondering why Belle kept such a hard cushion in her soft, bright room, but the pain left no space for reasoning. Eventually, even this stray thought was banished behind the dancing amber lights of pain. She became used to it, made friends with the hurt.

A sharp sound beat at her head, making it throb again. Then the scream stopped. Then a voice, gentle, "Fay. It's Fay." And Belle's arms around her, as if she had been away forever. As indeed she had.

Fay opened her eyes and blinked the tears away. "Belle," she intoned drearily, "It hurts."

The arms let her go, and Belle's voice sounded half amused, half concerned. "Trust you, Fay. And you choose my embroidered cushion to sit on, rather than something comfortable. I'll get you some willow-bark and valerian."

Soon she poured a tincture into a glass for her friend, and topped it with a good dose of spirits. Fay heard this, and saw a generalised blur of it, but her eyes were not yet fully functional. And her time sense seemed to have dissipated. That's how she put it, as if she were some kind of faulty machine.

Eventually the pain cleared and she could see again. And what she saw was Belle, at the other side of the room, waiting patiently.

When she saw Fay look up, she explained, "I was scared to go, in case you disappeared again. We have a lot to talk about."

"Yes, a lot," murmured Fay. Then she looked straight into Belle's eyes. "But I have even more to work out than that and I don't... I mean... I would find it difficult to work out right now. If I promise to come back..."

"Soon. If you promise to come back *soon*," Bellezour said, "and come straight to me. It's terribly, terribly important, Fay. You could be in danger. I've been talking about it with... well, with one of your friends."

"Danger?" asked Fay, stupidly.

"No, we won't talk now," Belle said, "You are very obviously not yourself. But come to me *soon* and *don't* let yourself be distracted. Not by love, not by hate, and not by any story you might dream up. Don't dream. If you start to, then come and see me."

"You know about my dreaming," said Fay, even more stupidly.

"Of course I know," said Belle, maybe more sharply than she had intended. "I have known for a long time. And you knew I knew. We have talked about it, remember. Since then I've been talking to other people, and thinking." The sharpness in her voice faded to pure concern, "When you disappeared those two years, I was so very worried I had to investigate. Too much has been going on here. At first, some people blamed you. But now..." Belle drifted off, her voice deep with anxiety.

"Better if I were to blame, huh?" said Fay, brightly, trying to return things to a more cheerful normal.

"You just get some sleep. And come back, quickly."

Belle took Fay to Belle's own bed, and, making her lie down, covered her gently with a green quilt.

Fay woke up refreshed, in bed.

And a wonderful thought struck her. A tune was going through her mind. "Belle qui tient ma vie" - a Renaissance love song. She would give Belle some love interest. Real love. True love. But she had promised that this time she would consult. Besides Belle wanted to see her urgently, probably about something else entirely.

Fay was impressed, in a quietly contented sort of way, that everything came together so very beautifully. *Serendipity*, she told herself, *Happy meetings of fate.* Then she decided that it was her mind, harmoniously bringing necessity close to desire.

Desire was the wrong word. It made her think of Gilbert. And the thought made her get out of bed quickly. She was not quite ready to dwell on her thoughts of Gilbert. What had started to happen at the emotional level and had reached the physical had not yet reached the intellectual. Which didn't stop her categorising it, of course. She wouldn't be Fay if she did not categorise somewhat.

In fact, if she were being honest with herself, Fay was not quite ready to admit it had reached the physical. It was as if her dream world teetered on recognition. It was as if she had used Fred as an excuse for postponement.

Six months before, she had treated it differently. Her fantasy world had been imaginary: she had condescended to visit, for reasons of entertainment. Strangely, it was only when she had stopped visiting regularly that she could admit its reality. Fay realised that she was fleeing from two worlds, not just one. And that there was a possibility, just a possibility, they were both real.

The first world was the mundane one she had grown up in. It had certainly improved during the last few years, but it was still, well, mundane. Comprised of the ordinary stuff of everyday life. Nothing special.

Dreaming was better. And Fay sat down, ignoring the need to go to work, and she took up a pen and paper, and she did something that she had not done before. It had no apparent links to what she had been thinking, about reality and the two worlds. It was a purely intuitive connection.

She charted the pain she had been feeling recently. She wrote down the pain that had originally sent her to Gilbert's arms and that Belle's home remedies had cured. She noted the physical pain that had haunted her at work, a low level she hadn't even realised until it became heavy and hurtful. Fay was surprised at how much pain there was to chart. No wonder she was an unhappy soul.

The chart did not overlap with the fruiting reality of her dream world as far as she could see. Fay didn't know whether to be thankful or sorry. Fay rang up the doctor and made an appointment. Then she rang up work and excused herself for another day.

She saw the doctor, and came home, thoughtful. Then she dreamed, straight to Belle's tower.

# CHAPTER TEN

BELLE'S TOWER WAS SHADOW-STIPPLED IN SUNLIGHT. FAY sat there and shivered. It was spring and the bright sunlight was not yet warming.

On reaching the tower, Fay had become nervous. Whatever Belle had wanted to warn her of was obviously serious. It seemed much more important now that she was here than it had seemed at home, in reality. So she sat on her uncomfortable cushion and shivered, watching the patterns in the sunlight and waiting for Belle to appear.

There was no reason for Belle to appear, as Belle did not know of Fay's arrival, but the headaches and feebleness and general miseries Fay had been suffering had somehow transformed her personality. She had been shy in the past, and often had wished to distance herself from people, but each time it had happened, it had been an active choice. Fay had not wanted to see people, so she did not. Fay had chosen to stay away.

Now, however, she felt as if control of her life had been gently lifted from her by outside forces. It changed everything. It changed the way she thought, the way she acted. So she did not look for Belle. She sat and waited, mesmerised by the light.

Eventually the door to the tower room opened. Fay gently inclined her body so that she could impress upon Belle her virtuousness in returning as promised. She met the cheeky gaze of Persa Doucor. "Persa! What on earth are you doing here?" Fay asked.

"I could ask the same of you, stranger," retorted Persa, pointedly, "Especially as I am officially in the employ of the lady of the manor. And you don't talk to me."

"'Officially in the employ'—I like that phrase. It's the sort of sentence an economist would use." laughed Fay. It was hard to take Persa seriously, even when she appeared unexpectedly.

"What's an economist?" Persa queried.

Lost for an explanation that fitted the fantasy world, Fay said, simply, "Well, I'm one, at least, I'm employed as one."

"Oh, some sort of witch, then," returned Persa, with a mischievous look. For her description she received a volley of cushions thrown at her by an enthusiastic Fay. And she threw them back with interest, until one fell out of the window. Fay and Persa looked at each other, at a loss.

Fay was the first to recover, "You had better collect that before everyone accuses you of being a witch, too."

"How?" asked Persa, indignantly.

"Aren't flying cushions a form of witchcraft?" suggested Fay.

Persa flounced off to collect the cushion, nodding at Fay's request to tell Bellezour that she was here.

Belle was not the next person to enter: it was Gilbert. Fay sprung to her feet, her face an interesting shade of crimson. Gilbert looked towards her calmly, then took both her hands. He sat her down, himself very close. "You look ill," he said.

"That's a nice welcome," retorted Fay.

"I was worried," was the quiet answer, "but you seem happy enough."

"I'm happy because I'm ill," Fay smiled at the conundrum.

Gilbert smiled back. "Don't tell me you dosed yourself intentionally."

"No, nothing like that." She tried to find words. "I had all these headaches and thought there was something really wrong in the town. It was just one of those thoughts that hits when you are ill and you worry. It's as if the world is falling apart. Anyway, I've just been diagnosed as having a work-related illness."

"Like a carpenter hitting his thumb with a hammer?"

"Sort of. In my ordinary job I use a particular type of machine and the machine, and the conditions under which I used it, made me ill."

"A machine. An ordinary job. Fay, somehow you always manage to find a way of surprising me."

Fay opened her eyes to their most innocent. "It's not intentional," she reassured him.

"That's helpful." He grinned, and then looked serious. "But why are you here, if you're not well."

Fay looked him straight in the eyes, her concern showing. "Belle asked me to see her soon, and before seeing anyone else."

"Including me?" asked Gilbert. Fay looked confused at this, not knowing how to reply, and he laughed. "It's all right. I think I know what she wants to see you about. I've been meaning to talk to you about it, only I somehow got side-tracked when I finally managed to call you. It's certainly serious enough." His voice developed a tinge of mischief. "The last time I saw you, you distracted me very badly, you know."

"That's a lie," said Fay, heatedly. "*You* distracted *me*."

Gilbert looked at her speculatively, as if he was prepared to try the distraction again and see if its perpetrator could be proven, before his face grew serious again. "If Belle is going to speak with you, I think that would be better."

"Does she know more than you?"

"N-no," admitted Gilbert, slowly, "but I think she'll be clearer than me. The subject is somewhat delicate." Gilbert rose to leave, and Fay stood up with him. "Sit down, you idiot," he scolded, affectionately, "You're ill. You just told me."

"Doesn't stop me from standing up," Fay argued.

"Oh no?" asked Gilbert, maliciously, and pushed her into the piled up cushions left from the fight with Persa. By the time Fay had extricated herself, he was gone.

Fay sat there for a while, dreaming. Then she became bored and re-arranged the tower room. She started by putting things back in their proper place, then she shook her head at the tidy room and proceeded to pile all the cushions and furnishings together to make a luxurious nest. Fay had just settled herself in very nicely, when Belle walked in, carrying the cushion Persa had dispatched by the window.

"Fay! What have you done to my beautiful room!" she exclaimed.

Fay gave a sidewise smile and said, in an apparently aggrieved voice, "And this is the way she greets an old friend."

Belle chuckled and threw the cushion at her. Fay threw it back, with a couple more for good measure. Belle laughed again and collected the projectiles. After she had arranged herself to her own comfort, facing Fay, she was very quiet. Since Gilbert had walked out rather than telling her whatever it was, Fay understood the difficulty in finding words. She didn't let her sympathy show, however. She allowed herself momentary meanness.

Fay broke the silence with, "You'll never guess how busy your little tower room is today, first Persa, then Gilbert, and now you. All I need is Enlai and Flor and my circle of friends will be complete."

Belle frowned. "Enlai and Flor, yes. That's part of what I need to tell you, but I just don't know where to start. I don't know what you know, what you don't know, what you ought to know, or *anything*." The silence settled in the room again.

Fay broke it. "Why not tell me whatever you have to as a story—I can always ask questions."

"What made you think of that particular brilliant idea," asked Belle, mildly sarcastic.

"I feel so very comfortable that my ears are just wagging and begging for a story. Besides, if you give me a boring explanation I'll just go to sleep, and you know what that means."

Belle's frown returned, uncharacteristically, "You're very flippant today."

"Well, yes. You see, all my headaches will go, I have the doctor's promise. It's a work-related... sorry, I got it from overwork."

Belle's frown deepened. She stood up and looked out of the window for a moment, then moved back to her nest of cushions. "I see," she said. "I wish I had known you were ill. Unless the doctor doesn't know..." Then her face cleared. "Well, I'll tell you some of what's been happening here recently."

"In the castle?" asked Fay, interestedly. *Mind, behave. Fay, focus. This isn't a tale. Or is it? I feel so distant from Belle's concern. When you get down to it, I just can't seem to make it feel serious. I can listen though.*

"In the castle, in the town, all around. You can do your own interpreting. If I just told you it straight out, either you would disbelieve it or you would say you designed it."

"And you don't want to hear either of these?" Fay's interest was piqued.

"Well, no," answered Belle. Her eyes caught Fay's and held them until Fay was forced to answer.

"Go on then, I'm listening."

Belle started with her wedding: "I'm sorry you missed it, Fay. Before then, I found that if I thought of you enough, you'd come. You'd been there for all the crises in my life: you'd given me support and comfort, in your Fay-ish way. And when anything good happened, you were there to share it. You were a constant in my life. But for my wedding, nothing."

"You appeared again after my life had been completely changed. I didn't think upon it at the time, although of course I missed you," she added that last bit in quickly but one of her fists was clenched. "When you did come you were very surprised it could have happened without you. That was when I started realising your proprietorial attitude to the village and to my life. You had thoughts about how I should speak, and knew what was happening even before it did. And you expected me to talk as if I lived in a romantic dream, which I have not since I was a teenager. When I married, I could see it clearly."

Fay nodded, and said quietly, "And that is when you started letting me know it was your life, not mine."

Belle laughed and continued, "Of course, I hadn't put together the full picture then. Anyway, you know that, while I was pregnant, there were witch hunts?"

Fay grimaced. "I sort of know, because they were mentioned, and there was this man on the gallows. I don't remember when." Her hands spread out in a gesture of incertitude.

"The hunts and the fear lasted a long time. I found

them very testing." Belle's voice was strained and her eyelids hid her expression. "I was not comfortable in the damned castle, not comfortable at all. It took me a long time to adjust to being in charge. The Prince was actually a great help," she sounded surprised, "though we distrusted each other horrendously at first."

"Don't tell me, he treated you with disdain because you were a merchant's daughter."

"HRH has many quirks, but that, my friend, is not one of them. No, he came to see which of his friends could help out in my husband's minority. He found there were things only he could do, so he stayed on. After all, he had the power."

Fay couldn't resist teasing Belle about this, "He didn't stay on because of the chatelaine's beauty."

"Fay, that is not funny," Belle said sternly, then her voice softened and she giggled, "Or maybe it is, but not in the way you mean. Besides, I was married. Anyway, between us we calmed things down."

"Although I didn't know this till later, Enlai was re-cruited into the services of the prince's lieutenant, to try to isolate the cause of the witch hunt and the gen-eral scares of the neighbourhood. At first he reported to me, but then not."

"It didn't upset you?"

"Actually," Belle answered with a grin, "I think it preserved our friendship for a bit longer."

"I didn't know you were friends with Enlai. But I didn't mean him directly. I meant the Prince's lieu-tenant using villagers to spy on each other."

Belle's foot tap-tapped in the short silence. "Well, yes, it did," answered Belle frankly, "but I talked it all out with the Prince. He's very approachable, you know. And I know what you mean about Enlai—we weren't friends, but friendly acquaintances, and I was happy to leave it that way." Despite her foot, Belle's tone was reassuring.

Fay nodded.

Belle continued, her voice darkening, "And then we found out it was not just old superstition. There was some sort of witch or sorcerer. A powerful one. The Prince found his subordinates early on. They met the gallows tree. The sorcerer was far more elusive. He had been careful, very careful, up to then, and had only hurt people without influence. Interestingly enough—and this helped put me on the path to what was actually happening—none of your friends was hurt until my husband died."

Fay started to speak, and Belle lifted up a hand to silence her. "Yes, I know that my husband's death was part of one of your songs, and so did several other friends of yours. You have a habit of singing those songs to us before you do anything with them. It's as if they need time to jell."

*Oh ye gods and little fishes, what do I do to my friends? I destroy their lives. I play dungeons and dragons with their souls.* "I'm sorry," Fay muttered, mortified. "If it's any consolation, I don't sing you them all."

"It's a bit late for apologies," said Belle tartly, "if that's what it was. Besides, what I was about to say is that you might have had my husband dying and a green grave at sixteen, but you never put him through torture, nor did you have every part of his death cycle happen in public, as if it were an evil entertainment. Every single symptom. We had no secrets. He had no sanctum." Her foot stopped tapping.

Fay was aghast. "No, I never," she stuttered. "I would never do such a thing."

"I know," reassured Belle, "I know you. You are careless; you are occasionally a trifle callous when you're taken up with your tale-telling; you play havoc with all our lives: but you're not malicious."

"But I did mean to kill your husband, and I was wrong, wrong," Fay burst into tears.

Belle looked at her with surprising dispassion. "As I said, callous but not cruel. And even the callousness is going now that you're starting to understand we are real."

"Am I that obvious?"

"Not to the others, but I know you particularly well." Fay nodded and sniffed. Belle handed her a kerchief to mop up the tears and continued. "In hindsight, we should have worked it out earlier, but all of us were traumatised. None of us realised that, firstly, you were not there when you ought to have been, and secondly, someone who knew your plans could, well, change them."

"What did he or she do?" asked Fay, then retracted it hurriedly, "No, I don't want to know."

Belle was silent a moment. Her face and body were both intent on Fay, trying to communicate the size of the problem. "You have to know—it's too important not to. But I find it hard to tell you."

"First Gilbert, then you. What is so difficult to say?"

"He had trouble too?" Fay nodded. "Well, that's a relief," smiled Belle. "I honestly thought it was just me."

"Can't you tell me the difficulty," grumbled Fay, impatiently.

There was an awkward silence. Fay suddenly remembered Gilbert's bleak look and the frozen dancer. She wondered if this were the root of the trouble. *I am here: I am me. But I don't know where here is. I can see Belle and feel her room, and I can see my kitchen as well. I don't know if I am here, there, or everywhere. I just don't want to hear what Belle has to say. But I have to. If I focus on one thing, can I stay in one place?*

*A cushion. One tassel of a cushion. Look at that tassel and feel that tassel. Focus. This is sounding like Sesame Street gone wrong, but at least I am in Belle's tower again. And she has that look on her face; I must have faded. I am back, and I will stay back. But I want Belle's face to look happier. I do.* I am so scared of what she is saying.

"It's you," said Belle, bluntly. "I mean the difficulty in telling is *you*." She went over to the window again and her eyes were glazed, as if the town had stolen her words. Silence.

Fay's mood shifted. Belle was obviously perturbed and had to compose her thoughts. Fay waited. Patiently. She was totally determined to be good on the patience thing. In fact, she was determined to be utterly extraordinary on the patience thing today. Which made her sound very Californian, she reflected. She tried not to look Californian as she listened. Not that Belle would know or care if she looked Californian, Fay thought further. It was a very long silence.

"Even today," finally, Belle got herself together. Fay hadn't realised just how much emotion was behind it all.

Really, all these things had happened in a place she only half believed in, to people she thought were probably fabrications. But she was not happy that it was hurting Belle. Fay was a little surprised at how much she cared, and at how uncomfortable this felt. Caring wasn't supposed to hurt. In fact, nothing was supposed to hurt. That was the whole idea of fantasy.

"Even today," slowly continued Belle, still unsure of what she was saying. Still drained by the town. "When we've actually talked about these things directly, when you have as good as agreed that we are capable of independent action, when the two of us are being far more open than we ever have, even now I don't know, deep down, how you see us and how our reality looks from your eyes."

Fay bit her tongue. This was one question she was not going to answer. Not until she knew the answer.

"And I was scared to ask you. I'm terrified now, but I'm asking anyway."

Fay tried not to smile. Two minds with but a single thought—but what a terrible thought it was.

"I don't know if we'll cease to exist if you don't like what I say," said Belle, earnestly, "Or whether you are the one who becomes transparent and fades, as you just did. If we fade, the whole thing becomes academic. If you do, and we are an important refuge for you, then what happens to your life?

"We need answers. And one thing we have agreed upon, all of your true friends, is that there is no way out of asking the questions."

A knock at the door interrupted their thoughts. Belle called, "Enter," and a very sad face peeked through.

"Sorry to interrupt," the man said, "But I promised I would let you know if anything happened."

"What was it this time?" Belle asked.

"Dancers again," he replied. "Drowned."

"A dance club went swimming?" Fay interrupted.

"They were dancing on the green and two died—the doctor said that their lungs were full of water."

"When did this happen?"

"About an hour ago."

"Thank you for telling me," Belle finally said. She looked as if she had swallowed shattered glass. "Would you mind sending flowers to the families and telling them I will visit later in the day? And of course I will tell the prince."

"Thank you, ma'am," and the face disappeared, leaving a silence. Belle picked up a green cushion and punched it over and over and over. Then she looked across at Fay. "Now you know," she commented grimly. "And now we need to know."

"Who are you? Why do you come here? Why do you play with our lives? And why does this lead to death?"

Fay looked sombre as she asked, "Not how?"

Belle answered. "We know the mechanism. It isn't unique. Besides, you yourself have admitted you don't know. Lots of times. When things go wrong you just look sweet and lost and your mouth and eyes go round like a child's and you turn around and say 'but it couldn't have happened like that'."

"Oh," said Fay, glumly, and put her thoughts in order. She skipped over the hardest bits. Which led her straight into randomness. The words Belle had used overtook the sense of them. "Why would I come here for refuge?"

Belle looked surprised. "You don't know?"

"Truly," answered Fay, "I have no idea. I thought it was all for fun."

"Well," said Belle, slowly, her rich voice puzzled, "where do I begin?"

This time the pause was reflective, rather than disturbed. Maybe Fay was only as much to this world as this world was to Fay? Why was that such an *objectionable* thought, Fay wondered.

*Can't I wake up now? Can't I make all this go away before it gets worse?* And she tried to pay attention. This was important, even if she didn't want to hear it.

Belle finally admitted, "When I first knew you, you seemed very lonely. I was unhappy too, and that gave us a bond. It was very *easy* to give you friendship. You didn't visit very often, but there was always a faint appeal in your eyes. You were always a little scared of being rejected."

Now this was a thought Fay could understand. She could see herself very clearly in Belle's description.

"Given my, well, my ambivalent position at home," Belle continued, "it was warming that you never took my friendship for granted. Your cautious fear reassured me: I was necessary to you." She finally moved away from the window and sat down again. "Later on, the fear was replaced by friendship, but you always treated me like eggshell china. I discovered then that the china treatment was because you didn't think I was real. I could just disappear."

"One of my friends did," Fay whispered, "I visited the cottage by the sea and he had been dead for fifty years."

Belle nodded, "But that wasn't the point I was making. What I am saying is that, however scared you were, you kept coming back. You needed a refuge. In the beginning it was just the refuge and solace of friendship. But recently you have come to me when things have been too difficult, when you have been in pain or distressed. I'm a sanctuary, aren't I?"

"I guess you are," Fay murmured, then looked up straight into Belle's eyes. "You know, when you said 'refuge', I thought you meant something else entirely."

"What?"

Where are words when I want them? Why do they always flood me when I can't use them? "I always come here on the edge of sleep, when I'm dreaming. I plan what I want to dream, then I lie in bed and pretend it out. Only it has never felt as real as this." She plucked at her tassel, anxiously, and was quiet for a moment. Even the cushion was too real at this moment. There were no shadows of her bed beyond it. Just the cushion.

"In the beginning..." with these familiar words Fay's voice grew less faded and distressed, "...In the beginning my life was so dull and boring. Nothing ever happened except for people picking on me, or ignoring me. My family would make decisions and leave me out. My mother would forget to collect me after school camp."

"I faded, and had no idea how I did it. The only place I was safe from fading was in my imagination. I was safe from fading, and boredom, and I was safe from other people. So my fantasy worlds were good places to be.

"They gave me tools to keep living, I think." She looked up again, defensive, "They were only stories."

And then she forgot her defensiveness and fell into truth again. She told Belle about books and worlds of the imagination. About dreaming and dreams. *I just told Belle about Tolkien. What an extraordinary thing to do— telling a piece of fiction about a writer of fiction. But I feel as if I am in the castle. I can touch this cushion, and feel the smoothness of the silk at the end of the tassel. I told her the truth. I told her that she was not real.*

"I thought to myself," Fay continued, "Why don't I make up a land? I could enjoy myself more. I could have more control. Control was important.

"I started listening to songs, and I realised that they told stories too. I started thinking of how the songs and my stories fitted together. Bit by bit, over a number of years, this country coalesced. When I did literature and history and economics, I just lifted what I learned and applied it to my dreaming, and I worked out what crops are produced, what metals are mined, and, oh, everything. I just added and added and added until it became real." Belle's gaze was absorbed. "Then I started using my fantasy world as a refuge. Yes," and she looked defiantly at Belle, "you had the right word. But my dreams were only an emotional refuge when I was a child. I really needed them. I did." *I sound defensive even to myself. "I did, I did, I did," —a child trying to prove something.*

"Since I then, they stopped my life from being terminally dull. I had friends but they were boring. I had work but it was mindless. I had a life that should have been full but was somehow empty. There's a wall between myself and reality, and this is my escape.

"You know, it's very strange, but in the beginning it was just stories. *You* know," her fingers made an impatient tapping on her left arm, "words I told myself and pretended were true. I held conversations with myself and pretended they were with someone else.

"But eventually it grew." As she said this, she sat up straight. "I found I could actually picture places in my mind just before I went to sleep, and I could make up faces and voices. It was like watching a very distant play, where I called out all the words, and they came back to me as movement and life.

"And I stopped analyzing it. It became real enough so that I could escape. And that's when I invented you and your world, Belle. Don't you understand?" and her agitation increased, "I invented you as a friend—I *needed* one.

"And now," Fay realised the magnitude of what she was saying as she looked round at Belle's room, at the door leading to the stairwell which led to the castle, at the window to the world outside, "there are no parts anyone is playing. I can dream myself in and out of here, but when I'm here I can feel things, and I can't predict what's going to happen.

"You are real now. I can't deny that you are real. When you give me medicine it cures a headache here and in the real world, and it tastes foul. And when I fall in love here," Fay looked almost surprised at herself, but bitterly so, "it affects my ability to act normally in the real world. I overcompensate and try to fall in love *there*, to prove that *here* is not real." *I am so truthful I am scared witless by my own speech. I must be lying. Lies must be emerging from a deep and unknown part of me. Aren't they? Because this can't be happening. It can't be real.*

"And is it?" Belle's golden voice asked. "Are we real?"

"I don't know," said Fay wretchedly, "I just don't know."

Belle nodded, and there was a very long silence as she thought through what her friend had revealed.

"Fay?" she asked, hesitantly, "Can you do me a big favour?"

"What, Belle," Fay asked, her voice faded with drained emotion.

"Can you suspend judgment on whether we are real or not? Don't just say—'I won't decide' but consciously suspend us between reality and imagination."

"Why?" asked Fay, "What would it achieve?"

Belle's voice became earnest, "It would mean that we could focus on the actual problem."

"The actual problem?" Fay was querulous. There could be no bigger problem than what she had just described to Belle.

"Fay, there is far more wrong than you not knowing if the cushions you fling at people exist. Or if I am real. Even if the cushions don't exist, and I am imaginary to you, I could get hurt if you threw one the wrong way. No, that is a bad way of describing it." Another pause. Belle was good on pauses. During this pause came another knock at the door. The same sad face appeared.

"Can it wait?" snapped Belle.

"Sorry, ma'am," and the face disappeared into the stairwell.

"You're a random factor at the moment. Too many people are trying to influence you, and only a very few know it's you they are trying to influence.

"I have a feeling that the chief actors in our little drama are going to be those you know because, whether you created us—whether we created you—

whether we exist independently—whether we are figments of your imagination—you have been key to all the major events in this region for a long time now. Even the dancers are linked to you, somehow."

Fay shook her head roughly, shaking off the headache caused by those ideas. "No, Belle," she said, "I can't suspend judgment, nor can I sit back not knowing what happens.

"Whether all this," and her hand spread out to encompass the world, "is real is not the point. You're right in that. The point is that it has a tangible reality to *me*." Fay continued, sharply. She didn't mean to be sharp—but she was still very fretted by the thoughts she was thinking and the thoughts she was hearing, and the worry came out in her voice, which trilled like high-strung wire.

"It's no use me being a 'random factor'. No use at all. I have to be committed to you all or to give up entirely." She took a deep breath. "If something is wrong, then me backing out will hardly help. And if whatever wrong comes from me, because I've not committed myself, because I've never broken down the glass wall around me and learned how to care, then we have to know, don't we. As you said, if I throw cushions, they will hurt someone, whether I think they are real or not." Fay wasn't sure that this made sense. But she was almost beyond caring.

Belle nodded, then denied the agreement. Maybe she didn't think it made sense either? Fay was almost hopeful. But her hope was very soon lost in another new thought. "No, Fay, it's not that sort of wrong. There's a person that's wrong. The fabric of the world is right."

"How do you know?"

"I feel it *here*," said Belle vehemently, placing both hands, fingers spread, over her heart.

"And if it's a person," Fay finally managed to ask, "if there is a sorcerer in the town and if it could be someone I know or who knows me, how does it help if I just appear at random?"

They were down to bare bones now. "You know I need to change my behaviour, otherwise you would not have been so very insistent that we have this talk. And it's more than my behaviour that needs to change. For all we know this person could be stopping me from coming *because* I have some sort of power in this world, *because* of all the things that are driving you silly-scared."

The tassel became an anchor. It became a weight holding her down. It chained her to the dream-reality. "Belle, I think I need to stay here. I'm not going away. Even when I sleep I will keep telling myself that I'm here, in this world. Maybe my dreams can be of the real world for a change." She smiled a little smile at the thought before she continued soberly, "If this person has got *you* scared, and Gilbert concerned, then you can't leave me out of it. Especially from this moment!"

"Why this moment?" Belle whispered. "Because of our conversation?"

"No," said Fay disgustedly, "because it's probably Enlai. I just worked it out."

Belle's eyes widened. This was not where she had been expecting the conversation to lead.

Fay explained, "It's someone close to me, you say. And I had nightmares about Enlai. Now, if my day-dreams affect this world, then why can't someone reach into mine?"

"Reach into yours," murmured Belle, aghast.

"I could still be wrong. But I think I saw Enlai's eyes in someone else's head—in my world. And I saw his re-flection in a window, several times. And there were nightmares. I kept telling myself that Enlai didn't exist.

I even had a little mantra about it. It didn't do any good, though. He still haunted me. Not in any big way. But not just in my dreams."

"In your world." said Belle, quietly, "That does change things. So what will you do besides stay here?"

Fay grinned, "Play the innocent. You keep Enlai quiet, and get him to keep quiet about our relationship. Almost no-one has seen me here for ages, so I can come in as if I were totally ignorant."

"And then?" Belle breathed. "We'll see what happens?" There was silence. "Can't you try another song?" Belle asked, tentatively.

"Huh?" was Fay's intelligent response.

"Don't wait for things to happen," her friend urged. "Set up a song which will bring you into the circle of things, innocently. That way you can find out things faster, I think, and we can work out who it is and what to do about it more quickly. Fewer people will be hurt. After all, we have no proof it's Enlai."

"But I just told you he haunts me!"

"Would you send him to the gallows-tree on that?" asked Belle, very quietly.

Fay was suddenly scared. Could she be responsible for doing anything that would lead to another human being hung? Maybe she should give up now. Maybe it was all a dream. It had to be. But Belle's distress was real.

Fay was caught between the need to just leave her dreams behind and all the nastiness, and her desire to help her friend. There had to be a way of putting off that decision. And maybe Belle had just given it to her. "Hmm," mumbled Fay, distractedly, and wandered round the tower room looking at things and out the window, searching for ideas. Finally her gaze fell upon the distant green of the fields.

"I know," she said, brightly, "The seeds of love. It's

an English folk song, I'll choose who I want to love. And I get to reject everything people suggest to me and go for what I want anyway." She grinned, wickedly.

"Sounds as if you're after something you've already determined."

"But the townsfolk don't know that, and it gives me an excuse to stay."

"How does the song go?" Belle asked.

"Well, I sowed a garden, but didn't have time to choose. I asked the gardener for help. He made some suggestions, but I refused them, and finally chose exactly what I wanted."

"At least it gives you a chance to review the single men," commented Belle, doubtfully.

"Yeah," said Fay, enthusiastically, "and won't Enlai be absolutely delighted. Besides, it could be fun. Oh, Belle, I just had a really mean thought. A really, really, really mean thought."

"What?" asked Belle resignedly.

"Well there's a little Japanese children's song about stepping on a cat..."

"And," prompted Belle.

"And I thought it'd be just the thing for Persa," smiled Fay dreamily.

# CHAPTER ELEVEN

*I sowed the seeds of love*
*'Twas all in the spring*
*I gathered them up in the morning so clear*
*When the small birds so sweetly sing*

*The gardener was standing by*
*I asked him to choose for me*
*He chose for me the violet, the lily and the pink*
*But these I refused all three*

*In June is the red, red rose*
*And that is the flower for me*
*I'll pluck and think that no lily nor pink*
*Can match with the bud on that tree (Traditional)*

---

"NEKO FUNJATTA, NEKO FUNJATTA," SANG FAY, CHEERILY, "Neko funzuketara hikkaita. Neko hikkaita. Neko hikkaita. Neko hikkaitara Naichatta. Neko Nyao Nyao, Neko nya nya nya. Neko Nyao Nyao.... " While she sang in bad Japanese, Fay was very careful to think out the meaning for the words in English just to make sure everything worked. That song was the first moment of merriment in an otherwise acutely depressing day.

*I stepped on a cat.* Fay thought, with glee, *I stepped on a cat. Because I stepped on a cat she scratched me.* She really had not thought she could be such a vile child. Fay continued to sing with a giant grin on her face, *The cat scratched. The cat scratched. Because the cat scratched I cried 'nya nya'.* As she sang, she strolled down the path to the cottage, the very first time she had ever walked all the way from the town. It felt good to walk that far. Tired, but good.

Now that Fay was thinking 'tired', her legs suddenly felt as if they'd drop off. So she raised her voice louder and sang through the song again. If Fay walked quickly, she'd reach the cottage sooner. Besides, it fit the beat better. And just as she reached the second agonising "Nyao, nyao, nyao," she also reached the cottage.

The door opened astonishingly quickly. There stood Gilbert, sword in hand. Fay blinked.

"Why do you want to kill me?" she asked, cheekily. "I though you cared."

Gilbert laughed and put his sword away. "I care for you, but not your yowling."

"It wasn't yowling," Fay said indignantly, "It was song most beauteous."

Gilbert ushered her in and said, "Remind me never to come to a concert by you."

"Actually," confided Fay as she sat down, "It's a part of an experiment."

"To see how badly you can sing?" teased Gilbert.

"No!" said Fay. "Belle and I agreed that we should find out if I can influence events, or if I'm a figment of my own imagination."

"I think you're a figment of your own imagination," said Gilbert, and handed her a cup of wine.

"Just watch," said Fay, immediately putting the wine

down, folding her hands in her lap, and looking at Gilbert expectantly. "The song goes 'I stepped on a cat and it went...'"

"No, don't tell me," begged Gilbert "I can guess the rest. But who is the target?"

"Persa," said Fay, happily.

Gilbert put back his head and laughed. He did not politely restrain his laughter: it echoed for far too long. Fay had her suspicions about who he was actually laughing at: she was forced to take action. Fay gave him his wine back. In fact, she gently and firmly force-fed him. Gilbert sputtered and recovered. He put down the goblet and examined his damp clothes.

"Hadn't you better get that off before you catch a cold?" asked Fay, her eyes wide with innocence.

There was not much of an interlude before a high scream came from outside. And a caterwaul. Then another caterwaul. And another. And another.

Gilbert put on a modicum of clothing with the efficiency of one used to answering emergencies. He opened the door. On the ground was Persa, nursing an ankle. Cats bolted down the street, round the corner of the house, slunk out of sight behind bushes. It was a very patterned movement, reflected Fay. Fan-shaped. In the centre of the fan was Persa. Still Life with Scream. And at the base of the fan, along the struts and right to the edges, were cats, all gravitating as far as they could get from Persa.

Gilbert muttered something under his breath then smiled sweetly. Fay had never seen so sweet a smile, nor so ambiguous a one. Persa looked up at him accusingly. He explained, "I've sent them home."

"But where did they *come* from?" wailed Persa, and then, "I've broken my ankle."

Gilbert leaned over and checked. "It's only

sprained," he reassured her. To Fay's fascination, he bent down and lifted Persa, as if she weighed nothing.

"Make some tea," he instructed Fay. Fay was chastened enough to obey. She was also still a bit dazed by the number of cats. A million. A billion. A trillion. A zillion. Well, at least two dozen. Lots of cats. Lots and lots.

She needed to talk to Belle about it. Or maybe to Gilbert. Which took courage. Belle was easier to talk to than Gilbert. She looked across, almost envying Persa the treatment her ankle was getting. Then she wondered how on *earth* Persa was going to get home.

———

*I didn't mean for Persa to step on a cat here. And she could have given me another ten minutes. Or maybe twenty. An hour would have been good. And two hours would have been better.*

*I am angry at Persa for doing it. I am angry at me for making it happen. I am angry at Gilbert for being so nice and charming. He should not have been nice and charming.*

*I am in a sulk.*

*I made her a cup of tea and I made us all dinner. And I only burned bits of it. I didn't burn the cup of tea at all. Wasn't that clever of me?*

*And here he is, making a bed for her, like a good little boy. And he will carry her to the bed, too, just like he carried her to the privy earlier. Do I really envy her being carried to the privy? I will have to think about that one.*

*I never thought I would be so annoyed with him for being so **nice**. He could have organised a way to get her home, surely. And her mother could have fussed over her. Storybook mothers do fuss, even if real ones don't. And I thought of Persa's mother as the gossipy, chatty, fussing sort, too. It is just not fair.*

*I could have had a whole night with him. Instead he is making me a simply **cosy** little bed on the floor, so that I can be there if Persa needs anything. Which she will. There is a 'How much can I milk this situation?' gleam in her eye. And she didn't even know I did the cats and that Gilbert is on a guilt trip. I wish he would drop the guilt trip. I am the only one allowed them.*

*Persa is thinking mischief. Look. Her eyes are moving around the room, spotting and cataloguing a whole evening's worth of requests.*

*I am going to add a nice fat cushion to my cushy little bed. And if she asks for more than two things an hour, I will suffocate her with it. Slowly. And then I will take the cushion right into the bedroom and suffocate bloody Gilbert. Less slowly.*

*Her ankle is not even very bad. I know this for a fact. When Gilbert was out getting firewood, Persa walked over to the kitchen and poured herself a glass of water. She did not limp. Not even a hiccup of a limp. And she sent me the most silencing look when Gilbert came back. It was such a strong silencing look I don't dare tell Gilbert. Or maybe I am easily silenced.*

*I am in a sulk. A very big sulk.*

*I bet he thought I got the water. I would have told him. Except... Except... I did send the cats. And her ankle might not be seriously damaged, but if I had stepped on squillions of cat tails, my nerves would be ragged. I would send my friend a silencing look when I went to get water. I would.*

*Actually, my nerves **are** ragged. It is those plotting looks Persa is sending my way. And she never told us why she came to the cottage. It's a long way to come for no good reason.*

*I am deeply suspicious. In fact, I am almost as suspicious as I am guilty.*

*Cat cries are so sick-making. All that pain. Then all*

*those hours of sulking. How many cats were there, really? And are they all at home now, engaging in graceful pique?*

*You know, until this moment, I didn't realise how much I miss cats. I miss cats, so I make Persa go out on a spree of cat torture.*

*Everything in this little world of mine is warped, including me. Very warped. Almost as warped as Fred. Not as warped as Gilbert though. Look at the way he has lined up on the table everything that Persa might ask for. I wonder what **he** is feeling guilty about?*

————

The sleeping arrangement was unusual when Gilbert was finished. Fay could see no sense in it. The bedroom was not in use at all. Persa had the couch, where she was nursing her wounded foot. This she did with aplomb: Fay wondered if the aplomb was as fake as the injury, but didn't dare ask. Fay had a little nest near Persa's feet, and Gilbert slept by the door. She had watched in fascination as Gilbert pulled everything together and turned the living room into a boot camp.

She wondered if there had been a secret message from Persa that had resulted in all this rearrangement. And when did she give it? The privy might be outside the house, but only just, so Fay would have heard anything. And apart from that, Persa and Gilbert had not been alone. It was very aggravating. Maybe Persa had a secret code of twitching toes and had communicated to Gilbert by twiddling her big toe three times then her littlest toe twice?

Fay took a close look at her friend's face. Maybe it wasn't mischief she was showing. Maybe it was relief. Hard to say. Persa had a three-expression face, and cultivated it carefully. It was very hard to tell if she was thinking something unusual. Unusual for Persa, that is.

Normally interpretation was straightforward, a sheer mischief face meant mischief and her sad face meant sad, serious or rare depression. And her other face was a kind of catchall for everything else. It was also the face she used to play poker with.

Fay knew third-rate actors with more facial expressions than Persa. Mostly Persa stuck with her merry, mischievous face. It was her natural state of being. So maybe she was just happy. But why were her eyes still checking things out then, and why was she playing sick?

Was she out to get Gilbert? A giant "NO!!" rose up within Fay. If Gilbert were a philanderer there would be trouble. And he would cease to be one. Immediately. Permanently.

Fay didn't claim easily, but what she claimed, she kept. If there was something between her love and her friend, then they had both dug themselves very big holes. If it were just Persa-sided, then maybe Fay would let Persa out of the hole. Maybe. Maybe she would throw soil and bricks on top of her friend instead. It all depended how long it took the grumps to go. And right now she had very big grumps indeed.

Fay dug herself a little hole in the bedclothes, and said a little mantra to remind herself not to go home. Then she fell into a restless semi-slumber.

There was something not right about all this. Her conscious mind was looking at all the wrong things.

---

For restless semi-slumber, it was very satisfactory. Not at all satisfying, but truly restless. The floor was hard, and it echoed. Fay's sleep never took her very deep. She kept on pulling herself back from anything more than a light doze, because she was afraid of going home. Her own bed was more comfortable than the floor, and that was a potential problem.

She was aware of Gilbert as she tossed and turned, though less aware of Persa. This was despite the fact that Persa kept kicking bedclothes onto Fay and retrieving them, which reminded Fay a great deal about what had been happening indoors when Persa had screamed on top of her pile of cats.

Her own restlessness meant she didn't at first notice the thumping. Or even the bells. Gilbert did. When Fay woke up briefly and turned to him to confirm her dream that he was there, on the floor by the door, she discovered him eyes wide open, focused on sound.

Jangle hop-*thump* thumpthump, jangle hop-*thump* thumpthump, janglethump, janglethump, thud thud

Jangle hop-*thump* thumpthump, jangle hop-*thump* thumpthump, janglethump, janglethump, thud thud

Jangle hop-*thump* thumpthump, jangle hop-*thump* thumpthump, janglethump, janglethump, thud thud

It took Fay a while to work out the pattern. She found the regularity and predictability soothing. Everything except the jangle and thud echoed through the floorboards. The thud was more like a clank of sticks, in the air.

Jangle hop-*thump* thumpthump, jangle hop-*thump* thumpthump, janglethump, janglethump, thunk thunk

Jangle hop-*thump* thumpthump, jangle hop-*thump* thumpthump, janglethump, janglethump, thunk thunk

Jangle hop-*thump* thumpthump, jangle hop-*thump* thumpthump, janglethump, janglethump, thunk thunk

The sound moved around. It bumped and thumped widdershins around the house. She got out of bed to investigate. Gilbert was at the window before her. He stopped her from opening the curtains. His face was a study of stern worry.

Fay gesticulated, "What?"

Gilbert looked over at Persa, fast asleep, and drew Fay into the kitchen.

"What?" she asked aloud. She didn't even bother to hide her peeve. She was beyond hiding such things. Which was a grand thought for a really irritable tone of voice. Fay resolved to try to be a tad more civilised.

"I don't know," replied Gilbert, "But I don't like it. I don't know what could be making those sounds, here, so far from anywhere, and I have made this cottage secure. I would rather not know, and maintain my security."

Fay wondered at this, wondering at things being her specialty. "I thought you were one of those perennially curious people?" she commented.

Gilbert sighed. "I am, but not by facing horror head-on. There are better ways of facing battle than with a drawn sword, and safer ways of finding out what is wrong than by seeking trouble."

Fay thought. It was not a big thought. In fact, Belle had already told her the answer. She wanted to hear it from Gilbert, though. In fact, she wanted to hear a lot of things from Gilbert. There had been a lot of seething emotions at her end, and not much communication between them. Voicing the obvious was a good start. "Has horror been happening a lot?" she asked.

"It was the disappearances that brought Persa down here, you know," was Gilbert's answer.

"The disappearances? What disappearances? And what on *earth* has that to do with morris dancers. Morris dancers do much more lunatic things than dance by the shore at moonlight."

"Morris dancers?" Gilbert asked, "You're sure?"

"No, I'm not," replied Fay, irritably, the pattern of thumps faded without her ear next to the floor, "It just sounds a bit like the noises they make dancing. Tell me about disappearances."

"We had some early on, with the first spate of sorcery. Persa was under strict instructions to come straight here and let me know if anyone else died. And she was to do it quietly—I don't want the whole town to panic."

"People faded from their firesides at night or on the way home in the early evenings. Which is why she faked her ankle, I think. She has a great deal of commonsense."

"Commonsense. Persa." snorted Fay, inelegantly, "Now I've heard everything. Hang on, you knew about her ankle?" Gilbert shrugged. "And you carried her... everywhere?"

He grinned and suddenly looked like himself again. Fay was inordinately relieved. Gilbert without merriment left the whole world an unhappier place. This resolved her to action again. "We have to do something. But what?"

Gilbert looked at her, silently assessing. It was a long while before he said, "We have to wait until morning. It's highly likely that this is a trap of some kind and our very best reaction is not to spring it. That's why I don't want to even look outside. As I read it, someone is anticipating our natural curiosity."

Fay was not happy, but she waited, because he had obviously not finished. "Tomorrow I will talk to the town council," he said, "and you to the castle, and we can meet and compare notes. We need to know a lot more about how and why before we can beard this particular predator."

"But *why*?" asked Fay, frustrated, "Your prince has been looking into this for *ages*."

Gilbert grinned, "My prince has drawn a dead end. He has a special talent in that direction."

"That's a mixed metaphor."

"Good." He turned to go back into the living room, then had a sudden thought. "Fay, how do you feel?"

"Scared."

"I can understand that. Not knowing is far more terrifying than facing monsters." This was something new for Fay, who was rather a specialist in not knowing. Had she spent half her life scaring herself silly? *Ye Gods*, she thought, *what a horrid idea*. "But one of the reasons we can't act is we don't know the source of the sorcery."

"That's a bad pun," complained Fay, "You are not supposed to make bad puns when you say world shattering things."

"I don't see why not," shrugged Gilbert. "Anyway, you are one possible source. If he or she is robbing you of power, you may feel it."

"*May* feel it?"

"Then again you may not," he grinned. Why did he always have that grin, just when she wanted to strangle him? It was conspiratorial, and wry, and funny, and banished all thoughts of strangling.

*Bother him*, Fay thought. "And how *might* I feel it?" she asked, acerbically.

"It feels a bit like someone having a window to your soul and the use of your hands and feet. The eyes. They are the windows to your soul. Shared power works through the eyes."

"Yuck," was all Fay could think of saying. "I don't want to hear any more. The thought of anyone doing that to me is… is… spiders crawling over me would be preferable."

"It is not something anyone offers lightly."

"Oh, go jump." He was being intentionally elliptic. Fay was annoyed all over again. The trouble is that Gilbert did precisely what she said, if walking back to his huddle of bedclothes and lying there could be called jumping.

And he didn't even cuddle me! Fay mourned her cuddle-freeness as she untangled her bedclothes and longed for the night to be finished. It was not a good night.

The half-explanation by Gilbert hadn't helped things. Suddenly the thumping and the bells felt eerie, and she did not at all enjoy having her ear to the floor, listening.

Although maybe Gilbert had planned everything. Fay on edge was Fay unlikely to return home. He could have given her a full explanation, but he had gone to sleep instead. And he could have given her his bed. It looked as if he wanted them all in the same room, with the floor clear for action. There was a great deal of space for Gilbert to move in, if he had to.

No, scolded Fay. I am thinking too much. And if I hadn't promised Belle I would stay I would be home in an instant. Regardless of bells, thumps, thunks or a very hard floor. This dream is becoming a nightmare.

Despite the echoes from outside, the night was very still. So the night remained a quiet nightmare, with the feet and the sticks and the bells of dancers echoing and anchoring it in eeriness. Sometimes closer, sometimes further, the ghostly echo seemed to be drawing a pattern. Suddenly it seemed important to break the silence. Fay whispered to Gilbert, "They're drawing a pattern."

Gilbert looked across the floor at her, listened, then nodded. He mimed, "Go to sleep."

Fay gave up on being irritable and sulky and altogether annoyed and actually did try to sleep. Eventually she drifted back into that restless half-slumber.

At dawn, her rest was broken by a sharp slap. Or a thunderclap. Or sticks hitting together. It was so hard, so loud, that it felt as if the house would fall down. She jumped up quickly, hitting her head on Persa's chin. Persa was also getting out of bed.

"Ow," said Persa, "Mind my head."

"Not your ankle?"

"Mind *yours*," was the reply. "It's morning and I feel mad. And your ankle is handy."

"Girls, girls," came Gilbert's voice. "It was only dawn."

"Dawn broke very hard this morning, then," commented Persa.

"We're safe," shrugged Gilbert, "which is all that matters. If whatever it was had worked, there would have been no magic residue to hit."

"What do you mean 'whatever'—I thought we would be safe here?" said Persa, suspiciously.

Fay commented that Persa had slept soundly.

"I *always* sleep soundly. The sleep of the just."

"And the terminally deaf."

Gilbert interposed. "Breakfast," he proposed, "then we find out what other remnants of the magic are left."

So they did this. Despite Persa's best efforts and Gilbert's clown-smile, breakfast was sober and efficient. And Gilbert was still untactile. Eventually, they were ready to check outside. It was as if all of them were putting off the outside world as late as possible— even Persa, who had actually slept.

"We have been left a truly charming calling card," Gilbert announced, as he peeked outside the front door. There was a morris dancer on their doorstep. In full costume. Drained of blood. Very, very dead. Gilbert pulled the body to the side of the house and covered it respectfully with a blanket.

# CHAPTER TWELVE

IT WAS A VERY LONG ROAD TO THE CASTLE. FAY HAD never walked the whole path with such urgency and she never wanted to walk it again. Especially not with lingering echoes of the dead dancing.

Gilbert left Persa at her house then walked Fay partway to the castle. He would not go past the common, however. "I have to face the town council," he pointed out. "You only have to face Bellezour Anma. I will meet up with you afterwards."

Only. And no kiss. But she was almost too tired to care. It was a one-sided romance in any case. She should give up. That was the closest she could come to caring.

By this time even Fay's legs were too tired to drag. The lack of sleep, the long walk, and the constant tension had all caught up with her. It was quite likely that Gilbert had given her a concerned look, she thought, but she was too tired to see it. And sleep was the last thing she could do. Because her friends needed solutions.

Except Enlai. Should she be afraid of Enlai? Or was she so tired she was turning him into a villain?. Had she *really* seen him looking through someone else's eyes? Or were they all getting paranoid?

Belle met her at the front entrance. Fay did not have to brave stairs. "Gilbert told me to tell you things," she said, launching straight into what counted. She was too tired for most words, anyhow, so she had to get out what she could while she could, "Only I haven't slept properly because I was trying not to get home, so I have to speak quickly."

Belle's mouth quirked at Fay's logic, but she walked Fay to a room with wooden benches, and sat her down. "Now you can speak as quickly as you like," Belle suggested.

Fay tried to sag in relief, but the wooden bench wouldn't let her. If she was really magical, she could make it sag, her mind thought, inconsequentially. "I don't remember what he told me to tell you," Fay said. "And I don't know what you know. But Persa found out something about people disappearing. And a morris dancer died outside Gilbert's cottage last night. Persa and I were both there. Persa pretended she had a bad ankle and slept like a log. It isn't fair. And someone must really hate morris dancers. Why are so many people stupid about morris dancing? There is absolutely nothing wrong with it. I should take it up."

"You're babbling," said Belle, and handed Fay a hot drink. Fay looked around for a stove, but only saw servants. She gave up on thinking. It was too tough.

"Will this put me to sleep?" Fay asked suspiciously, "Because I can't go to sleep. Not ever. Because if I go to sleep I won't wake up. Or I will wake up in my own bed. And I promised. I promised someone. Was it Persa? It wasn't Gilbert, was it? I don't promise him things. He doesn't tell me things. He has lots of secrets. Too many secrets. And he doesn't like me anymore. His hair makes me want to run my fingers through it. It wasn't Enlai. I couldn't tell Gilbert about Enlai because he was trying not to tell me things. It was confused. It could have been you. Did I promise you?"

Belle laughed and said, "You promised me. And the drink will help you stay awake and to concentrate. I think I have a solution to your sleep problem. I was thinking about what happened when you slept when I should have been sleeping myself, last night. Everything else can wait."

"That's good," said Fay, "Because I don't sound like myself. I don't think like myself. I sound like I'm drunk. Or, like Persa, I'm babbling. And I can't use long sentences. My brain is rewired. It isn't just sleep. It is like those headaches I had. The work-induced ones. I am not me. Or I am only half me. Maybe it started when the morris dancer died. In the cottage. I don't know. I don't know anything anymore. Or I know everything. They feel the same. Someone has smashed the window into my soul. Gilbert used that phrase. Not smashed. Just window to my soul. The smashing is how I feel. Not smashing, smashed. I feel smashed. Do sorcerers make me babble?"

"You need sleep, first and foremost," said Belle. "But there are a lot of sensible things in what you are saying."

"There are?" Fay looked around, "Where?"

"Were you like this last night? Or this morning?"

"No, I was all together. But silenced. I should have told Gilbert about Enlai. Or did I tell him and forgot? I forget."

"Fay, listen to me. Focus on what I'm saying. Think of that window to your soul. Take some wood, and board up the hole that has been left there. One plank at a time. Hammer them in firmly: make it secure." Belle waited a moment. "When you feel it's secure, and you can think without babble, then just nod at me."

Belle's instructions helped. Fay was still tired beyond belief, but that strange feeling of being out of control of her mind and of thoughts jumbling and playing games dissipated. She told Belle so, "I can't think why it helped, but it did. I'm still tired and if I sleep I go back home, and I promised you I wouldn't. Not until we have sorted things out. Gilbert has gone to argue things with the town council, but he didn't tell me exactly what. He really didn't tell me much of anything."

"I wish he would," sighed Belle. "It would be a lot easier to sort things out if he would talk to you more openly. He has his reasons not to, but..."

"You said you had an idea about sleeping?" This was said wistfully, rather than hopefully. Fay felt quite extraordinarily sleep deprived for only one night without slumber.

"I should have said it earlier, because time is probably different between our worlds."

"It is! Of course it is. That is why I feel so bad. I'm not used to the time here—I've never been here for so long at a stretch."

"It may not be the only reason, but it could certainly be a part of it. You need sleep."

"I need safe sleep. At home people talk about safe sex. And here I am worried about safe sleep. But how do I get it? A sleep condom?"

Belle sighed. You could see, however, that she was relieved that Fay was making bad jokes. "When you visit here, you are on the verge of sleep?"

"Mostly. Sometimes I am walking or taking a shower and it is only my mind that is disengaged."

"When you just visit here and then get up again for... oh, for some reason or other—"

"If the phone rings?"

"Who is the Phone?" Fay opened her mouth to explain, and Belle hastened on. "No, leave it for now. If you get disturbed before you actually sleep, do you feel rested?"

"Of course. It's like awake-dreaming, in a way. That is how I know if I have had a really good imagining. Because those are the ones I feel rested from. When things feel real."

"That is what I was hoping. I've been doing some research, you see, and piecing together things you have told me. I think you can do the same here," Belle hypothesised. "I think you can dream of your world the way you used to dream of ours. And that should give you enough rest, and shore up that broken window of yours."

"How is it you understand about windows?"

"We learn about them in school?" Belle answered. It was obviously supposed to be a joke, but it was delivered tentatively.

"Ah, Magic 101."

"You *are* feeling better. You have more and more comments which are semi-nonsense."

"Not complete nonsense?"

"Try harder."

"Oh," said Fay, deflated. "When can I try to dream? How do I do it?"

"Build it up the same way you would here. Deal with problems the way you would here. If something unexpected comes up then try to deal with it there, where you are stronger."

"What do you mean by something unexpected?"

"No-one believes me, but I do think that the sorcerer is feeding on your magic. Until you came in, looking so tired, I didn't realise that this may have been going on for a long time. But you look dulled today."

"And this means I have been vampired?"

"What a charming way of describing it. But yes, to my mind. Although others don't think so."

"You have been arguing with Gilbert about me."

"Yes," said Belle, with a sense of finality.

"So why does he let me stay round? I am sure he could get rid of me if he wanted? He has magic, doesn't he?"

"He does indeed. And he probably could. But he loves you. He just doesn't see you as pivotal to anything except his love life."

"That's so... deflating," Fay said. "I almost wished that the drink and the boards thing hadn't perked me up. Because then I wouldn't have to admit you are right. I am not his little woman!"

"But you are his woman, aren't you?"

"I think so. Except that if he doesn't see me, all of me, then only a part of me is. And he gives me mixed signals. Very mixed signals." Fay was sounding querulous, "I am turning into a feminist. I refuse to stay home and do his laundry!"

Belle laughed and laughed at that. It brightened the room.

"I need that rest more than ever," Fay said.

"You do," Belle answered. "With artificial stimulants you are yourself, and you can be formidable if you will permit yourself that luxury. But we need you here and unconfused and thinking. No artificial stimulants. Testing your realities isn't enough. You have to be able to work within one."

"Which I can't do if I am stuck in babbledom," said Fay, sadly, "Which means I need to rest and drink lots of this whatever it is."

"Coffee," said Belle.

"Coffee?" Fay looked her cup. "It doesn't taste like coffee. It tastes all spicy."

"I'll teach you how to make it, if you want. It has

herbs that help centre magic and spices to relax weary muscles."

"So I'm not the first person to babble in your vicinity?"

"Almost everyone babbles in my vicinity. You are just one of those rare people who have an excuse," said Belle acerbically. "Now come, let us find you a comfortable bed."

Belle was changing. Changes upon changes. She was no-one's servant anymore. And she was capable of being very, very independent. This required thinking upon. However, at this moment, there were more urgent things to think upon. When Fay went to dream from her normal world, she planned things first, so that is what she must do.

She would be in her own home with dinner and hot drinks at the ready. A quiet time in front of the television would be good. Belle seemed to think that something might happen. So she would have all her emergency numbers under the telephone.

For some reason she trusted Belle on this. She trusted Belle much more than she trusted Gilbert. Gilbert knew a lot, but was not intuitive about *her* need to know. Fay was glad she had a friend as well as a lover —there were times when a complex world demanded both.

————

*I need some rules. I must dream effectively this time. If Belle is wrong and it doesn't rest me, then we will find another way. We must. I must.*

*Babbling scared me. It was like hyperdrive Fay. Fay on fast forward. I bet I could use it to stun Gilbert sometime, though. In fact, I could use it to stun anyone. Superfast nonsense Fay—lethal weapon. Babble people to death.*

*I have never in my life imagined a bed like this. It is so strange to be in my imaginary world with unexpected things popping out of the woodwork. And this woodwork most certainly should not be here. It isn't a four-poster bed. I could have imagined one of them. Four-poster beds are romantic, and this world is supposed to be full of romance.*

*Not much of the romantic at all in this world, right now. In fact, despite Belle saying that he loves me (he must talk about me more than he talks to me—**what** a cheering thought), the really romantic thing here right now is busy treating me diffidently. He is really beginning to annoy me. I might change my name to Kate and sing, "I hate men."*

*The bed is a two-poster. And the mattress is on a kind of leather sling thing. Belle called it a demountable. Said it was the prince's bed. She says that was the best she could do in terms of protections. I guess princes need protection. This prince is going to need protection from me. He leaves his bed in a spare room of Belle's and goes off swanning around the country with his knights. I know that is what he is doing because that is what Belle said he was doing.*

*Belle tells me things, at least. Unlike some people.*

*I can't see anything magical about the bed. I am not sure I can see magic anyway—that is part of the problem. I need to see it, like an aura or a halo or something. Because otherwise it does not quite exist.*

*Unlike this bed. This bed definitely exists. It lives in its own world of extreme gaud. The carvings are gilded, for God's sake. And everything is embroidered. Except the sheets. Only bits of them are embroidered. The bits that touch my skin are very soft. So that's something. The prince must have delicate skin. Poor fragile soul, I bet he only wears silk. I bet he has a harem too. Anyone who carries a bed like this around needs a harem, otherwise they would feel very small, hidden in amongst the embroideries.*

*Which is where I am, now, hidden amongst lots of green leaves and autumnal fruits. Strange theme for a bed—the dying time of year. Seasons of mists, mud, murk and mellow fruitfulness.*

*Focus, Fay! You are supposed to be dreaming, not wittering. I am good at wittering; I do it supremely well. So it is quite natural for me to witter. I am also supremely tired. Strange that.*

*If I weren't so super-tired then Belle would have hung off on her suggestion, I fear. She wants me 100% here. At least until these problems are solved. And to me, right now, those problems boil down to a bunch of murdered folk dancers. I assume it is murder and not just mysterious, gruesome death. That word 'gruesome' has such a lovely relish to it. I could eat it on bread, like a scraping of vegemite to give the world savour.*

*If I were killing morris dancers I would drown them in ink from Cecil Sharp's inkwell. I wouldn't kill them with strange lightning or make them haunt-dance all night. God, that was eerie.*

*So what should I do next? I'm going to put more boards up over shattered windows. I am sure my soul has lots of windows and I bet someone has been throwing rocks at them and peeking in. That feels secure. But I almost went to sleep then. I must remember that hammering cedar planks is suitable replacement for counting sheep. Nicely soporific. I guess I just don't want to dream about home. I want to be there, safe and bored. But I need to be here, for Belle.*

*What should I do?*

*How about I be there, but with boards over the windows? That will remind me that it is not really home, but a dream. And if the boards waver I come back here, instantly.*

*Nice thought, Fay.*

*I will put more boards up (maybe I had better hammer my thumb occasionally, to keep myself awake) and then sit in my living room with hot cocoa and a good TV program. Reruns of Bugs Bunny cartoons or Gilligan's Island. I really hate Bugs Bunny.*

*But first, those windows. My poor thumb—I am thinking sympathetic thoughts at you in anticipation.*

―――――

Fay woke up and immediately switched on the lights. All the lights. Not just the ones overhead, but the small lamps she kept for mood lighting. And she lit candles. A gardenia one, and a lavender one and a rose one, because those were the only candles she had. She found a rose-scented oil lamp when she looked for more candles, so she lit that, too. Her cupboards were full of surprises.

It was very dark in the room. Her lounge room was normally light and bright, and her kitchen open and welcoming. Even the blinds didn't shut off as much light as the boards.

When everything was lit, she felt a bit brighter. Fragrant, but brighter. *A few hours of this,* Fay thought, *and my place will smell like a flowerbed. Next time I buy candles I will get some unscented ones. Just in case I ever get boarded up again.* Not that she planned to. Once was too often. Belle and she would find a long term solution when there was time. She trusted Belle, even if she did not trust herself.

It was a very strange feeling, to be home, but not home. Fay was beginning to doubt that she had magic as she made herself some tea. The whole thing was just a dream. She was a victim of her own over-lively imagination.

For a moment she felt sheets soft on her skin. Then she looked up at the fresh wood hiding the light and she shuddered. She was in her kitchen again. Hot drink in hand, she turned the television on and sat down. It was not Gilligan's Island: it was a weather report. Not even the real world did was it was told anymore! She put her chocolate down to watch. If it was a nice day, she might go outside. She wondered how long it was since she had actually breathed real air. Did dream real air count?

The weather report was worrying. Fierce storms were predicted. Some people had evacuated and everyone else had boarded up. She saw the camera panning down a street of boarded houses. It looked like a derelict's dream. And the wind was picking up. The trees waved frantically to get the camera's attention.

Her waking world had become her nightmare while she was in her dream world.

There was only one possible set of actions left. While the electricity was still on, she made herself a giant thermos of hot chocolate. And she filled some bottles with cold water. Then she made herself a thermos of hot water. After that she blew her candles out, but left matches next to them, ready.

In the background whispered the omnipresent wind.

Finally she did the most important thing of all: Fay went to her cupboard and extracted all the snack food, all the fragments of chocolate and crispbread. She took out the single, solitary muesli bar. Now she was ready for anything.

When all this was done, she watched the weather report. It seemed to have replaced normal programming. Outside the day was dark as night. She peeked out the door, and shut it again. And double bolted it. And pushed a chair against it.

Fay then did what all sensible women do in a crisis. She got out her favourite video and watched it, nibbling chocolate and drinking cocoa all the while. She got through it one and a half times before the power failed.

*Such an interesting way of resting,* she thought as she

relit her candles. *I wish Belle were here to relax with me.*
Fay smiled.

She remembered her battery-operated reading light.
She found all her favourite detective fiction and piled
the books next to her big brown armchair. With the
help of the reading light and the hot chocolate, she
worked her way through three paperbacks.

In the background the wind howled and gusted and
the wood rattled. Sometimes the house felt as if it was
going to be blown over. Sometimes it just felt like a
snug little hole, away from the elements. Neither way
left Fay crowing with delight. But she was determined
to stay there as long as possible, and do restful things.
To not think about magic or dream worlds or morris
dancers. And never, ever think about windows to the
soul.

Ten hours, she lasted. Ten hours before she got restless. Ten hours before she found herself back in the
prince's bed, with no howling wind, and a whole heap
of embroidered acorns somehow twisted up under her
right elbow.

———

*Well, that was a time and a half. It worked, though: Belle was
right.*

*But I hate this bed with a vengeance. I am not tired now
so I don't have to stay here any longer. Simple. Not so simple.*

*Someone has taken my clothes. They were right here by
my pillow. I piled them specially, so I could grab them three-
quarters asleep. Damn Belle's servants. I can't get out of bed.
I refuse to creep out naked. My clothes were right beside the
bed where I could get them. I should never have taken them
off. Damn. Damn. Damn.*

And with that thought, Fay opened her eyes properly and saw Gilbert, smiling from across the bed. He

was sitting upright and alert. She damned him, too, mentally. Just for good measure. While she was in the mood. "What are you doing here?" she asked, grumpily.

"We were going to talk, remember?"

"Not till I have my clothes back."

Gilbert eyes widened as he looked more closely at her. He could not have been there long, if he had not realised just how complete her state of undress was.

"This is like one of those nightmares," Fay grumbled, "Where things go wrong and wrong and wrong then you wake up without clothes."

"Can't you wrap yourself up in the bedclothes?" asked Gilbert.

"Maybe," conceded Fay. "But not with you watching. I'm shy."

"Now you tell me," he said.

At that moment a servant walked in with Fay's clothes, all clean and fresh. This was Fay's first indication that she might really have slept in her dreamworld, or at least that significant time had passed. Gilbert left, so that Fay could get dressed.

"I will be in the next room on the left. With breakfast," he promised.

"Breakfast?"

"You have slept a night and a day and another night," he said, without a glimmer of humour. "You should be hungry."

"All I can say is I must have needed the sleep! Now go and let me dress!" Gilbert bowed and left. While she was putting on her miscreant clothes, Fay noticed that there was a dent in the pillow next to her. And that both sides of the bedclothes were in a state of mortal chaos.

Had Gilbert slept in the prince's bed too? What futility. She had wasted two whole nights with him. It was just the sort of thing he would do, though, to sleep in someone else's bed. He was full of cheek.

She was glad, retrospectively, he hadn't gone back to his own house. Not with what had happened there. Him alone with the danse macabre—it just didn't bear thinking of. He could deal with it: that wasn't the issue. It was Fay who couldn't deal with it. So she was reassured to see that dent in the pillow and the rumpled bedclothes. And that was another thought. Maybe she wasn't reassured after all. It all depended.

He had not noticed her nakedness. So maybe it hadn't been him asleep next to her. Or if it was, it was a totally exhausted him. But Gilbert had looked perky when he smiled at her across the end. What had happened while she had slept? Why, whenever she saw Gilbert, were there more questions than answers?

Not knowing where to find food, Fay let her feet drift her somewhere. Maybe there would be food; maybe food was fictional. Anyway, she wasn't hungry. Fay was too bemused to be hungry, and still three quarters asleep. Her feet drifted her out a door and into a little courtyard. It had grass. Good, green stuff. Green stuff was nice. Green stuff was a positive. Fay smiled a little smile and thought a little vindictive thought. A very little thought. She would practice the seeds of love song and really grow plants. Get her magic up to speed, and make sure Gilbert came when he was called when she did the magic in earnest.

"I sowed the seeds of love," Fay sang, blithely, "I sowed them in the Spring." Little seedlings sprouted from the garden. They grew to nearly six inches while she sang. *A bit like film on fast forward. And a bit weird.* She didn't like it, and nearly stopped singing. *I can do this,* she thought, *I don't have to terrify myself, either.* And resolutely she continued, "I gathered them up in the morning so fair, while small birds do sweetly sing." And it was morning, and the birds were singing, and she found she could deal with the garden growing.

Fay let the garden grow for a bit without her assistance, very proud that she had actually started some magic working with good intent and without problems. She looked around and found a stick buried upright in the ground. Near it were bouquets of fresh flowers on piles of dead ones. There were bells, and handkerchiefs, and a full morris dancing outfit, once white, now soiled by rain and dead flowers. Next to the stick was a hand-drawn sign, "In memory of our lost friends. Good hearts will prevail over evil."

Fay felt suddenly a bit ill. A whisper of an ache fluttered past her left temple.

*I can do something. I can. Something simple and creative and positive. And I will not hurt. Not. Not. Not.* Fay carefully wiggled the stick out of the ground and planted it firmly in the flower bed. She chose the healthiest little seedling from the ones that had sprung out of her little enchantment, and she tied it to the morris stick with the cleanest, whitest, newest kerchief. There, that should place her on the side of good. And she sang a bit more of her song and watched the skerrick of green cling supportively to the stick.

Feeling safe, and protected, and without even a glimmer of pain, she went inside and asked someone where she would find breakfast. She was a hungry tyke now she was fully awake. Damn Gilbert for being right yet again. He smiled when she sat down, and turned quickly to his own plate of bread and sliced meat.

Fortunately there was no hot chocolate with the meal. Fay had really overdosed on chocolate during the storm. Although, if she were to ask Belle, Belle would say she had taken no hot chocolate at all. The mysteries of otherworldly travel. Which was true? Had she had chocolate? Or slept? Fay sighed. She needed breakfast. Quickly.

Over breakfast, she started worrying again. The minute she had carefully collected a nice plateful of food and sat down, ready to bare her breast (or at least her soul—she had been physically bare enough today already, she thought) Gilbert was called away, which meant they never got their talk. Which was a worry. They never did get to talk.

It was like one of those bad comedy shows, where all sorts of crucial information is about to be imparted and never is, setting up a series of excruciating accidents. *I am an excruciating accident waiting to happen,* Fay realised. *Either that or I am a bad sitcom, and there is a secret camera filming all this.*

She paused with a piece of toast near her mouth, looking for the hidden camera. She put the toast down and smiled carefully at all corners of the room, just in case. *Life was already strange,* she decided. *If it's strange, I might as well act as if all things are possible. Including hidden cameras. Besides, there might be an equivalent of magic video. What if the evildoer can see what I am doing?*

She put her toast down again and smiled at even more corners of the room. The whole room was now accounted for and anyone watching would be suitably disturbed. Including the servants, who were looking at her oddly. It was good for them to worry. *People never worry enough,* Fay thought, cheerfully.

She wondered what it was like to be a servant, and what they were thinking. She made a note to ask Belle or Persa or Gilbert who had been asked what. People should be talking to each other.

All this might not have been very useful in the absolute scheme of things. But in fact, despite Belle's best wishes, nothing Fay was doing was absolutely useful in the scheme of things. Considering this was her world and she had created it, she was terribly uncentral to happenings. This absolutely annoyed her. Absolutely.

Until she paid attention to it, she could deal with it. But when she focused on it, she realised that her invented world was becoming like the real world. She was fading. People were carrying on their lives without her. This was the last thing she wanted to happen. If it weren't for her friends (and Gilbert, she reluctantly admitted, who was not a friend as of this minute because he was behaving like such a *male*) she would dissolve the world in an instant.

It was all very well to sleep on fancy beds and eat at a well-dressed table, but that was not what she had created the world for. She had created it for *her*. So that somewhere in her life she would be at the centre of things.

Which she patently was *not*. And if she was not going to be, then she might as well return home and earn some money. At least with money she could buy more videos. And there was that DVD player she had been thinking about. George Clooney on DVD sounded nice. And a lot safer than bloody Gilbert. And people on DVDs don't notice you in any case, so you can't fade any more than you already have, she thought, her peevishness growing.

Which brought up another aggrieved point. Gilbert. His appearance. Why didn't he look like George Clooney? Brad Pitt would do at a pinch. But a kind of soldierly goon? With that funny hair? No. It just wouldn't do.

When Belle finally appeared, Fay was sorely tempted to say, "That's it. I will put you and the people you want in another world where you can live forever in eternal happiness, but I'm going home."

It was really her friendship for Belle that had kept

her coming here. And if she put up boards in her place to deal with severe storms then maybe she had gone to work while she was in this world. *And I bet no-one notices. I bet Fay in a complete dream is no different to the Fay they have always seen. I bet I could go through to retirement without ever waking up fully.*

Which was a terrible indictment on her work colleagues. Or maybe on how Fay treated them. Or the sort of work she did. An indictment on everything. Except for her lack of centrality, the discrepancies between her worlds were big and growing by the minute.

Fay sighed, and pretended to nibble at her cold meal. Because she really had no idea what to do once breakfast was over. All she could hope for was that Gilbert would return or Belle would appear. And then they could do something useful.

The world was falling to pieces and she was stuck eating breakfast. She was eating slowly because she didn't know enough about what was happening to do anything else. Nothing. All she could do was shore up those bloody windows. So she did. Again. Her thumb was very sore, in an imaginary way (since the angrier she got, the more times she hit her thumb), by the time she was rescued from a never-ending breakfast. But those windows were very, very secure.

Finally, it was Belle who came. She did not look happy.

"Have you eaten?" asked Fay.

Belle shook her head, collected a mixed plate of comestibles and sat down. There was silence a moment, then, "You look rested at least," she said.

"Yes. It was very strange. My home was in the middle of a truly vicious storm. But I weathered it, and when I woke up, I felt completely refreshed."

"A storm?" Belle's forehead furrowed. "So you were under siege?"

"I guess I could have been. It all depends on the nature of reality." Fay pulled back to the memory of the storm. "It was pretty foul. I did what you suggested with the windows to the soul thing, and all my windows were boarded up. And I drank hot chocolate. I never want to see hot chocolate again."

"Good," said Belle, approvingly. The frown cleared a little. "Very good, in fact. We may be making progress. And maybe I can persuade the prince to stay at the castle for more than one night at a time and to actually do something useful."

"He's not useful?"

"He was. But then he started haring off on wild goose chases. He is just so certain that he knows everything, you see. So he does some things well, pats himself on the back, and misses all the big stuff that needs sorting."

Fay thought a bit more. This time with a bit of a sinking feeling, "Was he here last night?"

"Yes, he was. For a change."

Fay did not pursue this line of thought. She didn't want to hear. She didn't want to know. The thought of being naked in a harem bed with a complete stranger was too terrifying for words. So she changed the subject. "Belle, where have you been? And what is it that's so wrong?"

"You're more noticing than two days ago?"

"I'm more rested than two days ago. I was a complete mess. I think you were right about me not being myself. I feel as if I am more myself than, oh, since Gilbert turned up in my cove."

"I don't know your cove?"

"My special, private place. I invented it for when things went wrong, so I would have somewhere that was just for me. No-one knew about it except me, until

Gilbert appeared and nearly gave me a heart attack."
She smiled gently at the memories.

"And that is where?"

"Past the seal rocks."

"The witch's cove. Oh dear." Belle sounded seriously
concerned. This was not her friend making polite conversation. There was something bad.

"Oh dear? Have I done something wrong?"

"Not you, me. And Gilbert." One of Belle's pauses—
this time very worried.

"Tell me!" Fay demanded, imperious. She was suddenly sick of half bits of new information.

"When we were trying to find out what was happening to us, quite early on, we sat down and catalogued all the places with bad reputations, and that
cove was one. Gilbert went there to fix it up. He came
back, and told me everything was fine, and that it was
all a mistake. He did *not* tell me it was your special
place."

"He found me there. We talked. So?"

"I suspect that it was your way of protecting your
magic. All magic users have them. And whatever else he
did, Gilbert would have taken down any barriers, just
to get there and to combat the evil he thought he was
facing."

"But he would have put them back up, surely?"

"Yes, and in almost any other circumstance that
would be fine. But not in yours. Because it was your
soul-place. So only you could put back the barriers.
And they have been left too long. Damn." The last word
shocked Fay into worry. Belle did not swear.

Belle was silent a moment, considering. Finally she
continued, "What you need is a new place. A heartland.
But these things take time to make." She shook her
head. "This is such a bad piece of news. But it confirms

what we were thinking—someone is using you. There can be no doubt of that."

"That is a ghastly thought. On both fronts. I mean on all fronts."

"It is."

"Damn Gilbert."

The women sat in sombre silence.

Fay broke it eventually. "How long does the boarding up last? I never thought about that."

"I don't know how long, but it sounds pretty solid. It isn't as good as what you had, though. Bother."

"Belle, I have to ask. Seriously this time. Do you have magic? Because you never used to talk about these things. No joking this time." Fay was stern. "Where did you learn it all?"

Belle smiled. "It's all your fault, you know."

"My fault?" Fay was genuinely puzzled.

"The chatelaine has to know about a vast number of things so I had the biggest crash course when I was engaged. Until then I didn't know anything. I had my own small world, and was just struggling to get through it. Magic was definitely an optional extra. In fact, most things were optional extras," and Belle contemplated her own past with obvious dissatisfaction.

"So that's why you've changed so much," was Fay's next thought, "Your world is much bigger."

"And I'm in charge of it. At home I was an unpaid servant, almost a slave. I didn't know just how repressed I was and how much I wasn't allowed to be myself until I left. It was like a whole new life for me, even with the tragedy."

"So you are being good to me because I helped, even if I did it for all the wrong reasons?" Fay asked.

"No, I'm being good to you because you're my friend." The thought caused Fay to give a mental blink. "It's what friendship is about. It doesn't hurt that I think you are key to what is happening here, either," Belle gave one of her old, warm smiles, "but it really is for you. You matter to me."

Fay was completely silenced. This was not the sombre silence of earlier. It was a stunned silence. "I don't think anyone has said anything like that to me before. I mean, suggested I was important to their lives." Her voice was almost a whisper, as if she were scared she would break Belle's resolution. "I invented this world because I was so much not part of anyone's life. And suddenly the world is real. And you care."

"I always cared."

"But I didn't know that it wasn't me just wanting someone. You're not the person I invented, Belle, you're *real*. It's not my decision that you care, it's yours."

"You have really never had that sort of friendship or support, have you?"

"No," Fay's whisper was a dwindled one, a shameful admission. How does anyone admit to no-one really liking them that much? Fay didn't like herself that much at this moment.

"More fool your world then, for missing out on seeing you."

Fay gave a watery smile and there was silence again. A companionable one. "Thank you," Fay said, eventually.

"For what?"

"For being you."

Belle smiled again. "That's easy. I can be me anytime." Then it was Belle's turn to think. "Bloody Gilbert."

"I'm sorry?" The comment came out of nowhere. It was more Fay than Belle, if the truth be known. Fay wondered at Belle today, truly she did.

"He's so focussed on proving me wrong, that he isn't paying you much attention, is he?"

"He is in a way, I mean, I'm seeing him a lot. He was here when I woke up."

"That's not the same as paying attention to you."

"It isn't. And I was thinking that. But then I thought he didn't care and was just keeping an eye on me. Then I thought he did care but didn't want to say. Then I thought he didn't know what he was thinking, and so was being ambiguous. Then I thought I was just a casual fling. Then I thought…"

"You thought a lot and it was all unhappy," Belle concluded the sentence for her.

"Yes," Fay was back to a whisper.

"We need to sort this mess out. Not the emotional mess Gilbert has created. That's for you and he to sort out. I refuse to be a go-between. But we need to sort out the sorcerer mess. We need to free this region from fear. And then you can choose."

"Choose?"

"Decide if you are going to stay here or go home: you can't live in two worlds. This is another thing I was thinking about," Belle explained. "You end up not living in either. You need a friend all the time, not just when you have a story to tell."

"I need to think about that," Fay admitted.

"Of course you do. And I didn't mean to say it so bluntly. I want you here: I really do want you here. I want you to live in the castle and be a part of my normal life. But that may not be what you want. Or what you need. You need to find your life. *Your* life. Not mine, not Gilbert's, not someone else's from your world."

"But we can't do that until we have sorted out who is killing all those morris dancers, can we?"

"They are doing a lot more than killing morris dancers."

"But they're fixated on the dancers, aren't they?" Fay was surprisingly certain of this.

"Yes," said Belle thoughtfully, "I believe you're right. We should talk to Flor."

"Enlai's girlfriend?"

"Enlai's' very ex-girlfriend. I'll tell you about that one the way down. The story of what happened to me while you were asleep. It wasn't at all pleasant."

"Why Flor?"

"Because she's part of a women's side. She's a very good dancer, in fact. And she might have some insights."

"I used to know her really well, you know," admitted Fay. "But just before you got married, I lost touch with her. Last time I saw her, she didn't really want to speak with me at all." Her mind went straight back to that shaft of searing heat that had so narrowly missed her friend.

"Interesting," mused Belle. "That's about when she took up dancing, you know."

And Fay started thinking about the fact that Flor had not been dancing at the fair in the castle grounds. Then she realised that Belle was not talking about then —she was talking about the time of her marriage.

When in doubt, be confused, Fay thought. And if in real doubt, confuse others. Fay suddenly laughed, her thoughts making an almost-logical jump. Almost logical for her, anyway.

Belle looked across at her, a query in her eyes.

"In fantasy books, with all sorts of doom and gloom and end of world nigh, everyone is a hero or prince or a descendant of heroes or princes. They do all sorts of things that have nothing to do with everyday life. Big stuff. Magic stuff. Saving the world with a sword or a secret inheritance." She paused for effect. "But here we are, old friends, going to talk to another friend about morris dancing."

Belle took Fay's comment seriously. "That's how the world operates, you know, people talking to people they know. The prince is into the larger than life stuff —and he misses the wood for the trees."

"I only just realised that, though. That the real events and the core of everything is the everyday. I always saw the everyday as boring. I wanted the big stuff —the glory, the swashbuckle." Fay gave a lovely yearning smile, as the back of her mind thought of the joy of swashbuckle. Then it fell into its normal groove and wondered how on earth buckles swashed?

"Let's see if Flor still makes a good currant cake and can tell us about morris dancing. That is the closest to swashbuckle I can get today."

More food. Fay's stomach threatened to drop as far as her big toe. But she hid her great torment, in true swashbuckling fashion. "And on the way down, you will tell me about Enlai and what he has done to make you so miserable?"

"Yes" sighed Belle, "I will."

And she did.

———

"I heard about Persa and the cats," she began once they were through the castle gates, "And I need to ask you something about it first. Did you start the other thing you talked about—the gardener and love sequence—yet?"

Fay shook her head. "Not with people—I just played about with the idea in the garden."

"Damn." Belle was unusually full of expletives today. She was normally so mealy-mouthed, too. Maybe that was her way of showing stress? Or maybe she was being supportive of Fay by using Fay's own style? Or maybe life was just strange?

"That means all this happened without any encouragement from you. I do not like it. I just do *not* like it."

"What don't you like?" Fay was frustrated. She was hearing yet another segment of a story. She wanted the whole thing. In Technicolour. And instantly.

She had a theory about stories, but she hadn't quite worked it out again. Something like them looking like a bunch of unravelling half-knitted knitting. If the ends were left loose for too long, she would never know if the knitting was a scarf, a jumper, or both. And she would freeze all winter long. It didn't make sense yet, but she was working on it. So she pushed, "Tell me!"

Belle laughed. "I didn't really want to," she admitted. "It's not horrific or even magic-ridden. Since you didn't have a hand in it, there was no magic at all, as far as I can see. It's just downright embarrassing."

"What *is* it?" Fay's frustration caused her to spit the words out, so they landed a full thirty metres away.

"Enlai has been courting me."

"Oh, that's nothing," Fay dismissed. "Persa said that he was making eyes at her ages ago. And then he made eyes at me for a full five minutes."

"I doubt if this was quite the same thing," was Belle's answer. "The night before last, after you were asleep, he appeared at the castle with a bunch of roses and a love poem. It was very sweet. Very, very sweet." Belle did not say this with admiration.

"Oh," said Fay. "I guess he was courting you then."

"He was," said Belle grimly. "And he wanted to make up to me, he said. He told me this in great detail. He said he had thought ill of me and had been entirely wrong. I was not anyone's lapdog. I was the proud chatelaine of the castle. And then he presented me the roses and went home. I found the love poem after."

"Did you argue with him? I didn't know."

"I did not argue with him. We have never known each other well enough to argue."

"Then there's a whole lot of thought at his end that bears no relationship to anything going on at your end."

"That's exactly right," said Belle.

"And that means..." Fay tapered off as her brain raced to obvious conclusions.

But Belle didn't let her finish thinking. "That he has borne a grudge. And you think he might be the sorcerer. And one set of lightning wasn't aimed at morris dancers, it was aimed at me. Or I think it was."

"I know it was," answered Fay. The truth was finally going to come out. She wasn't sure if this was a cause for celebration, or for hiding under the nearest table. Not that there were any nearest tables. "I deflected it."

"Please explain," came the curt instruction.

"I saw it heading to you, so I tried to think it in another direction. I sort of moved it with my arm. And so it missed you. I didn't realise it would hit anyone else."

"It seems to me that, while things have been very bad around here, I personally have had a very narrow escape. And that this is not going to last."

"But all he did was leave flowers, so he doesn't know you don't like him? You don't like him, do you?" Fay suddenly wanted reassurance.

"I dislike him intensely. And he knows it. Or probably guesses."

"How?"

"He came back yesterday. With a lute."

"A lute?" Fay couldn't restrain herself, she broke into giggles. Belle watched, unsmiling for a moment, and then a small lightness crept across her visage.

"Can he play it?" was Fay's over-riding question.

"No, he can't."

"Then *why?*" and she burst into giggles again.

"You know, Fay, Enlai has some things in common with you. He thought he was a romantic hero. And romantic heroes play lutes."

"That's exactly like me—I can do all sorts of things in my stories that I can't do in real life."

"Except that when you do those things successfully, you have magic backing you. You can do them, or at least you look as if you can."

"To a point."

"When we are children it's dinned into us that we have to work at school because even magic is never a replacement for solid work. Magic *plus* a real skill, properly trained, is worth a fortune. But magic by itself is not much."

"Oh," said Fay, enlightened, "That is why I'm getting the sort of treatment I am. I'm a magic user with no real skills."

"What would you say your real skills are?" Belle asked, curious.

"Administration, I suppose, though I hate it. Flute playing. Telling stories. And I am okay at art—I can draw."

"An unusual set, but useful. Can you read?"

Fay laughed. "Of course I can. I can read in two languages. I went to university."

"University?"

"Haven't we had this discussion before?" Fay was positive they had talked about all these things. They were so basic.

"Probably, but now more hangs on it, I need to understand."

"Oh. In that case, I have advanced education. Past school level."

"And Gilbert doesn't know."

"I don't know if he knows. He should know I read.

We've talked about books. But I can't remember if we talked about educational systems. Why?"

"Because it makes a big difference. Trained intelligence and magic are formidable. If you're good at learning and self-motivated and have advanced skills, then it matters less that you know nothing about magic. Which is what I've always thought about you. But no-one else could see it."

"Not even Enlai?"

"I never discussed it with Enlai."

"What happened with the lute, was it bad?" Fay was suddenly desperately curious.

"It was very ugly. He didn't know he couldn't use it until he started playing."

"Which is why you are so very certain he was taking magic from me?"

"Yes" and Belle smiled. "Your boards held. He was outside my door and played. "I kept the door shut and told him to go away, that I was busy. He didn't. He stayed there and made... noises.

"So I opened the door a little and peeked and his face was nearly apoplectic. He was muttering under his breath—some kind of incantation, and nothing was happening. He didn't look up at me. "He started muttering more loudly, something different.

"I recognised the words. I looked them up afterwards, to be certain. It was a strong incantation. It should have shaken the foundations of the building; it should have started an earthquake. It was a stupid thing to do." Belle's voice was caustic, then turned to wonderment. "And a gentle breeze swirled around in the corridor. My guess is that this was the storm that hit your house, in your world. A gentle breeze here and a storm near the source of the magic."

"But my wooden boards held."

"Your wooden boards held." They were silent a moment in appreciation. "I was standing there, watching him. The breeze was tugging at my hair, but very, very gently. It felt like a nice spring day. He gave up. Something inside him crumpled. He threw the lute at the wall and ran away."

"He didn't swear vengeance or anything?"

"He just ran. I sent people out to find him, and no-one could."

"You sent for the prince?"

"I sent for him. And he came, but I was out when he came. And so he went out again and didn't hear."

"And no-one gave him a message?" Fay was surprised.

"I wanted to tell him myself, which I now think was a big mistake. He's off haring after some mythical sorcerer two towns away, I'm told, when the problem is here, with Enlai."

"So remind me, why are we going to Flor's?" Now Fay felt very stupid. And not very useful.

"We can't do anything ourselves except find out more. So we're finding out more."

"What are we finding out? That Enlai is a bastard?"

"I had thought we could find out if he really has an obsession with morris dancing. Or if all the other deaths of dancers were also mistakes. If we can't get help in dealing with him now, at least we can prepare the ground for when we do get help."

*Oh*, Fay thought. *Make-work*, but she guessed it could be useful. Maybe. "What about Gilbert?"

"Didn't I say? He has hared off two towns away, with absolutely anyone else who has training in magic."

"Which leaves us with two people who have no training."

"That is the sum of it," agreed Belle.

"Well, I need a white hat," Fay stated categorically.

"Why?"

"I don't want to be mistaken for the bad guy again. We can give Enlai a black hat, to replace his lute.' She rolled on, full of resolution. "And if you will excuse me, I will spend the rest of this walk checking those boards in my brain. I want my brain very boarded up!"

"That's fine with me. I am going to dream of currant cake. The castle staff have put me on a diet, and I *miss* it." Suddenly Belle's obsession with cake was explained.

Fay discovered, when they reached Flor's, that Belle's dreams were not as powerful as her own. Flor offered them seedcake.

Flor was flustered to see Belle, but very pleased to see Fay. She was very open about why she was pleased, "I thought you were one of the friends who dumped me when Enlai did. I was so angry at you, you know. I just didn't expect it of you."

"I didn't dump you. I just didn't visit anyone at all. I'm sorry if you missed me though—and if I hurt you."

"So it was just you being absent-minded," laughed Flor. "I should have guessed."

Fay wondered why she hadn't guessed. Why was it so hard for these friends to know her? How could she know something forever and Flor not know it at all? Just what did people *see* when they looked at Fay's face? And why would one friend dump another, in any case? Friends were too valuable for that sort of ill-treatment. Too rare. "Who dumped you?" she asked, curiously.

"Everyone except my dancing friends."

"But *why*?" asked Belle.

"Enlai started working for the prince, and everyone decided he was important, I guess." Flor shrugged. "It doesn't matter. I don't need friends like that. I am absolutely pleased that you are not one of them, Fay. It would have been nice if you had said so earlier. I would have given you some of my herbs."

"I am not," Fay defended, vigorously. "Enlai is not in

my good books at *all.*" Belle laughed. "I'm terribly, terribly sorry. I've not really seen anyone except Belle and Persa for a long time."

She omitted Gilbert. Intentionally. Fay told herself she wasn't sure that he counted for anything right now. Besides, she had not invented him—he had just kind of appeared. And she was certainly not going to talk about her putative love life to anyone but Belle. "This cake is lovely," she said, as a distraction. She was nibbling it gently round the edges.

"It's mother's recipe. Very old."

"The cake is very old?"

"No, the recipe is."

Flor suddenly cut to the heart of things and lost all semblance of proper politeness. She was not quite accusatory in tone, but it was close, Fay thought. "Why *are* you here? What made you remember you forgot me?"

If Flor could be blunt (which didn't fit her fragile pale gold beauty at all) then so could Fay. "Partly because Belle reminded me I haven't been very good to my friends and I wanted to make it up," she admitted, "And partly because we're trying to find out about morris dancers. Belle said you had taken up dancing. Things seem very bad for them—we thought maybe you might know something."

Fay suddenly wished she had thought before she had spoken. She had been too direct. Really she had. There should have been an hour of polite everydayness before anything so horrid was mentioned. No matter how Flor had seemed to lead to it, she could not have known what Fay was planning to ask about. Or how painful it would be. Fay would never be a normal human being, she sighed about herself. She completely lacked any social skills; if she had not set the situation up herself, then she didn't know how to handle it.

Flor looked considering, but not repulsed. Fay held her breath. It was a while before she answered. During that time, Fay cursed herself three more times. She was very thoroughly cursed by the time Flor's reply slowly emerged.

"Within our little group of friends, we have long thought that someone hated us." The tone was almost wistful, as if it were not possible that anyone outside could understand, "While there have been many incidents, over half of them have involved morris dancers. But when we tried to tell anyone in authority, we were told off. Or nothing happened. It doesn't matter how many times you report something, if nothing happens you know no-one cares.

"And then you both come here. Suddenly interested. So why are you so interested?"

Fay fancied she heard a wisp of suspicion and a sense of desolation, but didn't know if she was imagining it. She wondered what Flor really thought, underneath the words.

"Fay has also seen the link, and we decided to check it out. It can't be dismissed," explained Belle, gently.

"Well, I'm glad to hear you say that. Even though it's very late in the piece. And we could have done with some support a little earlier. Everyone who has ever danced walks round in fear. And those of us who are still dancing are dancing with bravado—we refuse to be threatened." There was definitely some aggression in her tone, or was it defensiveness? Fay just could not sort it out. She worried about it and let Belle do the talking.

"I can understand that," said Belle slowly. "But this is the first I've heard that you're walking in fear. No-one reported it to me."

"I told Enlai as soon as it started happening," Flor was not pleased. "We may not be going out, but he used to speak to the prince directly so I thought it was best. So it was all reported. And reported. And reported."

"Enlai did not pass it on."

Fay gave up being pensive and went straight for the jugular. "Tell me, Flor, what does Enlai think of morris dancing?"

"Oh, he hates it," instantly replied Flor. "Which is one reason I took it up. I was certain I wouldn't run into him there, which was of prime consideration in a town this size. I've stayed dancing because the people are so nice and the dances are fun, but I took it up originally because of him."

"How does he hate it?"

"He was a member of a side once, and they were unkind to him."

Everyone was silent until she was forced to expand. Flor was not comfortable talking about it. "It wasn't here. It was before he moved here. He told me about it once, when he was drunk. If I had not got him so very drunk, I would never have known—he detested talking about it. His arm was nearly dislocated because they bashed so hard."

Flor seemed contemplative. Whether it was of Enlai drunk or of his unhappy experience Fay was not certain.

"They bashed him up?" Belle was trying to clarify.

"Not literally; they hit with the stick in the dance—it's called 'bashing'. Normally the weight balances the bash and it's just fun. But if someone very strong hits too hard, you can suffer real damage. It never happens because dancers are careful. Here, at least. But if someone hated Enlai and wanted to get rid of him and wasn't prepared to say so, they could make his dancing life really uncomfortable."

"And so they did?" Belle was so carefully inquisitive, trying to open every door and check out every angle.

"They did a lot more than that. I don't know what, but he gave dark hints. But I was horrified when I heard. It is just so unlike anything anyone would do here."

"And yet you reported the deaths to Enlai."

Flor seemed unmoved by the path the conversation was taking. Fay guessed that if she had dated Enlai for so long, she was used to the strange and gruesome. And people asking questions that led odd places.

Enlai loved finding out things. For Enlai, secret knowledge was a treasure. It always had been. That was why they played riddle games. More food for thought. He might have spotted her as what she was earlier than anyone else.

"I had to report it to someone. Enlai reported directly to the prince's lieutenant. Why doesn't he now? Do you know why he was sacked?" Not 'Why didn't he tell anyone anything?' but 'Why he was sacked?' And she didn't wait for an answer, either. "He should have passed it on, but Enlai likes his secrets. I will never understand how his mind works. I would really like to know who else had the good sense to dump him, though."

"You dumped him? He didn't dump you?"

Flor laughed a very wicked laugh, "Oh, absolutely."

Belle said that they had no idea why Enlai was sacked, and it didn't fit with what they knew.

"Tell me if you find out?" asked Flor.

"We will," promised Fay. "How is your garden? It's far too long since I have seen it."

And the rest of the visit was spent examining Flor's very orderly and fragrant herb garden. Fay and Belle left loaded with various sachets of mint and thyme and lavender. Curious, Fay thought—not quite the scents she had used herself in the thunderstorm. Very curious. All these new twists and turns.

# CHAPTER THIRTEEN

There's a trade you all know well,
It's bringing cattle over.
On ev'ry track,
To the Gulf and back,
Men know the Queensland drover.

Chorus:
Pass the billy 'round boys!
Don't let the pint-pot stand there!
For tonight we drink the health
Of every overlander.

As I pass along the roads,
The children raise my dander
Crying "Mother dear,
Take in the clothes,
Here comes the overlander!" (Traditional)

———————————

FAY WAS SO BUSY THINKING ABOUT TWISTS AND TURNS
on the way back to the castle that she tangled herself.
She had reminded herself that she had to sing the *Seeds*

*of Love* again and start being courted. She had discussed it with Belle, therefore it had to happen. No questions and no doubt. Even though so much had come between her and that little experiment, the experiment was still worth making. Add the results to Belle's store of useless information perhaps.

And it might be useful in other ways. For example, it could help get Gilbert into line, perhaps. Very much perhaps. Then again, maybe it wouldn't. It all depended on why he was behaving the way he was behaving.

Fay sighed. If Gilbert was determined to act exactly like a man, then maybe it was not so surprising that she herself was thinking like a woman. Did men *ever* get themselves into these tangles, she wondered. Or did they just think in straight lines? She bet for Gilbert there was no great love and no great problem. No agonies at all, in fact.

Belle was walking silently, obviously deep in thought.

*'Bout time!* thought Fay. Not about Belle, but about herself. Time to add to Belle's supply of futile facts. "I sowed the seeds of love," she hummed, "Twas all in the Spring."

"I am going to leave messages for everyone everywhere," said Belle, abruptly, cutting the tune off, "Can you catch up with me? I think that will be the fastest way out of this morass."

"Sure," said Fay. "I have a song to sing, anyway. I promised you."

"Sing away," smiled Belle, "But keep those windows boarded up!"

"I will." But the song no longer fitted her mood. Her mood was not sweetly adoring. Or even gently loving. Frankly, she did not even feel Sherlock Holmesian. In fact, she was full of energy.

And the street seemed so wide today. Maybe the

gutter crept and squiggled closer to the houses when she was not paying attention. How did they *know* that Fay was not paying attention. Where did gutters keep their eyes?

How did Enlai know, for that matter? And then how had he not realised that things had changed when he tried to play Belle love-songs.

Fay giggled and the tune changed. She burst into full voiced song, raucous and attention-grabbing.

"There's a trade you all know well and it's bringing cattle over

On every track to the gulf and back men know the Queensland drover.

Pass the billy round, boys! Don't let the pint pot stand there.

For tonight we'll drink a health to every Overlander."

It wasn't until she was well into the song that her brain cells kicked into gear. As usual, her brain cells were too slow. They delayed until she had sung,

"As I pass along the roads the children raise my dander,

Crying 'Mother dear take in the clothes here comes an Overlander'".

Because she had been humming with intent to practice magic a moment before. And she really didn't want to see a lot of drovers down this street. Which looked so nice and wide. Wide enough for cattle or sheep? For a crawling mob of them? Oh dear.

It was happening. Bother.

Folksongs notwithstanding, she had never met a drover and she wasn't quite sure she was up to it today. Fay gulped the rest of the song down and looked innocently around, as if she had never been guilty of anything.

It was too late. Fay stood there in the middle of a

wide, dusty road and looked around. This was not the cobbled main street she was supposed to be standing on. It was the Australian outback, and red dirt spread from beneath her feet.

The houses to the side were mixed: some were three bedroom cottages with verandas and patches of green. Redbrick or weatherboard. Very outback. Others were the English cottages she had invented for the village. She looked at the ground in front of a village home and saw the cobbles fade into bulldust. *This is not good,* Fay thought. *This is very not good.*

She looked around for people. Inside the house she was looking at she caught a group of frightened faces. As she looked at them they hid. "Damn, they are scared. Why are they scared? Magic must happen here all the time. I never invented fear here," and Fay rambled to herself as she walked down the road, trying to think the town back into existence and get rid of rural Australia from her mind.

Lurking in the back of her brain was what Gilbert and Belle had told her about foul sorcery and deaths. Fear. What if the morris dancer who died was killed because of her? What if it was not Enlai's unthinking grudge, but Fay's uncontrollable magic? Fay shuddered.

She thought about cobbled streets and the old pub and the mayor's house. She concentrated on them with all her might. But none of them were visible. The gallows tree. That would stay. Nothing could change its stark permanence. So Fay walked to the gallows tree, along her outback road. She turned her back on its length, and headed towards where the green should be.

As she walked, a sheep butted her from behind. "Get out of the flamin' way, girlie," shouted a broad Australian accent. Very male.

When she turned her head she saw a mob of sheep, battling down on her, surrounded by a film of red dust.

Something pushed her aside. Fay stumbled and fell. Her hands hit the red dirt, and so did her knees. She wondered if blood would show from the fall, masked by soil-red. It was so very dry, she just brushed her hands off, and there they were, white again. Her brain seemed to have gone to mush.

Not again. Her brain had been mush very recently. And she couldn't remember. She couldn't remember what she had to remember. All she could do was stare at her messy hands and feel their grittiness. And the giant rustle and crying of a flock of sheep with dog-sounds nipping at their heels completed her little world.

And then it changed. The world hushed. Enlai was there. He had come between her and the mob, his hands outstretched. From those hands streamed beams of light. And where the light touched, the world transformed.

At first Fay watched in wonderment as the green light turned the red dust back to cobble and faded the sheep. Then she was aware of her head. There was a sharp pain behind her left temple. It grew until Fay's body was soaked with waves of hurt.

She tried to sort out her mind, so that she could sort out this overwhelming agony. It had started by niggling, she thought, a small distraction from the grit of her knees and the foul feel of her hands. But it had grown. The pain grew as the light from Enlai's hands grew. Her thoughts came back to her a little, and she wondered if Enlai had stolen them. And then she realised that the green light was the light of her eyes. And that the power Enlai was using was not just her power, but her life.

Fay screamed "No!" and consciously willed the world to fade.

———

She woke up in bed, and at home. With great weakness. With a migraine. With no mental force to combat either the migraine or the weakness. She could not move for an hour. She could not think for an hour more.

Even when she could move and made herself some tea; even when the pain relievers had dulled the agony to a roar and then to a quiet thud-thud; even after she had warmed her soul with a hot bath; she refused to face the reality. That Enlai had forced her from her own world, using her own power. That he had crippled her. Effortlessly.

She was alone. No Belle. No Gilbert. No Persa. And no understanding of how it had all come about. Fay cried. Gently, softly, inexorably. She could not stop.

Nor could she think. The power of thought had gone from her, along with the light from her eyes.

# CHAPTER FOURTEEN

*WHEN I GROW UP, I AM GOING TO BE A... SOMETHING. I
don't know what any more. I used to know. Mantra of my
childhood. That I am going to grow up. That I am going to be
a something. A fire-fighter. A mathematician. A dancer
on MTV.*

*And here I am, a pot of coffee on, and not something yet.
I am still myself. I still have green eyes. Leeched of life,
leeched of light, but green eyes. We were so clever with that
windows bit. My home was protected, but not my eyes.*

*How did Enlai do it? Why did he do it? Why didn't he
just give me a few minutes to sort things out inside my head?
I should have been able to do that. How did he do it?*

*If he does that again, I'm dead. Or if he does it too much,
I'm dead. I don't know why it would kill me, but I know it
will. I know it would, if I hadn't woken up. If I had not come
home, I would be dead.*

*I was safe when I got out of bed. Away from dreaming. I
was tottery, but Enlai could not get me. I checked the windows here, at home, and they weren't boarded up. They had
never been boarded up. That is the eerie thing. I was
dreaming the big storm. I don't know what's real any more.*

*Ouch. Pinching myself proved something: that it hurts to
pinch myself. I think I might have known that already. But*

what can I do? I can't go back. Not the way I am now. I just can't. It's not possible. I mean, look at me.

Sam, Fran and Pinch Me went down to sea in a boat. Sam and Fran jumped out. Who was left? Ouch.

Maybe I am awake. Or at least awake in bits and pieces. But the chocolate tasted real last time and I thought I was awake then. And that road was real. It was. Even when it changed, it was real. The sheep were real. One butted me.

Two sheep short of a paddock. No, not sheep. Not now.

And I could have got it all back to normal, if Enlai hadn't stolen shards of my soul. And how do I **know** that? How can I be certain of any of this?

Funny. His eyes should have glowed, or his fingers should have twinkled. Glow and twinkle to show he was making magic. And how could that light be the exact same colour of my eyes, and so clear and so glowing?

I need Gilbert. I really do. I need Gilbert. He knows more than Belle, but he won't talk to me. He keeps running off and saving the world. Or hiding out in his cabin by the sea. Bloody men.

There has to be some good in this. There has to.

Number one: I'm alive. I hurt, but I'm still alive. Enlai didn't attack me, he just grabbed at me to get things normal. That was a pretty big 'just' though, because he grabbed really far into me. It was agony. I never want pain like that again.

But I've hurt like that before, haven't I? Think back, Fay. Remember. Oh yes. When I saw that frozen dancer. And there was a faint echo of the same pain in the castle garden. And, and... too many times. My brain is strained.

I've left friends behind. They need me. They're scared. I'm scared. We ought to be scared together. I should not be here alone.

If I go back, what happens to Enlai? Damn. I hate it when I think of things like that. The other sorcerers were hanged. Gallowed.

I saw a body, hanging. On the gallows tree. Even if he

was actually hung for poaching. Poaching magic. From me. And I don't know this Prince-guy. I can't turn to him and say, "Just stop him, don't kill him." I can't change the law. I am wittering again. I'm sure I'm wittering again. I can't just roll up and say "Hey, I may not know what to do with my magic, but look, Enlai does, so let's kill him." Bad idea. Very bad idea.

And besides, all the boarding up has gone. My windows are smashed. I just checked every single bloody window to this house-of-my-dreams and they are all sound as a bell. They still feel smashed. Fuzzy thinking. Maybe I am imagining they were sound as a bell. Maybe there is shattered glass and splintered wood all over the house. Maybe. Maybe just imagining everything. And just woke up from a nightmare. A nightmare that I had been having nightmares.

Except it was all so real. If it was a dream, it was a damn convincing one.

Stop, Fay. Recoup. Rethink. Start from the other direction. If I'm not sure about what is real and what isn't, then maybe I need to be sure within myself. I bet that is why I'm vulnerable – I don't even believe what I'm seeing and hearing and touching. I could be kissing Gilbert (wistful thought) and thinking I made it up. Or filing papers at work, and not even know I was there. Both of which are happening. Have happened.

Can they happen at the same time? My brain is wittering again, I am sure of it. On and off, it witters. Sometimes the wittering fades and sometimes I fade.

Enlai has declared himself. What a funny way to do it. In fantasy novels the villain kills everyone for miles around. Enlai turns sheep back into paving stones.

Like a dream. A kind of waking dream, where you try to wrestle control back from your own mind. It was all a dream. No. And I sort of know it. Or do I? Whether it was, or wasn't, I have lost control. That is the problem.

*I can do it. I can't do anything useful in the dream world, unless I am a bit more grounded here. Less fey and more Fay.*

*Maybe that is why the boarding up didn't hold. Maybe that is why I dreamed of being awake, and wasn't. And I should have known I wasn't awake. Because Canberra has never, in all my time here, had a storm warning like that one.*

*It was like a childhood dream, in a way. No, not a dream. Bad choice of words. Very bad choice of words. A memory turned into a waking tale.*

*Fay. Fay. Stop it. Now. Slow down and start again.*

*Make a nice clear aim. Committee of silly thoughts rattling in my brain, come to order. You have had enough time to argue, now you need a clear and firm goal. A mission statement. No, too Mormon. I am not a Fay on a Mission. I am just Fay.*

*But who is Fay? Where does she live? I have to consolidate myself before I go back. That is absolutely what I need to do. I hope the world doesn't fall to bits in all that time. Because if I don't work out a bit more of who I am, then I will fall to bits. I will lose all my light. I might as well gouge out my eyes and give them to Enlai on a platter.*

*Ooh, I do like that image. I think I'm getting my brain back. I am sure it was a head on a platter though. So where does one put the eyes?*

*Besides, I need to be able to not come up with sheep when I really ought not! It should have been sexy guys walking down that street, not a bloody drover. Although maybe he was cute. I never actually saw him, you know. I don't care. He called me "Girlie". No man what calls me girlie is cute.*

*When did I last go to work? What am I doing at home anyway? TV. Music videos. This means it is Saturday. So I may not be out of a job yet. That's something.*

*But what happened to the other days? Was I really going to work as a zombie? Did anyone notice? What does that say about the Australian Public Service? It probably says more about me than about anything else. How can any time have passed without me being aware?*

*It is one thing for time to lapse in a dream world and for me to miss weddings and things. It is quite another for time to lapse in the waking world.*

*Damn. Double damn. Triple damn. Too many dams and not enough rainfall to fill them. Quadruple damn. I am worried. And stuck. I can't think. So what else is new? Quintuple damn. If this goes on for much longer, I will have to use worse language. Like the drover did. Damn drover.*

*It is Saturday morning. The Television Tells Me So. So I have two days. I can survive without sleep for one night. Just one night. And I can find out who I am, what my world is made of, how I live my life, in two days. I must. Because I can't think of anything else. And I want to go back to the dream-world and sort bloody Enlai out. Damn Enlai too.*

*In fact, damn everything.*

———

Two days and one night. Not a long time, Fay reflected.

And it wouldn't be an exciting two days, like her recent dreaming time. This was because she had worked out one important thing: that excitement didn't really help solve inner problems.

She saw her current problem as an inner problem. It wasn't Enlai's fault that he had been able to breach her defences. It was something to do with the defences themselves. Boards got knocked down when you didn't know what they were protecting or how they were really doing anything at all. They just *looked* nice and tough and secure.

And if you don't know who you are, how can you decide if anyone else really exists? And if you don't know someone exists, how can you help them?

Big questions, but not big time to solve them. Fay

thought she might get a philosophy book from the library and let someone do the thinking for her. That was what she had done most of her life, after all. Even her imaginary world was based on other people's ideas. It had just grown a great deal from what she had read and heard. So maybe she needed to grow.

She could ring her family. Maybe. Maybe later. Maybe sometime. Maybe never. The thought of ringing family at this moment in time left Fay entirely unmoved. In fact, the thought of never ringing her family again left Fay more than entirely unmoved: it left her quite happy.

That was something she hadn't known about herself. She wasn't a family reject—she was someone who rejected family. Who did Fay actually like of her family? She didn't know. She genuinely didn't know. This was a revelation. Fay had assumed she liked them because they were family. One loves family, doesn't one? But if she met, say, Uncle Bill or her mother on the street, if she ran into her cousins at parties, would she strike up a friendship? Or even her so-charming siblings?

The answer had to be no. Not ever. They were small-minded people living in their small-minded world. Or maybe they were fine except where she was. Perfectly charming people until they came within a certain radius of her. And where she was should never be where they were. And she was getting all kinds of tangled again.

Did she like the *idea* of family? Surely that was an easy 'no'. Since she was single and almost beyond the pale in marriage terms. But it wasn't. It wasn't simple at all. Fay had a sudden longing to sit down and talk with a seven-year-old girl with her eyes and Gilbert's funny hair.

Her eyes. No trouble giving away her eyes, or at least sharing them with someone she loved. How odd.

Fay did not like the path her thoughts were taking. So she decided she had to find herself a different direction to find herself in. Even the thought made her brain get dizzy. It had to be done.

How about I question what the world is, from the ground up? This was another of those thoughts that hurt just to work through. Not an atomic dissection—too explosive. Also too bloody theoretical. No, what she needed was to know how she fitted in with the outside world. Her outside world. The real one. Fay needed to walk down the street and do some shopping.

She nearly marched straight out the door on that thought. Then she realised just how disconnected it was from reality. Where was her handbag? And what did she really need to shop for? She didn't even know what was in her refrigerator. Fay shut her eyes and tried to remember, her hand still on the doorknob, half turned to go outside. She was inanimate, her lists scrolling down the computer screen of her inner eye.

Cheese. A stale loaf of bread. She always had cheese and bread. And margarine. There had to be margarine. Pickles. And chocolate sauce. Milk for tea and coffee. It wasn't possible to have a refrigerator without all these things.

Finally inanimation found life, and Fay walked to the refrigerator. When she opened it and a wave of cool air hit her, as something else did also. The smell of decomposing beans. And sprouting carrots. No chocolate sauce. No margarine. And an amazingly mouldy jar of mayonnaise. When on earth did she buy mayo? When on earth did she *eat* mayo? A stranger had invaded her refrigerator? Maybe she should go back to the inanimate thing — much safer on her sense of smell. Also very ornamental.

She sniffed the milk carton and decided to do an entire spring clean. The coagulated milk went down the sink, lashed liberally with water. That smell was so intrusive. Everything else was bundled up in plastic and went straight into the garbage bin. She put the bin straight out the front, in the hopes that garbage collection would be soon. Very soon.

Fay then washed out the refrigerator, carefully, completely, cleanly. The only things left in it were two jars of pickles—one was green tomato chutney and the other was piccalilli. Everything else had to go. So that was her refrigerator. Clean and bright and empty. Almost as good as her brain. Not even an egg or some butter. No milk. She couldn't even have cup of tea if she wanted. What on *earth* did she eat while she was dreaming? Mayonnaise, apparently.

Fay went to the bathroom to wash her hands very, very thoroughly. She had not touched the acrid milk, but she wanted to be utterly certain that not even the thought of it clung to her hands. Then she decided to have a shower. Who knows how she kept clean while she was dreaming. Life was pretty much a mystery. As was mayonnaise.

She felt better for the shower, and was happy to see that the laundry was not nearly as badly off as the refrigerator. Maybe she did some things on automatic?

Fay had a thought and went back into the bathroom to look in the mirror. Her face looked the same. Green eyes, light brown hair, pale, pale skin. The skin of a redhead. Gentle and soft freckled and easily burned. Flushed with heat from the shower. Her eyes were not as dull as she had feared and her face was no thinner than it should be. If she was starving to death through her dreaming, it was not obvious at all. Mayo must be fabulous stuff.

She had a more serious thought. Complete connection to the world. No moments of drifting. Find out what it is like to live in the here-and-now. To get her off on a good note—one connected with her very sparse food supply—she made a shopping list. Old-fashioned. On paper. And remembered the usefulness of bags, and keys and purses. Especially purses. Money was such a handy thing for a shopping expedition. She was relieved to see that there was money in her purse. She had no idea how it got there, maybe she robbed banks while she drifted into the dream-world?

She would walk firmly up the street. Very firmly. Clomping. Feel the wind in her damp hair. Presumably there was wind. Wind was one of those real things that happened to real people, Fay expected. She just didn't remember noticing wind recently. Like the contents of her refrigerator, she took wind on trust. There was a frivolous breeze as she walked down the street. There was also light rain. Summer rain. When had summer come?

Or had she noticed the change of seasons and just forgotten it? *It was really like Sleeping Ugly waking without the help of a prince,* she thought. One day she would forget to breathe, if she wasn't careful. *No, not even I can be that stupid,* thought Fay, bitterly and clomped a bit to remind her she was walking.

*Damn, getting bitter again. I promised myself not to.* Fay wondered if bitterness were part of her soul. She really did. And not liking people. Especially not trusting people. Like her family. Like anyone.

Except Belle. She did trust Belle. Which is why she was here, clomping carefully down the street. She needed to know who she was before she could even think about why she trusted Belle. Thinking. Fay used to be good at thinking. What happened?

*Damn, forgot to notice the wind again. And I just crossed a major road and didn't even notice the traffic lights. I am not run over, so I probably pressed the button and waited for the light to say, "Walk," but I don't remember doing it. Why don't I remember? When did I start to live my life on automatic? How far on automatic have I been?*

*Notice your footsteps, Fay. One in front of the other. Walk. Walk. No thump-thump-thump. This is not a dream of dead dancers. It is Hindmarsh Drive and you are walking to the shopping centre. To the supermarket.*

She crossed into the Plaza and noticed a sign outside an estate agent, "We look after you." I don't need you, dammit! She thought angrily at the estate agent. I need to learn to look after myself. I need food. I need to know where my soul is. And who I am. *And then I can start worrying about higher level problems. Like whether Belle exists. Whether I have fallen in love with a figment of my imagination. Whether Enlai is stealing my soul. Whether I am magic.*

*Look at yourself walking, Fay, don't drift. It is life and death here. Soul-life, soul-death.*

But she had drifted. Not far—simply across the street. She had missed the entrance to the Plaza. The price of being on automatic. It took you in the wrong direction. If someone else directed things for you, it took you in their direction. Into, in fact, the Public Service, instead of into art or music. And then where did you go to hide from unhappiness? Into dreams. Into make-believe. Into...

Fay tripped over the corner of a shopping trolley; so busy was she savaging herself. The pain was so sharp she had to sit down for a few minutes. It was a good pain, she decided. Any pain was a good pain if it brought her back into her body. It was impossible to ignore a calf that damaged. Even if she limped all day, Fay was pleased she had walked into that shopping trolley.

Maybe she should try a brick wall next? Banging her head into a brick wall to prove she was alive. Not so that it would feel good when it stopped, but so that it would keep her here, in this world. Hurting, but connected.

Bad thought, Fay. And other bad, bad, bad thoughts. If you only connect to the world through pain, then that world is a world of pain. Better to invent a new dream world. Better even let Gilbert and Belle fade, than to live through pain and because of pain.

But wasn't that what she had been doing, emotionally? In the real world. Doing things that ached her because without them she doesn't feel she was a worthy human being?

I am not really alive, Fay thought. *I guess it is not really banging my head against a brick wall, though. It is being an ostrich. Hiding my head in the sand because everyone tells me it is the normal place to put ones' head. Only the sand clogs my sight and numbs me and I no longer live. Besides, didn't someone famous say, "Don't bury your head in a nuclear testing ground"? Flanders and Swann: that's who said it.*

*A nuclear testing ground describes Enlai pretty well.*

*So no pain. Or rather, pain is not my solution. I am allowed to not suffer. I am not allowed to suffer? I wish they were the same thing. So what is my way? What is this soul-thing? What is the inner magic that my friends are so worried about? My imaginary friends.*

*My actual friends don't even know I am magic at all. Or that I am in pain. And that is part of my problem, isn't it? I have hidden so much of myself from the world for so, so very long, that the person I look like isn't the person I am. And I do not know how anyone will take the person I am.*

*Except... Except... Belle knows who I am. She knows the worst of me and still calls me her best friend. I have put her through hell. And she still calls me her friend.*

*I have been so bloody good trying to conform that I don't know what I am capable of. It is at this point in my life I guess I should take up bungee-jumping. Isn't that what people do when they are proving themselves? Or write a novel. Or act in a play. Except that none of them is me. Not me at all.*

*What is me is my inner world. I have heaps of inner self. If my inner self were snow, I could start an avalanche. Maybe I started an avalanche in the dream world. Except that I didn't start it. Enlai was playing in my snow, without permission. Making snowmen and snow castles on the slopes of a mountain. I bet he is as surprised as anyone that he started that avalanche. I bet that's why he did that drover thing.*

*Look at the flower seller, and the newsagent and the chemist. I don't notice them normally. I have to learn not to walk on by before I go back and save the world or whatever. I have to learn to live. I have to learn to care. That is a lot of learning.*

*The first step is where I am now. Because seeing is the root of all of this. The heart of my soul-corruption. I don't look: I don't live. I just drift and dream.*

*It was drifting that caused the drover thing. And I bet it was drifting that caused the dragon one. So I don't need boards cluttering up my soul-window. I need clear, clean glass. I need to learn to see, and to notice what I see. Every minute of the day.*

*That's almost impossible. But I can try.*

*I know what I'm doing: I'm buying loads of food from the supermarket and getting it home delivered. I'm going into the candle shop and buying scented candles. (I never want to smell sour milk again.) And then I'm going home. I'm going to cook a gourmet dinner out of the things I'm buying. I will watch TV, have a bubble bath. And I will stay awake all night.*

*Time to stop dreaming and start seriously shopping.*

Fay did just that. Every time she bought something, she noticed she was buying it. Every moment of time was carefully catalogued and chronicled and narrated.

She told herself continually, "I am living." And wondered why it hurt.

She forgot things. She had been so busy reminding herself that she existed, that she forgot that bread goes with butter and that coffee takes milk. Treasuring each moment had its drawbacks. The biggest drawback, she discovered, was one she had realised early on. It was the banging her head against a wall, and her leg against a shopping cart. It was pain. It had crept up on her insidiously the further her expedition progressed.

When she returned home, and was tired and hurting all over, Fay was at a loss. She had firmly decided that life should not be full of pain and incorrect decisions. But a negative decision is not the same as a clear path.

I am falling into a cheap philosophy junket, she thought, as she put the kettle on. Maybe a hot drink would help. Maybe a codeine would help. But would it put me to sleep?

*If I give up the pain, do I stop living? Is pain really the only thing that keeps me awake? And why do I keep having this thought? Simple question, simple answer. I need painkillers. Lots of them. Blaming Enlai and knowing where the pain comes from doesn't stop it being painful. It still needs treatment.*

So Fay turned off the kettle and went back up the street again, noticing the wind in her hair because it hurt, noticing Hindmarsh Drive and the traffic lights because they took too long to change and the sun glared. She wobbled into the chemist and asked for the strongest non-prescription pain relievers they had. She didn't even wait till she got home, but took the glass of water the chemist offered her and gobbled them down instantly.

She was in tears with the sharpness of her head and the tautness of her neck. And she was in tears because it had seemed such a simple solution—just living life from moment to moment.

Fay didn't go straight home. She knew that if she did, she would go directly to bed (and not pass Go or collect $200). And she hurt too much to face Enlai now. She hurt too much to face anything now. Besides, she had solved nothing.

Not a scrap. Not a tittle. Not a jot. And she needed coffee. So she bought a coffee and the biggest piece of chocolate cake in the universe and she worked her way through it. All of it. I need to put chocolate cake in Belle's world, she thought.

*Belle, and Gilbert and Persa and maybe Flor and chocolate cake and life would be perfect. Does Flor have an ancestral chocolate cake recipe? I wonder if I could somehow magically transform Enlai into a big piece of chocolate cake? That would solve everything. Except I would be a cannibal. But I wouldn't care – not if it was nice chocolate cake. But Enlai wouldn't be nice chocolate cake. I would ache to my inner core if I ate him.*

*Maybe that is what him taking bits of me does. It is like he leaves an aftertaste of himself in my body. I have hurts where I can't get at them.*

Finally, the cake and coffee and codeine were doing their little bit of magic and her eyes were starting to work. The shops were also shutting. It was time to go home. Even the flower shop was being taken down, pot by pot.

She focused on the present on the way home, too, just for the hell of it. Fay realised this little trick might work as a short-term stopgap, but it was not a way of solving all life's problems. She sighed. At least she had a stopgap. That was more than she had a day ago. But it wasn't enough. She sighed again.

Fay went to bed and curled up. It seemed the right place to be, and the soft blankets were so comforting around her. Just before she drifted to sleep, she caught herself. She was giving into Enlai, just to avoid pain. That was just as bad as hanging onto the pain just to remember the present. No good. Not at all. Very bad, in fact. Reluctantly, Fay hauled herself out of her cocoon. She took more painkillers. Probably stupid of her; she should have waited four hours. But it had been long enough. Surely. Long enough so she could just get rid of the pain.

Fay grimaced as she tried swallowing too much water at once. Nothing was going right. Nothing. Nothing. Nothing. Nothing. Would it make things better if she said "nothing" a few more times? Nothing. Nothing. Nothing. Nothing.

At least there was less pain.

And the living in the present thing wasn't her. There was something wrong with it. Very wrong. Very, very wrong. Very, very, very wrong. And what was it with all the repetition? It was like the pain. It haunted her, but was not something she wanted.

*What **do** I want?* Fay wondered. *I know what I don't want. I don't want my job. I don't want pain. I don't want Enlai mucking round. I probably don't want my family. What **do** I want?*

*I want friends. I want instant answers. I want control over my life. I want a world where I mean something. I wanted the fantasy but Enlai poisoned it.*

*Right now there are no foundations underpinning any-thing. It is like one of those horrible dreams when you are standing on a cliff and it is crumbling underneath your feet. I think I need to make my fantasy world solid again. I need to make me solid again.*

*I want to be with Gilbert. I want him to trust me and to ask me things. I am not the love interest in a Star Trek episode. I am me. Fay. Central. Not peripheral.*

*Peripheral. That is **it**. I am far too peripheral for far too* *many things. Me in the centre of my own life. So it may not be a matter of experiencing every single second. It may just be a matter of inside happiness. The art of effective dreaming . Ah. What a lovely thought.*

*But what about my normal life? If I haven't really lived it, how do I know if it is really a complete monotone? Maybe I haven't given* **it** *a fair go either?*

Fay found her purse and her keys and her car and went to the video rental place. There she hired three videos: one romantic comedy, one old-time musical and one fantasy. Well, she nearly hired three videos. She put the fantasy back at the last minute.

She wanted to see Fred Astaire dance and to cry at the romantic comedy. She didn't want to think. She wanted simple happiness. And the shop was open all night if she decided to change her mind and go for tears or philosophy.

Fay watched her films, twice each. It was like the night of the storm all over again. Except instead of battening down the hatches she relaxed. Her throbbing neck soon developed softness and her head felt as if it fitted on her neck. She lost the need to snuggle in bed.

Fay was happy.

When the videos were finished, she put some music on. At midnight, Fay's shadow could be seen dancing vigorously round the lounge-room.

# CHAPTER FIFTEEN

FAY WAS TERRIBLY IMPRESSED WITH HER OWN STUPIDITY.
Acting from the heart was all very well in theory, but
she had told herself it was stupid time and time again.
And look where it had got her now.

Fay looked across at the green and pleasant hills and
wondered where the hell she was. Nowhere she had designed, at any rate. Charming view though. Nice place
to live, if you were rurally inclined. Rich grass and dark
soil. Wherever she was, it was not Canberra. Since her
name was not Dorothy, she assumed she was not in
Kansas either. What a clever detective she was. Not
Canberra, not Kansas. That was start.

And wherever she was, if no-one was in sight, that
meant Enlai was not near. At least she hoped it did.
Maybe Enlai had gone invisible.

Nasty thought. Also a stupid one. Fay tapped the
side of her head and made sure that there wasn't even
the hint of an ache or a pain. Unless her tapping gave
her one, there was not.

Her head was whole. Her soul was safe. For just a
moment Fay was tempted to act celebratory. Twizzle
herself round in a 'Sound of Music' way, and declaim to
the hills, "I am safe".

But she didn't really want these hills to be alive. What she truly wanted was to be out of them. Talking to Belle and Gilbert. Or did she? If there were one thing, just one single thing, that she could do, what would that be? Board up the window to her soul? No. Make her little cove safe again? Not that either.

Gilbert had been there, and other people. Now that she knew that, it was just not the same. Not that she didn't love it, but Belle was quite right: it was no longer her soul-place. She needed a new one.

Fay looked at the pleasant hills and wondered if this was it. Did she come here because her inner self was yearning for hills? No. Definitely not. She had come here because she was stupid and had gone to sleep without working out where her dreams would take her. Which theoretically was an empowering thought. Throwing destiny to the winds. But in practice it meant that she was stuck in the middle of nowhere. And no matter how pretty the flowers looked in the middle of nowhere, it was still the middle of nowhere.

And suddenly Fay knew exactly what she was going to do. She was going to build her soul-place in Belle's old house. That small one with the big, solid shutters and the thick textured glass that was Alberc's first big investment in pompousness. The one with the fine oak door. *Alberc hasn't sold it*, Fay thought. She had a half memory of it being given to Belle as dowry. Either that or a bribe to get her to accept the marriage. It was Belle's anyhow. She knew that Belle would not grudge it to her.

But it had to be hers outright, and she needed someone to help her while she sorted it out. There would be a lot of sorting out, Fay feared.

Fay needed Belle. She had to trust. To trust that Belle would and could help her, and that no-one else would interfere. That Gilbert would have the sense to keep out of it. And that she was right in designing a soul-place that would allow other people in.

Fay admitted then, to herself, that she had been disturbed at the thought that her little cove had been thought of as wicked.

Belle would know if the house could be used. And Gilbert could bloody well help her set it up. After all, he was the one who had broken down the last walls. Fay smiled seraphically. She was going to make Gilbert feel so bad about that. It was going to be very good for him. She was going to go to town on it, in fact. Going to town in town. Better and better.

Fay lay on the grass and thought about it, the sun warming her right through. For the first time in a very long while she felt at peace within herself. She didn't want to move. She justified she ought to spend some time thinking – make everything come out right in her mind before doing things. Get to the right places and do the right things. But this is what she had been doing all her life, at everyone else's behest. So Fay decided she would simply do what she was comfortable with. Not much thinking at all in it.

And what was she most comfortable with, besides lying in the sun? She dwelt on that for a moment. Even in her dreams, she normally let things run their course once she had set up a basic set of premises.

Inspiration struck. Maybe, just maybe she had been thinking about the whole thing from the wrong direction. Just as she should not be banging her head against a wall and staying alive through feeling pain, she should not be doing too much planning. She would live in the instant. Or she would instantly live. Or something. Because if she didn't Enlai was going to butt in.

She would go with her heart. Fay smiled sweetly. She really liked this thought. And she would have a house. A house with shutters. People could come in and have a fine time. Or they could all be barred from entering at all. And the sole determining factor in all this was her internal needs. Fay was very happy to see herself turning into a greedy power-monger. Selfish. Heedless of others. So very much alive.

Fay was so delighted with this thought, carried down the most logical path possible and for as long as possible, that she fell fast asleep. Not a dream-sleep, but an ordinary, healing one.

When she woke up, the sun was low in the sky. And when she looked around she found the pasture looked familiar: Fay was near the town, in dragon country. Only now it was all green; no desert, no whisper of wings. She stretched happily, no longer needing dragons or wanting to live in their shadow. Fay walked to the main street leisurely, as if the world had not been falling to pieces just the day before. She was so contented that she didn't rush to see Belle, as she would have just hours earlier. In fact, she remembered how alone Flor had felt, and dropped in to see her. Flor welcomed her and fed her dinner. They renewed a friendship.

It was nice to be able to knock on a door occasionally and get fed dinner and nice conversation. It reminded Fay of why she invented the village, and the nature of the village she had invented. Somehow, in its growth to a town and in the gentle rise of terror, Fay had let herself forget what everything had been like. That friendships were everyday and fine and comfortable. That dramas could happen, but seldom lasted more than a storm of tears.

She knew that her old village memory was invented; that her world had not really been alive then. But she wondered, by working hard, if she could at least take the horrid deaths out of the equation. If people could walk the night alone in safety and without fear. And if she could live back here, with her friends around her.

Not all her friends: Enlai was a puzzle. She could understand him wanting to steal her magic. Enlai had to be best and biggest and centre. Without magic, in a magic world, he wasn't. He was an ambitious turd. She liked that phrase—it described him so precisely—an ambitious turd. So finding a way of getting magic was pretty much the Enlai she knew. He would not have considered the pain others might feel.

But the deaths? And the ring of sorcery? How could that be Enlai?

———

Fay pondered as she walked to the castle. She pondered so hard that she ran into someone. *Not again*, was her first thought. It was her second, also, as she looked up and saw Gilbert. This time, he did not smile.

"I thought you were dead," he whispered. His face looked haunted.

He took her by the shoulders and looked her in the eyes, deeply, as if to check that she was actually herself.

"Stop that," grumbled Fay. "I'm not a freak show." Even that didn't get a smile. "And I'm not dead."

"But you have changed."

"Of course I've bloody changed. People do. Anyway, how could I not, with Enlai rampaging like a bull in a, in a barber's shop." Fay stopped in confusion, realising that the simile was a complete mess. "If you are worried about Enlai peeking out from behind my eyes he is not. And I'm on the way to make sure he never does again." This last was said without any bravado. Firmly. Collectedly. Fay was very proud of herself.

This produced the smallest, tiniest of unwilling

smiles. Whatever was eating at Gilbert, it was deep and woeful.

Maybe he had a dark side? Heroes with dark sides were supposed to be wondrously romantic. Right now, though, Fay just found it wondrously annoying. He raced off to save the world in places it didn't need saving, then when she had finally sorted herself out and knew what to do, he looked untrusting. Doleful. He stared deeply into her eyes as if she really didn't quite exist. Had he ever trusted her? Or had he just assumed she was a charming little accessory in his life? Was she even charming enough to be a charming little accessory?

Fay decided since today was a day for facing home truths she might as well ask. "Gilbert, stop looking at me like that. I love you dearly, but you have been mucking me around like anyone's business. You never stay for explanations, or to give me them. And now you wonder if I'm me."

"How did you know I was wondering if you were you?" This sounded more like the man of her dreams.

"Because you are looking at me like that."

Gilbert merged with one of his silences. A reluctant "You're right," emerged eventually from the silence, "And I'm still not sure about you. I am truly sorry."

"So am I," replied Fay tartly. "You don't know how reassuring it is to hear you say you couldn't trust me the length of a ten foot pole."

"I didn't mean it like that," protested Gilbert, feebly.

"Yes, you did. And get that poor hurt puppy look out of your eyes. I'm taking my life back."

This broke down his defences. Gilbert looked horrified. "No!"

"Yes. I'm going to build me a soul-place again, since you dismantled the other one. And I'm going to sort Enlai out." Fay said this very, very firmly. As much as to convince herself as Gilbert. "And then I am going home. I have a life to lead, you know."

That last was purely to annoy. Fay was not sure she had much of a life anywhere. And she had not really thought about the home thing properly. But by damn, she thought, I can create a life. Somewhere. She smiled brilliantly.

Gilbert, usually so ominiscient, misread this smile. He turned and walked away.

Fay was too delighted with the thought that she might have a life to lead to call him back. Then she realised that this had not been the discussion she was after. Not at all. He was supposed to tell her how to make a house for her soul. Or what Enlai was up to. And how Enlai might be defeated.

*Damn, damn, damn*, was Fay's eloquent thought. *Why do I always do this? Gilbert believes we have split up, and all I wanted was for him to stop a moment and think. And to bloody talk to me. Why do things never quite go right? And why can't Gilbert and I talk for more than two minutes about anything meaningful?*

Fay had her own sullen silence for a minute. Then she walked resolutely to the castle. She was going to talk to Belle. Belle was someone who would talk to her. Belle also listened enough so that Fay could get sensible words out. Gilbert and she never seemed to manage that. Fay sighed.

Then she realised. Fay said the little rhyme to herself as she walked. It summarised Gilbert's mood so perfectly. Even to the incomprehensibility of the ancient language. Gilbert was incomprehensible. Very busy being that, in fact. Turning it into an art form. It was like that time in the snow, by the gallows tree.

*Foweles in the frith,*
*The fisses in the flod,*
*And I mon waxe wod;*

*Mulch sorwe I walke with*
*For best of bon and blod.*

He took the sorrows of the world upon him. Almost Christ-like. And he was letting himself be over-run with the sorrow. Only human after all.

Fay smiled a little grimace, and wondered how she could have fallen so very deeply in love with a man who had to take on such a burden. To a man who never listened. To a man who could read her mind except when it counted. To a man who would walk away from her without question.

It had been easier to understand loving the merry clown who had seduced her. Those flashes of wisdom he had then were much more endearing than this tortured soul bit. It had been much easier.

Why did soap opera appear in the middle of real save-the-world stuff? And why was Fay being sensible and walking to the castle instead of being romantic and chasing Gilbert, to throw herself at his feet and to make up? Fay wondered this in a purely rhetorical way. Because the reason she was walking to the castle was because she had a soul to save—her own.

———

"You left," were Belle's first words. "You promised me you would remain here. We were working hard to help you. And you left."

"I had to," Fay tried to say, but Belle's opening words had led to more, and she could not be heard. Belle didn't have much to say, but she said it over and over and over and over again, increasingly upset.

Fay had no idea how to deal with this. It scared her that underneath the calm and competence and all the new skills Belle had developed to deal with her life lay this emotional turmoil. It was if everything that had happened to Belle—her unfortunate marriage, the death of her lord, the murders in the town, the sorcery, her loss of autonomy to the Prince—as if all this had been repressed and the tension had grown and grown. Belle's emotions were a volcano and had just erupted. Fay winced at the description, but stood by it. She also stood by Belle and accepted what her friend threw at her.

She was racked with guilt. Belle's words didn't flow over her and pass her by. Every one of them was like a sharp knife stabbing her. An ice-knife. Like the one she had felt on the green, when she had found the frozen dancer.

Because it was her fault. All this heat and torrent from Belle was the result of things Fay had done, or had not done. Her misuse of magic, her inability to keep promises. Her lack of self-knowledge. Her silliness. Fay was tempted to just give up and go home. Try to forget about it all. Run away from magic. Run away from broken promises.

She could fade. She would fade. Fay could not take standing there, with Belle's angry face upon her. She started to fade. The world swam around her. Then she stopped herself.

Fading would give Enlai a field day. He would take over here. Fay herself would probably die. She knew it. In her heart, she knew that there is a limit to how much of one's imagination and thought can be leached off before the self exists no longer. She might not die. She might live on in the real world, confined to a lunatic asylum. Incapable of thought. Incapable of speech. Fay could see that happening, if too much of her essence was stolen. She could also see herself living in a world of perpetual pain.

The dream-world firmed up around her. She was staying.

Fay half-fading stemmed Belle's tears. When Fay came fully back into the dream world she found Belle looking down at her ominously, silently. "I came back," said Fay, defensively. "I had to. And I had to go—Enlai was stealing from me directly. He took all my light from me, right there in the street. And my magic was out of control. It was bad."

Belle nodded and ordered drinks. "We need to talk then."

This was such a sudden change that Fay was bewildered. Belle had progressed from emotional wreck to lady of the castle in a bare instant. Fay had no idea if she was forgiven or not. Or if Belle was going to erupt again. This was the first time one of Belle's agonies of tears had been directed at her, and she didn't really know what it meant or how to take it.

"I didn't mean to fade," Fay started again. "But Enlai was taking huge streams of stuff straight from somewhere deep inside me. And it hurt like hell. And all I could think of was getting out. And once I got out, I was home. And I looked around and tried to sort out what I was and who I was and..."

"Did it work?" Belle's tone was cool.

"Yes and no. I worked a lot out. There are things I need to do. One of them is, I think, be more inside myself. Find out who it is underneath the dreams, or maybe who it is who makes the dreams. And I am not explaining this well." For all she knew, Fay might have been explaining it brilliantly, but Belle was giving her no indication. This was the problem. Belle's normally expressive face was a façade of white marble. *It's like talking to Dad,* Fay thought.

"Maybe I can do something and show you?" Fay thought aloud, since whatever she said was going to be received without any warmth. Fay cast around for something to show what she had been thinking. Or at least, how she had been thinking it.

It had to be something small, and from the heart. Something light perhaps. Wistful. Friendly. She needed to do friendly right now. She had to break down that alabaster façade. Unless she did, Fay could not see her way to asking Belle for anything. Not even a bed to sleep in, much less the gift of a home.

And right now she was wondering if what she was going to ask Belle would entirely break the friendship. Because the part of Belle's childhood that had been happy was the time spent with her mother. Most of her mother was embedded in that little house that Fay had so blithely assumed Belle would give her. Belle the rich. Belle the castle-owner.

*Fay is still Fay-the-callous*, she thought despairingly about herself. *But what else can I do?* Fay thought about things that might cheer her friend up.

She remembered back to a time when they had sat in the garden, chatting. Before the world had become so real. Fay had imagined the sun in her face and the waft of warm breeze in her hair. And she had imagined a beautiful butterfly floating over Belle's embroidery, mistaking it for real flowers. She had wished for a camera at that moment, and had taken a still picture in her mind. Because that was one moment of dream that had been pure happiness.

She saw, on the floor, a stray piece of leaf litter that someone had trudged inside and that had escaped the servants' vigilance. She picked it up and held it in her hand for a moment, looking down. "Hold out your hand, Belle," Fay ordered, gently, "I want to try something."

Belle suspiciously held out her hand.

"I am going to try and create you something small. I want to show you what has changed inside me, and this is the fastest way I can think of. I'm not going to sing or anything. Just try something out."

Belle didn't laugh. She didn't even smile a little.

Fay couldn't think of a better way of saying things. Her mind had not really reached the verbal stage. She had just known inside herself some of the things that needed to happen, and had found little codes, like the house-as-protection, that would help her achieve them. *I need deciphering,* thought Fay, *And at this moment, so does Belle.*

Fay directed Belle's attention to the crumbled brown leaf in her hand. It was not a thing of beauty. But then, nor was Fay, she reflected in self-pity. *Spectacularly strange,* Fay thought, *but not beautiful. But maybe transformation is possible. Maybe.* Fay put her mind to dreaming of it.

The two women together watched the leaf intently, their thoughts solitary. Both of them were surprised when the leaf changed shape a little, turned bright green (slowly, flushes of colour from the centre out) and then fluttered away, a leaf moth entire.

"Not a butterfly," reflected Fay silently, "but a start."

Belle commented, "This needs working on."

"Yes," agreed Fay, "But I have made a beginning."

"You have made a beginning," agreed Belle, and her brown gaze was thoughtful instead of stone.

"I was thinking," said Fay, diffidently, "About what you said about boarding up the window to my soul. And I don't think that's enough. I think the reason I hared off home when things got scary was because it wasn't enough. Not nearly enough."

"That might be," said, Belle, equivocally.

Fay sighed deep inside herself—this was not going to be easy. "I have thought and thought and thought of what I can do, and it has to be something already close to me. Something I already know. And it has to be related to who I am, deep down."

"Yes," said Belle, almost encouragingly.

"Belle, you are not going to like this," Fay had a note of desperation in her voice.

"So tell me."

"Do you know that the first house I built in this world was your childhood home?"

There was a silence. Not a happy one. "Something new won't do?"

"How much time do we have for something new?" asked Fay. "The reason I built it was because it was to be a friendly place. My friend's home. So I thought it might have the right sort of construct. But I don't know these things. I just don't know anything about them. So if you can suggest something that is better, please say. Because at first I thought, 'Belle will let me have it' and then I thought, 'But she shouldn't have to.' And now I don't know what to do."

"Your feeling is right," said Belle, thoughtfully, "As far as I understand these things. The only question is would you trust me with your soul? Because I would be the one person you could not keep out of that house. Ever."

"What about your father?"

"He left it behind long ago," said Belle, dismissively. "And not just physically, either. In redefining himself, he made it safe for you."

"And Gilbert?"

"Even if you spent the rest of your lives together, we can make sure it is your place, not his."

"I meant because of his magic, like he invaded the cove."

"Ah," Belle reflected for a moment. "I suspect the deed transfer will do the trick there, but I can check."

"If you don't mind. I just want to know if my windows can be broken again, I guess."

Belle smiled, gently.

"You have redefined yourself, haven't you?" Fay said, the thought striking her like sunlight. "You are not longer Bellezour Anma, you are the chatelaine of the castle. So how does that affect you and the house? I mean, given what you said about your father?"

Belle laughed. "We didn't redefine ourselves in at all the same way. I am still Belle. All this," and her gaze swept the castle, metaphorically, "expands on who I was before Mother died. It's as if I have resumed growing, reaching my potential."

"Oh. Oh," said Fay. "That makes sense. But I do trust you with that soul thing, you know. You do know that, don't you?"

"I didn't, but I do now," and Belle's frost suddenly melted.

Fay hated it the way the glacier suddenly ceased to exist and Belle forgave her. But it was Belle. And she was right in what she had said, she trusted Belle beyond anyone, solely. Which was in itself not a comfortable thought. Because she suspected she trusted Belle more than she trusted herself. What if Belle was a figment of her imagination? *Don't even consider going in that direction, Fay,* she scolded herself, silently.

"I'm not happy with you having the house, though," said Belle. Fay tensed. "You're not really committed to this world yet." It was as if her friend had read her thoughts. "But maybe you can't commit until we give you reason, and just asking you to stay is not really reason."

There was a silence as Belle thought. "You can have the house. More, I will be a part of making it over for you. That way there is an emotional transfer of title, not just a physical one."

"Thank you," said Fay. "You don't know how much this means to me."

"Well, you don't know how much that house means to me—so we're even," and Belle laughed again, not entirely happily. "I will have the deed transfer done immediately. Is this the first time you will have formally owned any land here?"

"Yes," admitted Fay. "I never thought of this world in terms of ownership and papers and things. I only thought in terms of stories. And of the cove as my sheltered place."

"Good," nodded Belle. "That might make a difference in several ways then." But she did not elaborate, and Fay was so relieved to have the decision made in her favour that she did not like to press.

She had another thought, however. "Belle, you know that even if I go back to my world, if my base is here then any magic of mine would still have a link here."

"True," said Belle, looking a little relieved.

"And," pursued Fay, "You would still have access to the house. That can only help you checking out if everything is okay. So I'm not asking you to give up the power-stuff, only the heart-stuff."

"Only the heart-stuff," Belle said, wryly. "But you're right. The house is a good way of sorting things out. It keeps our options open while making you more secure. Which can only mean that we're safer."

"No more lightning," said Fay wistfully. "And no more dead dancers."

"I most certainly hope not."

"So do I. I think the worst moment of my life was when I found that frozen dancer on the common. And my head hurt. Did I tell you about that?"

"Yes, you did," said Belle. "And I thought I had it all

sorted out then. I thought I had so many things sorted out, and they still all go wrong."

"Me too," sighed Fay. "I need to talk to Gilbert. He thinks I have split up with him."

"I know," said Belle. "I suggested he check with you."

"Don't tell me, he walked off?"

"I am afraid so."

"I told him I wanted to live my own life. And I need to. It doesn't mean I don't want him in my future."

"I can see how he would read that as you not wanting him," Belle commented.

"Well," Fay frowned, "Especially as I was not sensible in the way I said it. I need to explain to him. But he hates serious talking."

"He does, doesn't he," and Belle grinned. "Men!"

Fay had to smile back. "Men," she agreed.

---

"Fay," said Belle, diffidently.

"That's my name," answered Fay, determined to be cheerful and supportive and everything wonderful. One had to start being wonderful somewhere, after all.

Belle sighed. Fay being determinedly all sorts of great things was obviously not something she was enthusiastic about right now. "Can you see your way to staying around this time? Until we've sorted things out?"

"I can try," Fay said, dubiously, all her great hopes of personality reform instantly shattered. "I can do my very best."

"It's not enough, you know, "Belle was severe, "Not nearly enough."

"I know." Fay was defiant. "But I'm not going to promise. I promised last time and events overtook. If I had stayed, I think I would be dead." Fay instantly regretted not having made the truth prettier somehow. This was not a mantelpiece truth.

Belle was silent at this. It patently made her no happier. But then, nothing was going to make her happier right now. Nothing was going to make anything happier right now—not even the most determined cheer and the most cheerful determination.

"Then I guess you trying will have to do," was Belle's final acceptance. It was grudging. Even the way her fingers tapped was grudging. Belle was doing a very good job at making Fay feel bad.

"Sorry," whispered Fay.

"So you should be," said Belle, censoriously. She finally smiled. "It is not your fault. The rest of us only do what we can."

"Including Gilbert?"

"Especially Gilbert."

"I think... I think I would like to talk about Gilbert with you, if you don't mind. I really, really would like to. I know you don't like talking about him and that my love life is my own business and all of that. But..."

At this decidedly inapposite moment, a tornado burst into the room. Its funnel was called Persa, and swirling around that funnel was a gaggle of children. Grubby children. Nor was it an orderly tornado.

Belle's eyebrows raised to their very highest and she stood up, looking down from lofty height onto Persa's irrepressive cheer. Fay had never seen Belle quite so... head of class... as this before. It fascinated her. It was those elegant eyebrows. That arch said everything. Words like "What is this messy mob doing invading my lovely, tidy PRIVATE living room?" were wholly unnecessary.

Persa looked up at Belle, totally unrepentant. Of course. Persa never repented. It was not in her. Belle lost a shade of her formidability. But only a shade. It made no difference. Persa was still irrepressible. "I will tell you about my little adventure once I have taken care of the kids," she promised, and the tornado spiralled out of the room as quickly as it had entered.

Fay couldn't help laughing. "Why did she come in here at all? Since all she did was come in and tell us she was coming by later?"

"I think —but don't quote me on this—that this was her way of asking for permission. I'm not sure what I have given permission for. We'll find out later."

"Persa is a total entertainment," declared Fay, and they both laughed. Fay got to wondering at what had changed Persa from being a private entertainment to such a very public one. She guessed everyone was changing. Maybe that included her. Maybe. She could hope, anyway.

Persa's little intervention had caused Fay to completely lose her train of thought. Persa had derailed that train so thoroughly that the two had even lost their high seriousness. It was as if the last little while just didn't exist in their minds, and they started gossiping. There was not really enough time to blacken anyone's name convincingly before Persa returned, sans attachments, grubby or otherwise.

This time she was more communicative. Persa was in story mode, and, since she was the heroine of this little tale, she took the greatest relish in telling it. Her eyes were alight and she even spoke sequentially. Fay wished she herself could only think as sequentially as Persa was able to speak, when telling a story. Some things, she thought, are just beyond possible.

"The children were in trouble and I saved them," was Persa's simple, sequential explanation.

The actual tale-telling and bright eyes came when Belle asked for the whole story. But this was a part of story telling—being sure the audience knew that they wanted to hear the story.

Fay found herself wondering what Persa was like as a teacher. It seemed strange that her flightiest friend could do big things. Fay settled down to hear what on earth a gaggle of noisy brats needed saving from, and how Persa had cast herself in the part of saviour.

Persa explained that she was going about her own business. She had that glint in her eye that suggested her business was certainly none of Belle's or Fay's, and probably contained more than a skerrick of mischief. Belle wondered aloud if her business had anything to do with Alberc's new civic garden?

Persa spluttered. She admitted that she had sewn some curious new seeds in that new patch that ornamented the town. She had carefully harvested the seed-pods of all her favourite weeds and planted them in Alberc's proud new patch.. She was almost apologetic. Persa admitted openly she could not see the logic behind a garden where children could not play.

"And where you shouldn't play either, by the sound of it," said Fay, roundly.

Belle's eyes were crinkled in an attempt to look stern.

Fay wondered at Persa. After having been caught out so badly, you would think she would have at least the grace to show a little remorse. But she didn't. She probably wouldn't even fix the garden. In fact, being who she was, she would probably organise a formal expedition to the garden when the time came, to admire the flowers produced by all those weeds. She sighed. She wished she were as strong as Persa. Or as silly.

On her way home, Persa had heard a commotion and gone to investigate. It was at the pub. There were a bunch of the soldiers hanging around. These were not her soldiers, she said, but the new mob, brought in to restore order and all the rest of it. Persa's mouth gave a small purse of distaste at the thought. Fay wondered whether it was because Persa hated order so severely, or because these soldiers were not keys to the royal court as the earlier ones had been.

Belle was faster. "Cause trouble, did they?"

Persa nodded.

There had been just a few soldiers in the pub, bemoaning their lack of pay. A few, but very loud. They had been 'persuading' locals to buy them drinks, and had become a tad rowdy.

The children were employed by the pub from time to time, when big cleaning jobs needed doing. It was pocket money. Fay's eyes opened wider for a moment. She had not realised that the children were respectable infants who had been doing honest labour. Seeing grubby children with Persa automatically had her assuming that they were street children in need of basic succour. Apparently the polishing and scrubbing had got in the way of the drunken louts who called themselves soldiers. And apparently they had reacted violently.

Persa had stepped in and scolded the soldiers into silence. Fay could just imagine it, and smiled gently. Such a little person for such a big mouth, she thought fondly of her friend. Persa had whisked the children away from the pub, threatening retribution on the landlord if she didn't send them their pay and didn't protect them from being molested in future. And now the children were cleaning up somewhere, and getting ready to go home.

"Cleaning up, or being cleaned up," asked Belle also amused.

"Being cleaned up, I think, judging from the light in your housekeeper's eye," Persa answered. "Her nephew was one of the children, and she never seems to think he washes properly."

"Does he?" asked Fay, curiously.

"I don't know," shrugged Persa. "He's a friend of mine, and you don't ask your friends if they wash their ears or their big toe."

And that was that. Persa had rescued her friends from a beating. The whole thing now was obviously up to Belle. "I will have a talk about those soldiers," she said, resigned.

"You could at least be enthusiastic about it," cried Persa. "They need a good spanking."

"You give it," suggested Fay.

"I would," grinned Persa, "Except the bloody Prince would probably be mad at me for getting out of line again."

"Is he often mad with you?" Fay asked.

"Yes," she replied proudly. "He does his job much better when he's mad at me, you know."

"You wouldn't believe it," said Belle, resignedly, "but they work well together."

"Good," said Fay, for want of anything else.

Belle had one more question. "What exactly happened? The whole thing," she instructed.

Persa looked a bit shamefaced. "The reason they were out of money is because my cousin was so sick of their rowdiness that he put on what he called a soldier tax. Every time they broke something or were too rude, he raised the price of drinks."

Fay couldn't help but giggle. Belle frowned on her. "So what happened?"

"They took the children as hostages. For each round of drinks they were bought, they would release a child. If they weren't bought a round of drinks they would wallop a child."

"I will certainly follow that up," promised Belle. "With your cousin as much as with anyone else."

"And there is one other thing," said Persa, in a small voice.

"What?" and Belle's voice was as school-marmish as Fay had ever heard it.

"They chased us right to the castle. They won't go away. The soldiers are at the gates, waiting."

"Damn you, Persa," Belle said, without rancour, and left to deal with the soldiers.

———

So much happening, so little time.

The episode with the soldiers triggered a general alarm in the town. It was not a matter of magic, since there had been none. It was panic. Innumerable upright citizens were moving themselves and at least a part of their possessions into the castle. This created an instant scurry.

Fay found herself wondering which of the people with bags and blankets were those she had seen hiding at the window when she turned the street into a scene from outback Australia?

"Only for a few days," every second family seemed to be reassuring Belle. "Only until things settle down." Fay was quickly bored. She rather suspected that Belle's reaction to the number of people appearing and to the sheer quantity of their possessions was not boredom.

Fay looked around for Gilbert and did not see him. Nothing unusual about that, she supposed. But she needed to speak to him. There was so much that needed to be said. Not the personal stuff, Fay found herself thinking, though that was essential too.

Gilbert needed to know about Enlai and about what was happening with Fay's magic. Gilbert needed to know so much. Fay sighed and started to explain this to Belle. Belle was good at getting messages to people. At least, that is what she had disappeared to do last time Fay had a magic crisis.

A servant came up with an interruption just at that moment, which might have explained the near abstraction in Belle's voice as she said, "When we get the house sorted out, maybe then we can deal with small things."

*But I don't think Gilbert is small. Even if I had only met him once, he would not be small. He is not even that short. Even if he is not six foot six. He doesn't make sense, you know. Come to think of it, I don't make sense. Nothing makes sense.*

*I am totally, totally miserable. And Belle hasn't helped. Which is strange, because she normally is there for me. It is like having a rock in a rough stream, underneath the surface of turbulent water. When I am in trouble she is there. Invisible. I mean, even in the real world, she is somehow there for me. If I try to ford the stream normally, Belle-the-rock keeps my footing entirely sure. And this time there was sand, and no rock. And I am struggling to stay upright.*

*I guess I just didn't realise how very much I relied on Belle having faith in me. I need someone to have faith in me. One person in the whole world. In both whole worlds. I need someone to trust and who trusts me. I am not even sure that I trust myself.*

*Damn, I have fallen into the slough of despond. Or was it the slough of despair? Bunyan was boring, any old how. And look what my despair or despond has produced. I guess even if everything else is a total, total mess, my magic is still with me. But what am I going to do with this thing? And what do I call it—the magic of self-pity?*

In her right hand, Fay found herself holding a deep red rose. It was a despairing rose, near death. The petals one by one drifted gently to the floor as she held it. She stood there a very long time watching the petals fall, transfixed by her own moodiness. When all the petals were around her like a light drift of blood-coloured snowflakes, Fay's brain kicked back into gear. Well, maybe only a little into gear. Maybe the sulk wasn't entirely through yet. She wondered why all her magic turned to gardening when she was not paying attention to its form. She hated gardening.

Nice rose though. Addams Family in form. Very morose. She should plant the stalk somewhere, she decided. *If the drooping rose grows, its official name will be the 'Mor-rose'—that will settle everyone,* Fay thought, in complacent misery. Fay was quite impressed at her talent for complacent misery.

She wandered through the castle grounds until she found her quiet corner. She planted the forlorn stem next to the morris stick. A decaying kerchief held a vine closely to that stick, so her first garden magic was not a failure. Fay's corner—hardly cheerful, but somehow things grew.

The walking gave her some measure of composure back. Still, deep down, she hurt intensely. There was something in her that had never quite hurt like this before. It was as if she were unthawing. Maybe she was in a fairy tale, with that rose and its lost petals. Maybe she used to have the iced up heart that only the Snow Queen could give. It was the essence of pain: it hurt to connect with the world. *Better to be frozen,* Fay thought, *than to hurt like this.* She sat next to her dead rose, planted surreal-life in the ground, and wept. It did nothing useful, but it felt good.

It felt so good that she felt almost energised. What could she do with new-found almost-energy? She could investigate the house, Fay supposed, doubtfully. She was feeling so foul for stealing Belle's childhood happiness that there was no enthusiasm in this thought at all. Fay thought of herself as the thief of happiness, the murderer of dreams. All in all, she figured, she was obviously the bad guy in this film and should have died two scenes ago. Or something.

Buoyed by this thought she obtained the key and directions from Belle.

While she was at it, Fay borrowed Belle's most comfortable shoes. If she was going to steal all else, she might as well have comfortable feet, Fay reckoned. And then thought back to the days, early on in her dreaming, when Belle didn't really even have a face. She had thought it was a great idea then to give her new friend the same sized feet as her. She had never anticipated that Belle's shoe would ever feel real on her feet.

"If you want to know someone, walk in their shoes," —that was the saying. She really needed the high heels of the elegant lady of the castle. These old, low heels belonged to the Belle Fay had created. At least, she thought that Belle had been created and not born. Maybe. More maybes.

Always maybes.

———

Fay happily jangled keys as she walked along. Keys had a good feel to them. They felt like security. The future. Predictability. Control.

The biggest element of unpredictability was unfortunately standing at his front door as she walked past. "Enlai," Fay hissed.

Her mood changed again, mercurially. Suddenly, she was very angry. Fay dropped the keys and ran up to him, furious. "Stop it," she yelled. "Leave me alone."

Enlai held out his hands openly, mockingly. "Stop what?" he asked, all reason and light, "I'm not doing anything."

"You do things," Fay said. "You hurt people. You take

things from them. You leech their life and their substance. Stop it!!"

"Why?" asked Enlai, still sounding reasonable, his hands filling with light, "You started it anyway. Or one of your mob did. I nearly have it, you know. I'm nearly there," and he laughed, his hands awash with Fay's light.

Fay's head was icy, and agony. She turned inward instantly. She wasn't going to let Enlai do this to her. She willed herself to fade.

\*\*\*

*I hate, I hate, I hate migraines. And I detest knowing that they are Enlai's fault. And my own for not safeguarding myself. And Gilbert's for just dismantling my cove without asking. And for promising me the world in recompense. And not delivering. On anything.*

*He did not give me protection. He did not give me love. And that is the migraine speaking, young Fay, because you never asked. Not for protection. Not for love.*

*What can I do? I can ask him for that help he promised. And I will.*

*But not yet. Right now I can only think because I am on the strongest pain relievers I have ever been on in my life. And this is not good. Very not good. Like my English.*

*I did recover here before, so I will stay here till I recover now. I protected myself from Enlai before, too. So I can do it now. Somehow. I can. I must. And then, when I am better, I will go and do all the things I need to do in the fantasy world. Every single last one of them. I can. I must. I shall.*

*I thought saving the world would be so dramatic. Questing. Rescuing people. High sorcery. Well, the closest I get to high anything is high dudgeon. Because each time Enlai takes a bit of me I end up so mad and so sick and so weak.*

*Damn Enlai. Can I damn him to smithereens? I never*

*did work out what a smithereen looked like. But I wonder. I wonder if I can really think him out of existence?*

*Enlai Devers is imaginary. Enlai Devers is imaginary. Enlai Devers is imaginary.*

*Enlai Devers is imaginary. Enlai Devers is imaginary.*

*Enlai Devers is imaginary.*

*I bet it doesn't actually fade him. But it makes me think he is faded.*

*I am going to bed until the worst of this migraine is over. And then I am going to do whatever it was I was going to do before. I can't remember it now. I can't remember anything much now. But it will come back. And I have a lovely new charm to put myself to sleep with.*

*Enlai Devers is imaginary. Enlai Devers is imaginary. Enlai Devers is imaginary.*

# CHAPTER SIXTEEN

FAY WOKE UP BEFORE SHE WAS QUITE READY. SHE WAS muzzy and unfocused. So unfocused was she that the telephone was a huge surprise. It startled her almost out of existence.

She could not work out what the ringing was. She thought it was the doorbell, and answered the door. Then she went back to bed and turned her alarm clock off. After that she got really clever and turned the smoke detector off. When this didn't work, she went to the stove and banged hard on the oven timer. Her hand hurt then, as well as her head. But still there was still ringing. Finally she picked up the telephone.

"Hello," she said, spaced out and sore.

"Fay?" asked a familiar voice, "Is that you?"

"No, it is her sorcerer's cat," answered Fay, grumpily. It was a stupid question. And the only thing she knew at this moment was that she was probably Fay. She wasn't even sure which world she was in, but she was Fay.

"You sound sick," the voice said.

"I am sick," came the honest reply, "Go away."

"I will be right round," promised the voice, and it hung up on her.

Fay looked at the dead receiver in her hand and let it drop. This brought her feet to her attention. She looked at her feet and tried wiggling her toes. They seemed to be there, but dysfunctional.

She wondered about the necessity of clothes for a disembodied voice. Or if she could even walk to the wardrobe and pull something on.

In the end, she made it to the wardrobe and to a pair of jeans, but left her nightgown flopping over the top. She could not manage any more. Not if her life depended on it. She barely made it to the door and just waited there, ready to tell whoever it was that she wasn't home. Or didn't exist. She desperately wanted to tell someone she didn't exist. Not existing would solve everything.

It was a very tired waiting. Very still. Very cautious. She was shell-shocked from the pain and the rambunctious awakening. Whoever it was, she did not want to see him. She thought it was a him. That was about as far as her thoughts could take her, too. It was not a good morning.

It turned out to be Fred. A surprisingly practical Fred. He took one look at her, and sat her down. He made her a hot herbal drink. It was so hot it hurt her hands. He made sure she drank it. Then he made her another.

When she could move enough, he helped her dress and took her to the outpatients of the hospital. She was whisked into a bed somewhere. All cold and clinical and starchy. She was given an injection and for a while it didn't matter how clinical or starchy anything was. Even the funny smell ceased to matter.

She had a day in bed at the hospital, doped up so high on medication that she couldn't dream. Which was a good thing. It was also a good thing that Fred came to take her home again. He cooked for both of them. But she couldn't eat. She couldn't face food at all, so he left dinner for her. A plate to be heated up in the microwave.

Finally Fred programmed his number into the telephone, in case it should happen again. He put the short cut code in big black texta on a piece of paper, and pasted it next to the phone where she could not miss it. And then he left. No fanfare, no questions.

One day she might be surprised at this nice, kind Fred. *But not today,* Fay thought. And went to bed for some ordinary sleep. She got it too. By late the next morning she was almost herself again.

————

She was herself enough to ring up work and explain about the brief hospitalisation. By the sympathetic noises made at the other end, Fay gathered she had made these types of excuses before. She vaguely remembered a piece of paper from the hospital and so she read it out to them. It was apparently enough to give her a day off work. That was nice.

It wasn't that she was still full of hurt. In fact, hurt was all gone. Bye bye, pain. The problem was that she was really not in the world. She was yearning to get back to her fantasy land. She couldn't remember feeling this strongly about it, or this disconnected from her daily life. Not ever.

She was so worried about the world she had left. There were things to be done. Things only she could do. So she rang up her regular doctor and explained about the day before. Within an hour she was in there, being checked.

He gave her a prescription and two more days off work. "That should do it," he said. "If you get the headache again, though, we might have to do scans."

Fay agreed politely, collected her medicine from the chemist, and went home, content. She rang work again and said she would be back in three days. She remembered her dinner from last night. She ate the noodles Fred had so kindly prepared. Then she took off most of her clothes and just curled up in bed, ready to dream again.

Somehow she appeared right in the middle of a conversation with Belle. And Belle didn't even blink. Very Alice in Wonderland, Fay decided. "Do you want to know what I think Enlai has been doing, Fay?" asked Belle.

"I would love to."

"I don't know if you will like this. And it is only my view."

"Why do people say this sort of thing when they have bad news?" Fay's tone was aggressively cheerful. She was determined nothing would get on top of her this time. And no-one except her was going to know how much she wanted to recall what she had said to Gilbert. Except Gilbert himself – when he had the decency to heave into view.

She wasn't sure about Fred yet in any way shape or form. Did he have a form? Maybe she could pretend he was a figment of her migrained imagination? That would solve a whole heap of conflicts somewhere in her brain.

"Because we do," smiled Belle.

"It's unlike you, though," answered Fay.

"Yes, it is. I just get this feeling you would rather know than not know."

"Well, I would—I forgive you in advance—does that help?"

Belle laughed, and looked a bit reassured. "Enlai is copying you in several ways. Firstly, he is trying to be what you have been—which is what you are not."

"Huh?" said Fay, intelligently.

"You were hiding from yourself. I think Enlai sees that hiding as key to your power. When it is not key to it at all—in fact it is the biggest restriction on it."

"You've been talking to Gilbert."

"About what makes up magic, yes. About you, no. So don't even think it." Fay grinned, sheepishly. Belle continued, almost fiercely, "And I think that Enlai is not just trying to be you, but has somehow found all the worst in you. That is why he tried to get into your world. To see you. And he only saw the negatives."

"When I was bored and fading. Which made me callous. Which meant I managed other people's lives for them without them knowing, as a private entertainment. About the time when I saw the town as a giant playground, when none of you were at all real."

"Exactly," nodded Belle. ""And the fact that his magic comes out so evil shows how powerful this negative can be. You and I know that this is only a small part of you. Enlai thinks it is the source of your power."

"So how do we change that?"

"In an ideal world, we gently persuade him of the wonderful person you are, and that he has it all wrong. And that he is allowed to be himself—he doesn't have to be Fay and he doesn't need magic to make his mark on the world. But I suspect that we are going to have to take far more drastic action. I suspect he is too far gone in his delusion."

"It's my fault," muttered Fay.

"It is NOT," Belle rounded on her. "He did this himself." She calmed down a little. "You are learning how to deal with it. You didn't tell him to copy you – or to steal your magic."

"I guess not," mumbled Fay.

"What did you say?" Belle's eyes glinted.

"I did not," said Fay, clearly.

"That's better."

"Yes, Mum."

They both laughed.

"I can't help you with Gilbert, though," said Belle wistfully. "That is a problem you will have to sort out yourself."

"You mean he is my problem," retorted Fay, "I should talk to him, I think. In fact, I know I should. But he is never where I am to talk to."

"Please," answered Belle.

———

Fay didn't know where else to go, so she went to check out her seal-friend's cottage. Gilbert had been there twice, so there was hope that he would appear a third time. Alas for her hopes, the door was shut, the chimney bereft of smoke. Fay went inside and looked around, and he was still living there, patently, but was not home. Not even under the bed. Fay thought she had to check under the bed. It restored her self-view, somehow.

She also skirted around the area where the dead morris dancer had been, as much as she could. To do this she made an imaginary chalk line in her mind, like the ones used on detective shows. She hadn't seen a good cop show in ages, she thought, irrelevantly, as a way of distracting herself from the thought of that dancer, dead. One day she would find a use for that detective thing, she thought, as she desultorily wandered towards the seal rocks.

Fay just didn't feel like going back to the town or the castle. She wanted help and answers and all sorts of things. And if she wasn't going to get them, she might as well be alone in a place Enlai didn't know. She hoped he didn't know about it. She didn't want to see him, that was for certain. If she never saw Enlai again, it would be too soon. Far too soon.

Fay was surprised at how vicious she felt. Then she wasn't surprised. She was obviously not a nice person to know. She had a mean spirit, or something. The fact that Enlai had been a friend said it all. Everything. She had discovered a kind of peace. An odd sort of peace, but peace nonetheless. Peace streaked with mean.

It was a still day and there was no sharp wind to add to the grief. Which was just as well, because for once she didn't have any grief. Nothing sharp, nothing deep. Fay felt entirely shallow emotionally. Drained, even. There just had been too much to deal with and she had run out of steam. Even her metaphors were running out of steam, she grimaced.

But it was a strange thing to be going towards the place she always associated with great romance and with sorrow and to feel not much of anything. At least it was a lot easier than carrying some of the emotions she had borne in recent months.

To her great surprise, Gilbert was on the seal rock. He looked rather windblown and forlorn, actually. Which was pretty impressive on such a still day. She clambered up and sat down beside him. Not too close—she was still totally confused about any emotions she or he might have. He would have to reach quite far to touch her, she calculated. All they needed was a chaperone and their lives would be complete, Fay reflected. Or a complete mess.

There was a silence. Fay told herself it was companionable, like her sitting beside Gilbert, but the truth was, it was just a silence.

"Did you sort yourself out?" asked Gilbert. His voice was leeched of colour. Fay thought this was an impressive trick. One day she would ask how he did it.

"Nup," she replied, cheerfully. "I did all the wrong

things that day. Belle and I have some thoughts, but I needed to talk to you. And I didn't want you to walk away."

"What did you expect me to do?" This time the voice was quite colourful. Bitter, in fact. Acerbic yellow, biting mustard.

"Not to misinterpret me for one thing," said Fay, acerbically. If he was going to be stupid, she was not going to put up with it. "I told you I loved you and then I said everything else wrong. You could at least have heard the first bit the way I meant it."

Gilbert turned and looked at her consideringly. "Do you still love me?" he said, softly.

"You don't just turn love on and off like a... like a... something," Fay said.

"I don't, certainly," said Gilbert.

"Well, I never did. But I told you that I loved you and then you walked away."

"It didn't happen like that."

"No, it didn't," and Fay couldn't stop chuckling.

"What's so funny?"

"You are, we are. The situation is. I was not even sure we were a couple, and I made a declaration that sounded as if we needed to split up. And you acted as if we had been married for thirty years and I had cheated on you."

Gilbert tried to hide a smile. "So?" he asked.

"So what do you think?"

"Not much, right now. Except that yes, I love you. And I am not certain that we have ever been a couple either."

"Belle seemed to think we were," offered Fay.

"I gave her reason to," replied Gilbert.

"Nice of you to give her reason to and not to tell me a thing."

"I didn't need to tell you. I thought my actions spoke

volumes." Fay sighed. "What is it now?" And Gilbert's voice had some of its old merriment in. Just a hint.

"I really, really need to speak to you. Can we put whether we are one, or if we are two alone, or even if we are arch-enemies in disguise on hold and talk about magic?"

Another quiet. This one was reflective. At least Fay hoped it was.

"Fine," said Gilbert. "But how did you find me?"

"I didn't. I had given up and came down here because it's a good place to be miserable."

"It is, isn't it?" They looked out to sea together for a bit.

"And besides," eventually Fay felt impelled to complete her thought, "I was pretty sure I would not find Enlai here."

"You and Belle are fixated on Enlai." This was a categorical statement. And it surprised Fay. She was just learning that side of Gilbert's personality, she supposed. She had not thought of him as guilty of black and white thinking and categorical statements. It would explain the walking away, at least.

"Well, I have seen him take light from me, and it hurt like… like…"

"Cold hell," suggested Gilbert.

"That is exactly it," beamed Fay.

"I have suffered that one, once," admitted her friend.

This emboldened Fay to continue. "Whenever he does it I run back home until I am better. Then I come here and try to fix things up and something goes wrong before I can do anything. You wouldn't believe how frustrating it is."

Gilbert laughed and laughed and laughed. "I would believe it," he said softly. "Since something similar has been happening to me."

"So tell me about magic," prompted Fay.

"What precisely do you want to know?"

Fay explained about Belle's house. She got the whole thing backwards and explained first that she needed the protection.

Gilbert asked her if she didn't have some already. Fay was suddenly despondent. She just did not want to tell him about the cove. But she had to. There was no way out of telling Gilbert that he had dismantled her protection.

Fay could not look him in the eyes when she told him—she knew this before she even started. She picked up a pebble and was rolled it round and round and round with her hands. Gilbert didn't look at her either, as he listened. He watched the pebble. "So I need to redo my protection," Fay finished, "And nothing I have tried works. So Belle is going to deed me her house, because it was the first thing I built in this world. We're going to try that."

"It should work," said Gilbert, thoughtfully. "It's unusual to use a house like that. It may take some special measures."

"Can we do it all at once?" Fay was suddenly enthusiastic. Her idea had potential!

"Maybe, maybe not. All we can do is try."

"We?" asked Fay, wistfully.

"I promised you help if ever you asked for it, didn't I?"

"Yes," acknowledged Fay, disappointed. She had hoped for a bit more than help. But she wasn't going to say. She had put her heart on the line publicly just once too often recently. Fay pocketed her pebble and stood up. "Coming back to the town?" she asked.

"Yes," he answered. "You need a guardian while you and Belle do this thing. I can help keep Enlai away, and anyone Enlai might have working for him."

"So I won't get migraines while we are renovating?"

"Not if I have anything to do with it," and Gilbert's chuckle finally emerged. "Enlai is very strong now," he continued, "I wish I had known who it was earlier. I can't do it forever. He can hide from my magic, somehow."

"I don't need forever—I just need long enough to make me safe. Then we can stop him using me once and for all. None of this eternal guard duty. No more dead dancers. A lot of problems will be solved."

"A lot of problems will be solved," repeated Gilbert, wistfully. He stood up and looked down at her. "There is just one we can't solve yet," he said, looking her in the eyes. She read deep sorrow there.

Damn. Why was she always making him so miserable. She certainly didn't intend to!

"I wish," said Fay.

"What do you wish?" Gilbert's voice was very gentle.

"I wish we could solve it instantly. Happily. Wave of a magic wand and all of that."

"Would hope do?" asked Gilbert, taking her hand in both his and turning the palm towards his face.

"A magic wand would be better," admitted Fay, "But at this moment, I would settle for hope."

Gilbert smiled at her then, and kissed her palm gently. He let go of her hand and they walked together back to the town. Silent. Amicable.

Not lovers. But not strangers.

# CHAPTER SEVENTEEN

WITH GILBERT RUNNING INTERFERENCE, THEY HAD A very small window of opportunity to sort out the house.

"Oh what fun, oh what fun, home improvements to be done," sang Fay, somewhat unmelodically, in the hopes that it would cause a little magic to make things move quickly. Belle was managing the whole thing and it was very complicated, to Fay's mind. Project management was something she had enthusiastically fled throughout her life.

First, Belle sent down the castle carpenters and builders to finish up all the things that could be done quickly and professionally. Everything that wasn't sound was made sound. Everything that needed painting or polishing was painted or polished. While this was happening, Fay and she chose suitable furniture from the castle. A bed, tables, chairs.

It felt like a luxury shopping spree and a home improvement show combined. But Fay was very careful to only choose things that fitted with who she was, inside herself. It was a new experience, choosing furniture this way.

She was scared that Enlai would find her and do

something. Or that she would do something to Enlai. She didn't know what scared her more. She spent a lot of her daytime boarding up her windows—and checking that they were safe. That nothing could enter, that nothing could get out.

She also practiced her magic on little things. Lots of little things. Stray webs of enchantment appeared in the house whenever she found an excuse. Her biggest moment of pleasure was when she made a faint pattern in a window. It was in Belle's solar, and she called her friend to admire it. Belle worked frantically and the two only caught up occasionally, like ships in the night. Fay determined they would still be able to talk—people had to communicate.

"Look what I did!" Fay said, proudly.

"It's very pretty," Belle responded politely.

Fay laughed. "Look closely."

And as Belle looked, Fay talked silently, and the pattern in the glass resolved itself into a picture of Fay, and the words Fay carefully spelled out in her mind emerged, thinly, from the glass. "I can tell you things from anywhere now!"

"Can I tell you things back? Preferably rude things," asked Belle, tartly.

Fay laughed. "Of course not! But it is useful," Fay became wistful, "Isn't it?"

"It is very useful. Just a bit… light hearted for magic. Especially when it pokes its tongue out at me."

"I am going to do magic *my* way. That means coming from who I am. And if silly is who I am then that is the magic that gets done."

Belle smiled. "I can't wait to see what you do with the house, then."

"I can't wait for the house to be ready for me to do things to it."

And the two became suddenly serious. Even with

Gilbert watching Enlai, there was no guarantee that this time was safe. The sooner Fay's magic was completely her own again, the happier everyone would be.

The idea was to do it perfectly (at least from a protective point of view) in the shortest time possible. To simplify things for the various delivery people, Fay stuck up notices on each door. Persa was the one who suggested the notices and wrote them out. So they had a certain flavour to them.

Restoration zone 1 – anyone can enter as long as they are being useful or silly. If Fay is with you, do not be respectful.

Restoration zone 2 – friends of Fay only – politeness forbidden

Restoration zone 3 – beware: Fay only.

As each zone progressed and the notices were changed, the house moved from a huge bustle to a series of bustling and contemplative areas, to a quiet place where only Belle and Fay went. Gilbert dropped in from time to time, but wherever the third notice was posted, he would stand at the door of the room and make rude comments. Never about the house—always about things outside. And he never came in. Gilbert was taking great care not to despoil Fay's special place.

Gilbert did some magic outside at one stage, without any explanation. When Fay went out to see what had been done, she found that there was some kind of barrier up and that it let her and her friends through, but no-one else.

*Just as well all the big deliveries have already come,* Fay thought. *Shame Gilbert didn't ask before doing it. But it's a good idea.*

An ice-wind blew through her at that moment. It touched her left temple with faint pain. Enlai was watching, Fay felt, and shivered. The chill lurked until she had taken a pain reliever, then it went as if it had never been. From that moment she felt as if the house might work. She walked around it possessively, touching her new belongings and dreaming of peacefulness. In the corners of some rooms lingered a sense of darkness. It made Fay nervous.

Lighting. Lighting. Lighting. Fay repeated the word till ideas came. Right now, the house was lit to perfection. It was broad daylight and the shutters were open fully. She had just sorted them out with a bit of oil and a hard shove. The slightly opaque windows gave glorious sunlight the range of every room. The darkness she felt was not real. She still had to address it. *I would kill for some decent down lighting,* Fay thought, *Halogen would be nice.*

But electricity was just too out of keeping with this dream-world. Fay put oil lamps all over. Still not quite the same sort of thing as other people used—but not quite as twentieth century as electricity. Some of the lamps were glass—and some were like hurricane lamps. She snuck in a few kerosene lamps for her reading spots. Getting kero to fill them was going to be the killer, she thought.

Maybe they could run on magic? She wondered what sort of glow magic gave? She just did not know—she had never seen magic glow. Apart from the green of her eyes, of course. Out, damn thought. Banish. Instantly. Nothing miserable allowed in today. Nothing.

Back to lighting. And all those candles. All the rest was done by candles. The sort that magically never need tending. She was not going to make her hearthome any harder to upkeep than her normal home. All the mod cons of Alberc's luxury mansion plus a few. Magic-assisted.

If her magic failed, she would go visit Belle. A nice cheerful escape that would be! Head down, admitting failure. So don't admit it. Cheerful thoughts, only, she advised herself strongly. Banish dull care, and all that. This house would work. No matter what. No matter who. And no matter where she was. And if the magic failed? Unease kept on creeping back. Memories of chill. She put it from her mind again. Firmly. Because if the magic failed, then she wasn't in this world at all. The end.

Fay walked through the house again. She looked everything up and down proprietarily. At her bed, she stopped. Something missing. Something definitely missing. Linen? Well, yes, but it was an emotional miss, not mere sheets and blankets. Belle was going to give her bed linen in any case, with the kitchen stuff. Fay pondered. Then she looked hard at the wall above the bed, a blank space. And above it appeared, gently and without fuss, a dream-catcher. "Now I am trendy," she thought, "And now even my sleep is safe."

When this was finished, she thought of something else, and made herself a mood notice. "Like a mood ring," Fay explained to Belle. And then got totally tangled trying to explain a mood ring. "Anyway," she wound up, trying to ignore the fact that Belle was stifling giggles, "When I am in a bad mood, it will read "PMS witch inside. Enter at your own risk", and when I am in a good one it will say "At home today—cake and coffee and lots of chat". And it can make its own mind up what it wants to say in between that."

"It has a mind?"

"Of course it does! It makes life more interesting."

"Why don't you just forbid anyone from coming?" asked Belle, "It's safer."

"Not in the long run," said Fay, seriously. "Look what happened at the cove. If I'm going to live here, people need to know who I am."

---

She wasn't allowed to sleep in her house yet. Gilbert explained it would dilute the ultimate protection the house could give and Belle explained it would dilute the ultimate protection the house could give. Persa simply took her by the hand and dragged her back to the castle. Fay hoped she was doing the right thing in not arguing.

She was so tired, she couldn't argue. The minute she hit that sumptuous bed, she slept. She was definitely alone in it this time. She checked, very carefully. She also kept meaning to ask intelligent questions about the Prince. But Fay couldn't because each evening the world went a bit swimmy and she forgot the questions. No headaches. No soul rending pain. Just a bit swimmy.

If it weren't for the vagueness in the evening and the occasional feeling, just before bed, that she was ploughing through deepening water, she would have been perfectly happy. Nesting suited her. Security suited her.

Except. The swimmy feeling got worse. Marginally at first, then quite drastically. She wasn't just swimming, Fay thought. She was swimming uphill. Or maybe it was upstream. Fay gave up on metaphors and decided she needed to seek help.

Gilbert had gone about his business in true Gilbert fashion, so she had to talk to Belle about it. "Could I be coming down with some sort of illness?" Fay asked, "A virus or something?"

Belle checked to see if she had a fever, and took her pulse, and sent for the local physician. It turned out that she was perfectly healthy. Her arms were a bit stiff, and her shoulders were showing an incipient problem, but care and gentle exercise should sort them out, the doctor said.

When the doctor had left, Belle and Fay sat down

again and talked the problem through again. Finally, Belle hit on a possible cause. "Have you sorted out everything in your ordinary life? I mean, you didn't just come here and leave everything on hold, did you?"

"Of course I did: everything was in crisis here. And I don't know what happens back there when I am here anyway, so what could I do?"

"You might need to be there again."

"Like when I needed time there to act as sleep here?"

"Exactly," approved Belle.

"Damn." said Fay. "I really don't want to go back."

"I think you might have to."

So Fay did. She didn't just go. She went with great care and lots of warnings. She was to watch out for anything unexplained that could be causing strange feelings. She was to come back soon. This was quite different to most of her other interworldly voyages. Planning and cautions and care. Fay was amused.

On this visit home she was hardly home at all. She turned on the TV to find out what day it was, and it was a weekday. Immediately then, she checked for days off, in case she had been sick and hadn't known. *This alter life thing had its drawbacks in terms of confusion levels,* Fay thought, as she rummaged through piles of papers.

She would love to know what happened to her time when she wasn't experiencing it. Was her body zombie-like or did someone else get use of it? Did she go into some sort of stasis? Was the real world actually a figment of her imagination too?

She had no time off from the doctor as far as she could see, and no real need to stay home. She also was not really in the mood for speculation on how she dealt with being away in the fantasy world. It was a practical day today. Maybe it was the nesting carrying over, but what she wanted to do was go to work. So she did.

Fay was on time, to her surprise. She missed breakfast because of her paper-hunt, but that was all. On her way into the building she stopped by the café to pick up a coffee and a snack. As she stood at the counter and eyed her options, she found they were more limited than she thought. The hot snacks made her feel sick.

Fay bought a chocolate bar. Chocolate was something she had not had since the night of the mythical thunderstorm, so she thought she could deal with it again. Besides, chocolate for breakfast was classy. Especially combined with a nice frothy cappuccino. Frothy, but weak. That was the great virtue of buying at the downstairs café. She sipped it in the lift on the way up. She had also bought some Twisties, which were hidden in her handbag, for later on. She really had no idea when she had eaten in the real world, and what her body needed. Instant carbohydrates seemed a good emergency measure. Fay felt very clever.

It was just as well she felt clever, she reflected an hour later. She would need it. It was shaping up to be one of *those* days. With all the strange and wondrous happenings in her life she had entirely forgotten that *those* days were possible. There were some kinds of non-excitement that were more trying than others. This kind of non-excitement was draining and alienating and altogether awful, was her thought, as she raided those Twisties for moral support and contemplated dashing down to the café for more.

She was not hungry at all. Fay was just entirely frustrated.

The lift was faulty. There was a notice on it advising people to take the stairs. She had not read the notice—she hated reading notices just as much as she loved putting them up for other people to read. It had not broken down with her in it, fortunately.

Or unfortunately. She, at least, could escape into dreams if she was trapped. Which was more than could be said for the fellow staff member who was stuck in there for two hours. Every now and then someone got on the emergency phone to reassure him that help was on the way, but really, help was not on its way until fifteen minutes before he was rescued. And everyone knew that.

Everyone except the two officers who were off sick. Fay was not the only person with an extraordinarily wonderful collection of medical certificates that season. She looked at the leave roster and even the most recalcitrant never-take-a-day-off types had been ill. No-one was being permitted annual leave because half the workplace was off sick.

It was one of those days. The trouble with the public service is that the public did not necessarily know that it is being served. Deadlines happened frequently and viciously, despite the lift and the absentees. Fay frantically keyed in the data that had to be attached to the advice that had to go to the Minister in just under an hour. And this was just the start of the day.

When the advice was ready to get more senior approval, Fay was hauled over the coals for a typo. A tiny, unimportant typographical error. But it took four people fifteen minutes of scolding before they let her fix it. And so the advice was late.

*Everyone is on edge*, Fay reflected. *The new, modern public service.* As soon as she was out of the office where she had received her latest scolding, four pieces appeared in her in-tray with comments on urgent changes. She buckled down and prepared to work as hard as she had to and as long as she had to. Pretending joyousness.

It would have been easier if she had not found a sudden vacancy in the building at lunchtime. Everyone trooped back in at 2 pm. It was only then Fay found there had been a work lunch.

No matter. It felt lonely being left out, but she really preferred missing it. She wanted to get finished with some of this garbage. When everyone else had returned and there was someone else to answer phones, she dashed down to the café again for more coffee and for a sandwich. She received an icy stare from her superior for her dereliction of duty, since, of course, it was after the usual lunch hour that she did this daring thing.

Fay knew this was a normal day, from the lift breaking down to the overwork, but she didn't like it. By the end of the working day she was totally exhausted. Her defences were down.

Fay suddenly thought that the office had been so much of her for so long, she should take a bit with her to her fantasy world home. She slipped a couple of the things she liked from the office into her pocket, and went home. She truly hoped that multicoloured paper-clips and lurid sticky notes would do the trick in terms of integrating the different aspects of herself. Because she really did not want to take anything else from the office. Not even a bag of Twisties.

Fay admitted that she would be happy if she never saw the office again. Had her life really be that unfulfilling? Yes. She was not the right person for the life she had chosen. Or she had accepted too many people's ideas about a normal life. Fay was now firmly of the opinion she was not normal. *I should be proud of that,* she supposed.

Fay sighed and wished she could go straight to the dream world. But she couldn't. There were things to do still. The next thing was to check with the doctor about the headaches. She didn't want tests. She wanted another prescription for drugs. That would take some negotiating. She picked up the phone to make an appointment. This was followed by a thought. It was a good evening for thoughts. Did she really want to take that whole drug-thing to her dream house?

There had to be a better way. Fay smiled and dialled the number of a massage therapist instead of a doctor. This therapist knew natural therapies, according to the advertisement. She booked in for a massage immediately and instead of going home, she went in and had her back worked on. While she and her massage therapist chatted about the general impossibility of Fay's neck muscles, they talked about headaches and what Fay could do for them. Fay's face, upside down, poking through a hole in the massage table, still had her little smile. She even stuck her tongue out at the floor, to prove she could do heaps of things at once.

Not only was the massage relieving a lot of deep tension she didn't know she had, but she was going to walk out of this place with a bunch of oils. More importantly, she knew the properties of those oils. Her massage lady was very helpful and enthusiastic. Rosemary and marjoram and feverfew grew in her dream world, she was sure. All she had to do was make sure that her garden was sown with them.

Not quite the seeds of love—feverfew was not as romantic as roses and violets and lilies and pinks. Since romance sucked, though, she was not concerned. She had given up on romance. Entirely. Right now she was into pain relief.

Fay was proud of herself for finally getting her act together. And she wondered, as she paid her bill and took home her bag of oils and tinctures, why she had not obtained a massage earlier. The one Gilbert had given her had been such a help—why had she not thought of it since? *Fay, your mind is always mush*, she reminded herself, and went home.

Nothing gave simple answers. Despite the massage and the oils in her back she had an incipient pain by the time she reached home. It was probably Enlai, Fay thought, a squiggle of despair at the back of her mind. It could be just the long day. But she suspected Enlai.

Fay took a pain reliever to be on the safe side. They were not a solution, she knew. But at least she could get a stay of execution with them, and work through her problems a bit. The visit to work and the visit to the massage therapist had solved the worst, she reflected as she cooked dinner and the pain reliever did its work. She had material and even ideas to take back with her.

She had a thought about her bookshelf in the house that had been Belle's. Fay went online while her dinner was simmering nicely and ordered books on massage and on aromatherapy and on growing herbs and on the chemical properties of herbs. It didn't matter when they came—what mattered was that they should be in her world, waiting for her. A little reference library. Magic would make this so. Fay felt smug. She was finally getting the hang of this world creation business.

And she had defeated a migraine dead with only one pain reliever. She had a mental image of throwing that pain reliever at Enlai Devers and saying, "Vanish!" And he would vanish in a puff of smoke. Scented smoke.

The thought made her add some fiction to her book order. She needed more dream-stuff. She probably needed a bigger bank balance, too, if this is how she managed her dream world. It would take ongoing upkeep! Damn. That meant she had to have a paid job of the vile kind. Suddenly Fay was unhappy. She just couldn't seem to get everything to work together.

The biggest thing she needed to get together was her emotions. Fay knew that the battle with Enlai was for something at the very heart of her. She really did need to get rid of the bitter hell. *Which may have nothing to do with my soul and everything to do with tension and heart-misery*, she thought, *otherwise I would not be down to just one pain reliever after the massage.* Fay pondered more over dinner.

After dinner she checked her answering machine. A mistake. A big mistake. Fred was there. And Kath. She didn't ring Fred back. She totally refused to. He might have been nice to her that once. Okay be fair, Fay, he was lifesaving that once, but his voice on the answering machine had been querulous.

She knew her Fred, and he now wanted his payback. And his payback was going to be more emotional support stuff. She knew it. She knew it from the tone of his voice. She knew it from the, "Now you are over all those illnesses, it's time you were useful" statement. She really couldn't believe that anyone actually said such things. But they did. And their name was Fred. And they said them on her answering machine. She sat back with a kind of oomph of astonishment.

She didn't ring Fred back. She totally refused to.

Kath had just left her name and number and asked her to return the call. That looked a safer bet. Fay really wanted safer bets right now. Life had the feeling far too often of walking off a cliff and not knowing just how far it would be to the ground. And sometimes the ground had been a very long way away. Kath was safe. When Fay actually rang her, they had a pleasant chat about nothing in particular. Fay was pleased with the world and her part of it.

Fay then made her big mistake. Instead of staying just long enough in the real world to do what had to be done, she stayed several days.

She explained to her conscience that she was trying to ground herself, and felt that one day at her charming workplace was not enough, and one non-crisis night in her home wasn't, either. She also yearned for a second massage before she returned, and her therapist said she had to wait a few days. So she did. And tried to convince herself she was not making excuses. That she did not suddenly feel ambivalent about her own imagination.

Every day, however, was a day of grinding hard work and a test of physical endurance. And very night proved to be more of an emotional burden than she expected.

The biggest part of the problem was that now she had discovered she was not fit for the public service, every moment she spent there was agony. Bored agony. She would rather brush her teeth five thousand times than print out yet another draft of yet another boring briefing. She carried both the tedium and the pain with her twenty-four hours in the day.

Even the good things, the things she normally enjoyed, turned and bit her when she was not watching. She no longer saw any logic at all in security cards and in clean desk policies. Fay found herself unable to speculate on the idiosyncrasies of paper molecules or why Ministers did not like knowing that real people did all this work for them.

She was not interested in sport anymore, or politics, or the arts. She was not interested in Canberra. It was a fine city, a beautiful city, but it was fading. Not in the same way as she faded and changed worlds. It was not there for her and she was not there for it.

She might have hung onto the real world, pretending to be normal, but everyday, in her handbag, were Fay's little souvenirs, along with the tinctures and oils. Reminding her of alternate realities. Of Belle and of Gilbert and of Persa and of Flor.

*Worlds are going to be a tad less random in my future,* Fay thought. Fay wondered why the more lurid office supplies were so important, and why slightly illegal stationery meant more to her than, say, the latest staff joke. But it was the office supplies that hid in her handbag, ready for her return to the dream world.

Life was still pretty much a mystery, she reflected. Pretty much. She needed to sort it out before she did anything more drastic to sort out Enlai the imaginary.

She needed to sort out Kath, too. Every night that week Kath had rung, now that she knew that Fay was back in the world of the living. And every night Kath had increased the level of complaint. Fay couldn't just switch off and let it flow. She had to actively listen. Kath didn't let her drift: Kath didn't even know what drifting was. Nothing was going right in Kath's world. Small things, big things, all were equally horrendous. Kath wanted sympathy for everything, too. It wasn't enough to have the universe fragmenting and to tell Fay about it. She had to have Fay say how awful it all was, in exactly the right tone of voice. When Fay used the wrong tone of voice Kath wept and said she didn't care anymore.

Kath hated her job, and the shoes she had bought the day before. She had financial woes, and had turned atheist. She was thinking about adopting a child and breaking up with her de facto, all at the same time. The pot of rosemary at Kath's front door had just died: Fay found herself unsurprised.

All of these plaints were uttered with equal misery. There were no positives in her life to alleviate things, and no discrimination between the mildly sad and the very bad. Kath needed constant reassurance that she existed.

Fay found herself thinking that Kath had always been like this. Her high maintenance value had kept Fay anchored, to a degree. When it was too much, Fay simply forgot to return calls for a bit. But Fay's anchor was coming adrift or was moving elsewhere. Or something. Whatever the reason, Fay found herself not wanting to hold Kath's hand. She wanted Kath to get on with her life.

So she got on with hers. She went back to her fantasy world.

# CHAPTER EIGHTEEN

FAY IGNORED THE PEOPLE SHE LOVED. SHE WENT BACK TO her roots. She decided to do a little walking tour to ground herself, so that she didn't have to flee back to that drab office ever again. This was the heart of the problem, she thought. That she still saw life in an office job as real, and the life of her dreams as unreal.

The first place she went was the house of her heart. She ate dinner and washed dishes. She used her little window-image to leave a message for Belle, explaining what she was doing and why. Belle needed to know. Gilbert probably did too, so she asked Belle to tell him. That she was grounding herself. That she was trying hard to build a closer connection with the world that used to exist only in the moments between wakefulness and sleep.

She started with the house, and she would end there. She wanted to pull all the sources of her strength together. Bring her emotions into one place. Feel strong and secure within herself. This was obviously why she had pilfered office supplies. Obviously. Fay smiled her little smile as she stuck her post-it notes to a chest of drawers.

Through the town she walked, slowly, consideringly, past the empty gallows tree and over the common. She waved jauntily at the castle before she turned around and walked back again, passing the inn and Alberc's white stuccoed residence with its big oak door, down the main street then a turn and she was heading towards the coast.

From there, she went past Gilbert's cottage to the seal rocks. It was a long walk, but it was a very good one. Every inch of the way was part of her world now. Every step had memories that could be added to the tapestry of her emotional existence.

She went south east of the house past the rocks. She negotiated the wind-pulled shrubs and welcomed the drag of the wind on her body. She went inland a little, and finally reached her most important destination. It was a perfect sandy bay with the sheltered cave that is washed clean by the high tide of spring. It might not be the place of her soul anymore, but it was still her dream cove and she had lost her heart there.

She sat on the sand in quiet peace, thinking of the times she had met with Gilbert. She then went back in her mind further, to the first time the cove was really alive to her. When she would come here because it gave her a solace that nowhere else could, in any world.

She looked around at the limestone that framed her little bay. At the entry to the bay the cliff was fallen away at the base, as if nibbled by mice. She worked free a fragment of nibbled rock and put it in her pocket, to take home. She found some shells and took a handful of sand. All this was accompanied by the roar of the sea outside the little bay, and the gentle peace within it. And all these memories were placed in her pocket with the sand and with the shells and with the fragments of limestone.

As Fay walked home, she smiled. This time it was not quietude she had found in her little bay. It was soul-rest.

———

Persa raced up to Fay.

Fay deflected the shadow of a headache by thinking about Persa. Fay reflected that Persa could never just walk. She ran, or raced, or tumbled, or bounced. When she was angry, Fay betted that Persa fumed or even exploded. Except the times Persa had got angry in Fay's presence it had been more steely determination than explosion. Why weren't people simple?

Persa was definitely bouncy today. She tiggered her way to Fay and started explaining, very quickly, very enthusiastically, that she was going to leave home. "I have a new job at a school. They want a residential teacher who will be good with children. I've outgrown the town," Persa sounded almost reflective. As reflective as she could get, anyway. Thoughtful on fast-forward. "Everyone here thinks I'm lightweight. "

"Well," said Fay, almost tactfully, "you do tend to leave that impression. I always thought some of it was intentional."

"Some of it is," Persa's best cheeky smile emerged. "The Prince wasn't fooled though—he was the one who found me the job. He said I was undervalued," and Persa's eyes gleamed with hero worship. "And Belle was the one who said I could teach children. They both sorted it all out and made it right with my family."

"And you want to go?" asked Fay.

"Oh, YES!" shouted Persa, her arms flung to the heavens in joy.

Fay laughed with pleasure for her friend. "Are you coming to the castle?" she asked.

"No," answered Persa, with dignity. "I'm going to celebrate."

"How?" Fay was most definitely curious.

"I'm going to the beach and I am going to fulfill a childhood dream," Persa grinned complicitly.

"What dream?"

"I'm going to swim naked."

"Why on earth?"

"Because I've always wanted to, and if people see me I don't have to face them for the next twenty years." Somehow Persa managed to invest this with dignity.

Fay hooted with laughter. "Go and swim then – I will see you later, Ms Teacher."

"I will have clothes on," Persa promised.

———

Fay didn't go to the castle. She went to see Flor.

Flor needed regular visits, Fay had suddenly decided. Friendships had to be worked at. And besides, Flor made good cakes. Fay felt in need of comfort food. She was pleased that Persa was sorting her life out. She just wished her own existence were a tad simpler and was even capable of being really, properly sorted out. And, and... it was a comfort food day, for certain.

She wasn't sure how long she had left of this visit. There was the nagging feeling of a migraine that had almost come just before she saw Persa. The ache was sitting in the back of her mind, waiting to pounce. She might have days. She might have minutes. Best do the duty stuff of friendship while she could.

It wasn't as if the duty stuff of friendship was so hard. She would never have cultivated Flor so assiduously in the first place if she wasn't worth the effort, after all. It was funny, Fay reflected, as she knocked on

Flor's door, how much more fun her friends in this world were than people like Fred and Kath.

Flor was a bit preoccupied, but she still welcomed Fay in. Hospitality was very important to Flor. *It's strange*, Fay thought, *that I have to keep reminding myself about who Flor is and how she feels. It's as if Flor is still being invented or something.* Probably 'or something'. Fay felt that the longer she stayed around, the more confused she was. *Make that the older I get, the more confused.*

Flor was obviously aching to tell her something, and could not quite get it out. There were words to be said. Fay sighed and went into encouraging mode. It took two pieces of cake before encouraging mode worked. Fay was going to get fat, she just knew it. Too much cake in this world.

Flor admitted to having been violent. With her morris stick.

Fay was totally stunned. Of all things, this was the last she had expected. Flor was so tiny and fragile and gentle.

"It happened about an hour ago," Flor explained. "I'm still getting over it. Someone has to report it to the castle, and I was wondering if you would mind."

"I would be happy to," Fay said, "But please, can you give me some details. I find it hard to believe."

"Believe it," said Flor grimly.

"Won't you get arrested or something?"

"Not in this case," Flor said calmly, pouring tea, "Because Enlai attacked first."

"Enlai." This was a silencer. Fay began to understand the incipient migraine. "Did he use magic?"

"Not much. He tried, but he couldn't seem to sustain it. I got in with my stick and was… discouraging. After that I whacked him with my kerchief and he gave up entirely."

"How discouraging?"

"Not very," replied Flor, still inhumanly calm. It was her ex-boyfriend she was talking about, for goodness sake. Fay's mind fretted. "He's a bit bruised and quite battered and he had a very badly bleeding nose. I offered him ice."

"What did he do then?"

"Left me to clean up the mess."

"Where on earth did all this happen?" Fay could just not see it, any of it. Did Flor carry a stick around with her?

"Here," and Flor gestured to her beautiful living room. "I cleaned up the blood. The stick's a bit stained though."

"Can I see it?"

"Of course," said Flor. Like the rest of the conversation, she made the strange seem normal, even ordinary.

The stick was bloody, but otherwise intact. There was no dead body lying about. So Fay gave up. "I'll let Belle know." She gave the stick back to Flor, who stood it up in its usual corner. The conversation turned to food and plants and the weather. The weather seemed safe, Fay thought, a bit desperate. A pitched battle in this living room was just too... weird. And fragile Flor winning it was even stranger.

But Enlai had been beaten, that was the main thing.

In the end, she told Gilbert before she told Belle. She ran into him (this time not literally) on the way to the castle and they walked there together. He was as astonished as Fay. Neither of them could see Flor succeeding with Enlai where no-one else had. And with a morris stick, of all things. Poetic justice.

The oddness of the incident served Fay well, because Gilbert was obviously still a bit standoffish. No jokes. No fun in his eyes. He didn't stand too close. He didn't look directly at her, either. She didn't know whether to be sad or relieved.

They almost reached the castle when Fay reeled with sudden pain. "Damn Enlai," she said to Gilbert. "He's really attacking me this time."

Gilbert tried to do something. His hands waved, he muttered things. But the pain just got worse and worse. "Go!" he said. "Come back soon. And stay safe."

So Fay faded.

———

*Let me think this through. I know I don't have many words right now, but it really does need thinking through.*

*This migraine isn't as bad as the last one. I don't know if it was Flor's fighting that helped, or if I'm getting stronger. I hope it's the latter. Because my house has to start to work! It has to.*

*Mind you, little Flor was terribly impressive with that big stick. And I just loved the thought of her dropping the stick and whacking him with that kerchief. I bet Enlai was so surprised! I am sure the kerchief did him as much damage as the stick.*

*You know what I love the most about that whole episode. It is not that I had a little headache rather than the soul-stealing one I am avoiding now. I am happy with that, but it doesn't give me a bubble of joy. What gives me a bubble of joy is that Flor just gave her poor dead friends a bit of their own back. The morris dancers aren't avenged. Revenge is such an ugly thing, anyway. But things are a little more even. And I bet Enlai thinks twice before he attacks another dancer.*

*Which means. Oh damn. It means he will attack me. I know it. He has such a temper. He will stop thinking sensibly at all. Oh, Enlai Devers is so, so stupid. Enlai Devers may not be imaginary, but his brain certainly is.*

*The worst thing about him having such a big streak of brainlessness is that he doesn't distinguish between things that are good for people and things that are not. The second worst thing is that when he loses what little brain he has (like when he gets angry) you don't know what he is going to do. Except I think I will somehow be involved.*

*Damn. Damn. And double damn.*

*I need to make a full recovery before I go back. A very full recovery.*

*I also should think of new things. Ways to reinforce what I have done and how it was done. That home-thing helped. I'm sure of it. But it needs more. It needs layers. I need to find more things to take there from here. That was a good instinct I had last time. And from my childhood. I need to combine all of me there, and feel happy that I have done so. Face my nightmares and learn that they have helped create who I am.*

*Sounds fine. Bloody difficult in reality. The sort of thing I used to get a self-help book for. I remember all those books. They were really fun. Fun to read, and fun to ignore: I am back to helping myself.*

*I need to go through every cupboard and every drawer here and work out what needs to be put into my special home. My soul-home. And it must include pictures of the family, even if I never speak to them again. What a foul thought. Never speaking to them again. That is actually a giant weight off my shoulders. I would rather work in my current job than ring any of my family. But they helped make me Fay, so I need a photo album.*

*Maybe if I make one up? Didn't a little baby one come with my last film? I can make a little picture-digest of my life. Then I can move onto the drawers and things.*

*Bother it. This sounds like a task that will take several days. If it takes a week, then it takes a week. I can be a bored public servant during the day then work at putting these*

*things together in the evenings. It gives me a chance to check
my control, too.*

*If I have any migraines, though, I need to know what to
do. Racing back to deal with Enlai is not going to solve it. He
is going to be ready for me; besides he is already taking from
me. I need to be ready to fight the migraine here until I'm
ready to return. Stronger. More me than I have ever been before. Fay the Super Hero. Well, Fay the Super Fay.*

———

It had sounded simple. Fay had made one big error. She
had assumed that she could just leave work behind her.
She found she couldn't. There was so much to do. And
so little support. It was as if she lived on the very edge
of the workplace and got all the work and none of the
friendship.

She knew why that was so, too. The people at work
had never been dinner party friends. They had no idea
that there was an interesting person beyond the intense
exterior. That was the good side of being invisible; they
forgot her easily. No-one noticed when she was only
half-there. She remembered trying to be a part of the
workplace and always being on the edge. Never quite
noticed. Never quite accepted. Now she saw it more
bleakly and it hurt. Yes, it hurt.

And it kept on hurting while she worked her guts
out on meeting all the new deadlines. There were lots
of them, it seemed. Each harder to meet than the last,
because people forgot her and forgot she needed information. Fay's insides were a permanent sigh. Sighs of
frustration. Sighs of exhaustion. Sighs of loneliness.

She realised that in her was some kind of strong
work ethic. Because she continued with all the tasks no
matter what. No matter than they left her open to En-

lai. No matter that they kept her way from the fantasy world.

This is what had caught up with her before. Kept her away from dreaming. She had made a promise to do the work by getting paid and turning up to do it – so she did it. She knew it was the worst possible time, but she had done that lunchtime stint and had trapped herself inside her old habits. She hadn't forgotten what she was there for. Getting stronger against Enlai, however, had somehow taken second place. Even as she deplored her old habits, she still turned up for work every morning.

The same feeling of doing the right thing made her ring Fred once she had finished her little photo album. They had dinner together the second night. Fay was surprised at herself for doing this, and not at all surprised when Fred rang the third night to complain.

Fay had cried off dinner a bit early. She could feel an incipient ache, and was determined to beat it, and beat Enlai. Fred thought she was malingering. He had not said so at the time – he had dropped her home like a good and supportive friend. He made sure she knew the day after, though. One giant, hospital-level migraine was exciting and worthy of support: daily hurts were imaginary. Fay was quite surprised when she looked at the phone. She did not believe she had it in her to hang up on anyone. But she had hung up on Fred. She smiled.

Fred had done her a favour. He had jerked her out of her custom and her sense of duty. Fay found herself longing for her new home. And for her gentle cove. And for her friends. Fay slid open a drawer to find more mementos.

Life was not meant to be a waking misery. She reiterated that as she deleted a litany of complaints from Kath from her answering machine. She would not ring

Kath back. Fay did, however, ring a florist and have Kath delivered a pot of rosemary.

Fay made herself some celebratory hot chocolate, leaving the computer on and a whole row of drawers hanging open. She was not yet ready to tie up loose ends. She had changed her mind. There was hope in her real world at last. Give up on the hurting things and establish new paths, new patterns of living.

That night while she was asleep, she found that someone was trying to change her mind back. She had nightmares. Enlai's eyes again. Whatever she dreamed about, they were there. However hard she tried to escape them, they were there.

Fay dreamed of shades. Dancers in white on the common, with the gallows tree visible through their bodies. She drifted with the breeze, looking at them, wishing they were alive, hoping that her wishing would bring sound to the sticks and bells. But there was no sound. There was no sense. There was no feeling. She found herself forced to the ground and joined in the dance of ghosts.

Fay woke up in a cold sweat. She raised her chin. She would not be defeated. Fay went to work and slaved away until there was no pain except the pain of overwork.

That evening, when she came home, she thought she saw Enlai's eyes in the mirror. Fay covered all her mirrors with sheets. Her home felt eerie, but safe. Until she looked in the window by mistake. There he was, full face staring. Amber eyes glaring. Daring her to come and face him.

Exhausted by the demands of her job, shocked by the dissolution of the boundaries between her world, Fay consciously dreamed of her new home that night. Instead of waking up in her bed in the real world, she woke up in her bed in the fantasy world. She found some relief. For in the fantasy world Enlai's shadow could not be seen in the reflective surfaces. It was Fay's real world that was no longer safe.

Enlai had raised the stakes. Fay was determined he would regret this. Enlai should not have raised the stakes. Fay lay in her fantasy bed and thought: *This is endgame.*

# CHAPTER NINETEEN

---

*Okay, that's it. I'm going to investigate. Showdown at the Dream-world Corral. I'm sick of mulling round here, having my old life take me over as if it had never gone.*

*Enlai is a coward. It's strange to think he runs away, but he does. That's how he survived so long. He ran from Belle, he ran from Flor. And he seems to be continually half-hiding from anyone official. Not that Belle isn't official, but he was wooing her, which was different. I guess he thought he had the magic down pat and wanted a new power base and she was it. What an awful sentence. What an awful thought.*

*He started off nice. With a bit of an edge which made him fun, but a good friend. Like Flor. Flor is all warmth and hospitality on the surface, but always has that glimpse of sharpness. I do not like sweetness and light types. Pollyanna should have been strangled at birth.*

*That almost-hidden side to Flor makes her interesting. Enlai liked her. When he got bored, Enlai and Persa used to do the craziest things to keep the world swirling around them. Persa did them for fun and because they were crazy. Enlai did them because it made everyone turn and point at him. That's how I read it. As a real outsider. Strange to admit that. I thought I made them up and now I'm not even sure I know them.*

*So where did he go wrong? I guess it really started when the Prince came to town. Enlai liked the authority and the spy stuff. I bet, knowing Enlai, that he thought, "This is what I was born for," and started looking for ways to aggrandise himself. I do like that word. Aggrandise.*

*None of this is provable, mind you. It just isn't. I guess I can find him and ask him. I just wonder if he would talk to me now? I think the last time we had a good talk we didn't talk at all – we all played riddles. Silly games.*

*It wasn't a good thing that I beat Enlai. It was great for me. Made me feel all in control. But it can't have been good for him. I have done so many things wrong. Some of them have been giantly enormous things, like wrecking Belle's private life. Others have been little things with consequences, like besting Enlai in a riddle game. No wonder nothing ever seems to work. I'm just not worthy of things working.*

*Now that's a depressive thought. Get out of it, Fay. Recover.*

*Go and see what is happening and what you can do to help. That is much more productive than more bloody morosity.*

———

Fay got out of bed. She got out of bed in her real-world home. Totally virtuous, she finally finished the preparations to bring herself together in the one place. There was that little photo album, and a collection of other key items (an old bud vase, a cruet set, a Barbie doll given to her when she was ten). And she had her detective gear.

It was time to don that garb, she decided. Time to layer her clothing and get to the bottom of things – which sounded nicely contradictory. Which described her life just perfectly. Fay was edgier than she would admit, even to herself. The scarves and boots helped. As she donned each piece of clothing, she felt more like someone solving a problem and less like the person who caused all the problems.

Fay was prepared for anything.

She tried a new entry point into the world, just to prove her preparedness. She told herself she would be a few metres from Enlai.

———

Fay appeared in the middle of the main street, and in the middle of a crowd. Not only was she close enough to Enlai to talk at him or sing him into submission, she was right next to Persa.

Persa was surrounded by trunks and suitcases. She seemed to have a lot of possessions. The highway was a strange place to pile one's life, Fay reflected.

Persa was very irate. And very loud. "I don't care what you think," she scolded Enlai, "And I don't care what you think I can do. All I want to do is leave this town and teach. Children. Beings more mature than idiots like you."

"You can't go," said Enlai obdurately. "I will do whatever I have to—you will stay."

"Go jump," Persa cried, and threw her handbag at Enlai. It hit him in the stomach. The 'oomph' of losing breath did not remove the smug look on his face. "I'm not your girlfriend. I'm not even your friend anymore. You can't tell me what to do."

"Ah, but I can make you stay," this was Enlai at his most know-all, a little smile of superiority accompanying his words.

Fay started forward. It was too late. She found herself suddenly wrenched with agony, clutching her head. She did not flee though—she reached into her pocket and took those two painkillers. Oh please, she thought, let them work quickly. Very quickly.

She could see everything that happened after that, but she was oddly detached from it. Maybe it was the pain, Fay worried, and then stopped worrying and just felt it flow. Enlai wasn't going to kill her and he wasn't going to make her run back home either. She was here, and here she would stay.

There were other people there, too. Most of them were soldiers. They had been standing back, behind Persa's luggage. Maybe they had been helping her move? Now they stepped forward to attack Enlai, and they in turn, tumbled over in pain. Whatever Enlai was doing, it was hitting anyone who wanted to hurt him.

Damn Enlai Devers. Enlai Perverse. Fay found the pain dragging her to the ground where she knelt, refusing to let it take her further. The soldiers were less strong—all of them were in foetal position, hands over heads, hiding from the world. The only people left standing were Persa and Enlai.

Enlai radiated light. Demonic light. Her light. Fay tried to take back his nimbus, but all her effort merely made it fragment at the edges.

There was an impasse—the tableau of pain was unmoving until Enlai said, "I have had enough of this." With his right hand he formed a spear of his light. He did not pause to reflect. He threw it straight at Persa's heart. Persa collapsed.

Fay dragged herself to Persa to help her. It was too late. Persa was frozen. The air around her was midwinter. Fay looked around for Enlai but he had vanished. She slumped, holding Persa's hand, pretending that it was not ice-cold.

Fay sat beside her friend for a long, long time, totally numb, entirely unable to believe what had happened. It had all happened so quickly. So very quickly. She half expected Persa to sit up at any moment and say "tricked you." But she didn't. Persa was silent. Fay's heart was freezing over again. The ice of death-magic was spreading.

Eventually, one of the soldiers tapped her on the shoulder. Belle had arrived. All Fay could do was follow Belle and the soldiers and Persa's body back to the castle. Persa was laid out in state. Fay stayed with her. She couldn't cry. Even when Belle put an arm around her, Fay refused to be comforted.

I should have been able to stop this, was the thought going through her mind. I should have stopped Enlai ages ago. I delayed and delayed and delayed. It's all my fault. All my fault.

Someone gave her food, and she ate it in an uninterested fashion. It calmed her down. She found she could identify her emotions. One of the strongest emotions she felt was anger.

Her first thought was that she could use that anger. She had to. Sitting back and waiting to see what would happen was no longer an option. Fiddling with things at the edges was no longer sufficient. Finding herself was a luxury. She had been putting off and putting off and putting off facing up to Enlai. The result was that one of her best friends was dead. So now she would face him.

Angry. Other emotions could wait. Everything else could wait. Her anger was the controlled sort. Fay didn't just race out there and confront Enlai. When she met him, she would be ready.

Gilbert was very ready with advice for a change. Highly literate, terribly philosophical answers to Fay's questions. Fay was not sure how much use they were. But he needed to give them—this was his way of not thinking about the murder of the town sprite.

His answers were really not useful. Can you defeat

someone using the knowledge that they wish to control an aspect of the causal factors? And what were the causal factors, anyhow? The causal factors of what, was another. Gilbert explained that they operated the world (*I hated physics, too*, grumbled Fay to herself) and that the sectors that could be controlled by humans were largely those with creative or emotional components.

Fay commented that it sounded like five hundred years of thought by experts had gone into making a theory that was incomprehensible to people who had not studied it for ten years. Gilbert grimaced and agreed. But he could not explain it simply.

What was worse was that he was not apologetic about using jargon that meant nothing to an outsider. In fact, he was proud of it. Fay's instinctive response was somehow inferior. Fay wondered why Gilbert's highly expert view of reality had failed to deal with Enlai.

And then she thought of the results of their slowness. Neither Gilbert's theory nor Fay's gut reactions had been any use. Persa was dead. Slivers of ice knifed her heart. Even her tears were frozen.

Belle brought things down to earth a little, and reality a bit closer to being manageable. She said that people in the town had told her that Enlai had said once that he had got things wrong. None of them knew the context, but it was a surprise to hear Enlai say it that they remembered and had passed it on. Belle suspected that Enlai thought that Fay was not the source of magic. She said, "He isn't trying to isolate you—he's trying to get more power. If he thought you were the source of everything, he would have attacked you directly and differently."

"But what about the times he has sent me home—when he stole from my soul?"

"Did he know it was you?"

"I assumed so, but looking back, I am not sure he ever looked at me directly. I guess he might have thought I was Persa or Flor or even you. He has to have known I was female though."

"Why?" asked Gilbert.

"Wearing a dress mostly indicates that," said Fay, the idiocy of the question restoring her to her acerbic self a little.

"So he might have thought you were someone else, but we don't really know," asked Gilbert, still curious. Or still determined to spell out the obvious.

"Yes."

"We know that he thought it was me for a bit," Belle said. "Because he as good as admitted it by wooing me. He attacked Flor. And now he has killed Persa." This strangled the line of thought for a moment. It was still too new to deal with. Too horrific.

"He would know it's me by now," Fay finally said.

"I should think so," offered Gilbert. "There aren't a lot of other choices."

Maybe Gilbert was upset too, Fay realised, with a jolt. Because his words were certainly not well thought out. Which meant that the only one of them who had half a brain right now was Belle, who had no magic. Which meant Fay had better get her act together this time. Properly.

"I need to think about this some more," Fay said, and excused herself. Belle and Gilbert walked her to her home, then went about their various business. They promised to come back in a little while. Whatever they did about Enlai, it would be done together.

It was a couple of hours before they came back to collect her. They brought Flor with them. "Safety in numbers," Gilbert claimed, cheerfully.

During that rest time Fay had rested and thought things through. She had thought about the leaf magic and the rose magic and all the various things that had not quite worked. There was no simple solution. She had to trust herself. Like when she saved Belle from that lightning. It might not work, but it had a better chance than anything else. And she was pain free, which meant that Enlai was magic free. Both of them would be starting from scratch.

Then she had another thought. Words and music were on her side. She had no idea what to do with this brilliant thought, but maybe, just maybe, getting Enlai talking might give her time to react and focus. Enlai didn't know how her magic worked. Otherwise, how would he not have known it was her? Words and music gave her hope.

A small hope. A small hope is better than no hope, though, was her thought as she marched in serried ranks down the high street with her friends.

Words. She let them fly the minute she caught sight of him. Almost before they were within earshot. So loud that her voice reached across the street to the pub beyond. So loud that Flor covered her ears.

"Why?" she asked, "Why do you murder your friends and your neighbours?" He did not answer. As they came closer, her question changed from 'why' to 'what'. "What on earth do you think you are doing here? What do you hope to achieve? Not power, certainly. All this garbage you have done hasn't netted you any more power." She hoped it hadn't anyway.

"I can draw on power whenever I want. All I have to do is kill its source." Enlai was very confident, Fay thought. Worryingly confident. "So if whoever is the creator of all that magic will just step forth, I won't have to kill all four of you." A pause. "Don't you think there have been enough deaths?" His tone was threatening. And she was not happy at the way he was turning things round.

"Don't be so bloody melodramatic, Enlai," Fay advised.

"This is not melodrama," he told her, disdainfully. "This is real life."

"I would never have guessed it," answered Fay. "And if this is real life then I might as well admit to dark and dire truths. I am the creator you are after."

"No," says Gilbert, "I am."

Bellezour, "No, I am. Didn't you think I was earlier? Now you can be certain of it."

Flor stood up also and said, coolly, "You can all be. I have other things to do with my life than play children's games." She walked away.

This statement, more than any of the others, flummoxed Enlai. He paused. Enlai then did what he had done so often before. He tried to kill.

Every time something goes wrong in his theory, Fay thought angrily, he tries to kill someone. Like a kindergarten kid in a sulk, tearing down some game because he was not winning. She was angry. Her anger swept all her sorrow aside, swept her pain away. She reached out with her magic and fought back.

It didn't work. She and Enlai were so evenly matched, that it could not work. Fay was just beginning to realise this, when she also realised that she was not feeling any pain this time. She might not be winning, but she was holding her own. Enlai's face was frowning in concentration. Maybe even in worry. Maybe. Maybe.

The pale green light that was Fay's was joined by another shade. Straw-coloured light emanated from Gilbert. Golden and healing. Enlai fought harder. He made a light spear and threw it. Then he made a dagger. Both fell short. Fay exulted. Enlai didn't have enough magic to draw on!

Fay was tiring. She hoped Gilbert wasn't. But if she tired then Enlai could draw on her magic again and all would be lost. Fay kept fighting, but inside her was a little hollow of despair. And the hollow was growing with every minute.

Then, without any warning, the fight was over. "What happened?" asked Fay, surprised she was still standing.

"I threw a rock at Enlai," Belle explained cheerfully. "He wasn't watching me, only you two."

"You knocked him out with a stone?" Fay was surprised.

"Not at all," despite this, Belle was smug. "I almost missed him. He looked to see what had hit him, and all the stuff you two were throwing at him took over and he collapsed. Congratulate me on my superior intelligence."

"Congratulations on your superior intelligence," said Gilbert, who was examining Enlai's body.

"How is he?" asked Fay. She was not happy that all she was capable of was inane questions. But then, maybe she should be relieved that at least she was capable of inane questions. She was a bit astonished to be standing upright at this point.

"It looks as if I killed him," was Gilbert's final verdict. "Not you, and not Belle." Gilbert sounded oddly aloof. Neutral. Like an observer.

Fay, on the other hand, was hugely relieved. She had not had to kill. She still had to mourn though. Fay had to mourn the loss of Persa. Her loss of innocence. A commotion interrupted her dolour. Fay looked round to see what was happening. It was all over, wasn't it? Enlai was dead.

It wasn't that simple. Life is never that simple. Nor is death. Fay's magic had not just faded, or even streamed back into her. It was separating into its constituent colours. It turned into a soul-rainbow connecting her with Enlai. Complex. Beautiful. Fragile.

The rays of light disintegrated somewhere between her and Enlai. One section went back into Fay's eyes, helping restore their brightness and Fay's mind. She could feel words returning a little as the light blinded her. Blinded by her own soul-light—how ironic, was her first thought. As the blinding faded, she saw what happened with the rest of the rainbow.

The second coalesced into a luminous shape. Enlai-of-light. It couldn't speak. It poked out its tongue. It waggled its hands rudely, and then disappeared with an, 'I'm the King of the Castle' grin. Fay hoped that this was an end of it. Her hopes were very soon dashed.

"Damn it," Gilbert said, "I was afraid of this. He has gone into hiding again. Or his shade has."

"Why didn't you say?" She was supremely annoyed.

"Because I couldn't be certain. It all depended on if he had hold of you at the precise moment he died."

"Well he did," grumbled Fay, "I could feel it. And I want me back."

"We need the burial ground," said Gilbert.

They left Enlai's body lying on the cold, cold road.

The burial ground wasn't far from the coast. Fay shivered when she saw that it wasn't far from the cottage, either. This was why the cottage had been such an easy target for Enlai.

Why didn't she know everything? Why? Fay was totally miserable. She rummaged in her pocket for more pain relievers. She would need every bit of support she could get in this final battle. There were none to be found.

Gilbert turned to her. He took her by the shoulders, gently, and looked in her eyes. "I can't do anything more," his tone was bleak. "Only you can retrieve that part of yourself."

Fay said "I wondered about that," and fell to

thinking as they walked through the tori gate into the graveyard. Tori gate?

Fay looked twice to make certain. Yes, it was one. Just like a Japanese temple. Strange kind of graveyard. Except that she had mistaken her first Japanese temple for a graveyard—the shrines near the entrance had looked like memorial stones. This burial place still had links with her dreaming. She wondered if use could be made of that.

# CHAPTER TWENTY

FAY DECIDED TO GO WITH WHAT SHE KNEW BEST. WHAT she knew was songs. And she thought she knew two songs that might help. She told Gilbert, and Belle. Fay asked Gilbert if he could run interference again.

"Make sure that I have time to sing, since Enlai never allowed us time before."

"I can try," he answered. His face was a study in shadows. This situation was as new to him as to her. Fay felt a bit relieved by that. She was entirely sick of him having big explanations and no cures.

"Why don't you attack Enlai directly?" this was from Belle to Gilbert.

"Because if I do at this moment, Fay could die. It's her life that gives him this after-life."

"Damn," said Belle, softly. "Fay, what do you want two songs for? Why not one?"

"Can't you feel it?" asked Fay, her voice also soft. It was the graveyard through the gate that was hushing them. "Enlai has put up some sort of barrier. We can't get in."

Gilbert walked forward a bit and then stopped, suddenly, "She's right." He looked worried. So Fay smiled.

"I think I know a folksong that I can use to get me

in. And then another to send him on, leaving me behind. I hope, anyway."

"I hope too," said Belle.

"Sing then," Gilbert was impatient. "Let's get this over with." *Why is it so reassuring to know he is scared?*

A pair of songs, Fay thought. One to get me into that graveyard and one to get Enlai's spirit out of it. I had them on the tip of my tongue a minute ago, and now I have forgotten them entirely. Damn all this unnecessary talk.

The first song was very mournful and Japanese. "Tooryanse, Tooryanse," sang Fay. She didn't worry about melody, she worried about feeling. "Let me go through," she was asking, "let me go through."

It didn't take a second singing. A smaller gate opened up inside the tori gate, just big enough to let her in. It was a shadow gate, flickering red flame framing a well of sorrowful dark. Fay wondered where she was going when she stepped through. Into the graveyard? Or into the same place where Enlai was preserved as living light. Or maybe into hell.

The others tried to follow, but they could not. All they could do was watch from a distance, the light that was Enlai shimmering triumphantly over the dead.

As she walked down the path into the cemetery, Fay couldn't help comparing the graves of the dead, clustered together, with the living in the castle, fleeing Enlai's cruelty. Fleeing Fay's lack of confidence. Hiding together until the world was a safer place.

As she walked, Fay started singing her second song. And as she sang, Enlai moved closer. He did not walk. The light that contained him hovered a little, and moved sinuously and unnaturally down the path. Fay could almost imagine that they had guns by their side. Almost. Instead she focused on her singing. This song had to work. She abbreviated it a bit as had become her wont. The closer she was to the way she liked things, the better. She would need every bit of herself to banish this foul spirit.

———

*This ae night, this ae night,*
*Every night and all,*
*Fire and fleet and candle-light,*
*And Christ receive thy soul.*

*If ever thou gavest hosen and shoon,*
*Every night and all,*
*Sit thee down and put them on;*
*And Christ receive thy soul.*

*If hosen and shoon thou ne'er gav'st none*
*Every night and all,*
*The wind shall prick thee to the bare bone;*
*And Christ receive thy soul.*

*If ever thou gavest meat or drink,*
*Every night and all,*
*The fire shall never make thee shrink;*
*And Christ receive thy soul.*

*If meat or drink thou ne'er gav'st none,*
*Every night and all,*
*The fire will burn thee to the bare bone;*
*And Christ receive thy soul.*

*This ae night, this ae night,*
*Every night and all,*
*Fire and fleet and candle-light,*
*And Christ receive thy soul.*

As she walked towards Enlai and sang, she could see that the song was bothering him. He twitched and squirmed a little. She wasn't close enough to see any detail, though, and he was still there when she reached an end.

"Damn!" she thought. Fay started her singing all over again.

*This ae night, this ae night,*
*Every night and all,*
*Fire and fleet and candle-light,*
*And Christ receive thy soul.*

Now she was closer. When she sang the first verse Enlai smiled. *You can't get me,* said his smile. *I know this song.*

Fay grimly kept singing, and kept walking.

*If ever thou gav'st hosen and shoon,*
*Every night and all,*
*Sit thee down and put them on;*
*And Christ receive thy soul.*

Enlai looked down at his feet, uncertainly. It looked as if he wanted to do something and did not know what. Fay kept singing.

———

*If hosen and shoon thou ne'er gav'st none*
*Every night and all,*
*The wind shall prick thee to the bare bone;*
*And Christ receive thy soul.*

———

Enlai's feet were naked. They had not been naked before. Enlai was puzzled. He stopped and looked down again and then around. Hunting for his shoes?

Fay didn't know. All she knew was this time, the song worked. Enlai's feet shifted as if the ground was full of burrs and sharp pebbles. Maybe it was proximity. Maybe it was because Enlai was dead and just echoing what he had been. Fay kept walking, and kept singing.

———

*If ever thou gav'st meat or drink,*
*Every night and all,*
*The fire shall never make thee shrink;*
*And Christ receive thy soul.*

———

Enlai laughed. It was silent laughter, but his face lit up in merriment. Obviously this verse troubled him less. Fay cursed inside, but kept singing and kept walking. It was all she could do.

*If meat or drink thou ne'er gav'st none,*
*Every night and all,*
*The fire will burn thee to the bare bone;*
*And Christ receive thy soul.*

His laughter hushed. His green glow started to fragment and fade around the edges,. Red fire was eating it. The same red fire that had rimmed the entry to the graveyard. Enlai tried to focus green light with his hands, but found he could not. How could he, Fay reflected? He was the green fire himself now. And the red flames ate away at him as Fay sang.

Soon his face and body were being eaten by the little fires that surrounded him. The flame had burned him to the bone. Soon Enlai was gone. The graveyard was dark again.

Fay still didn't feel safe. She finished her song, just for certainty.

*This ae night, this ae night,*
*Every night and all,*
*Fire and fleet and candle-light,*
*And Christ receive thy soul.*

Then she turned round, to join her friends. As she came through the tori gate again, Fay collapsed. Gilbert caught her and sat on the ground with her and rocked her gently. Belle sat quietly with them, holding Fay's hand.

Fay found relief in Gilbert's arms. She even found comfort. But she could not talk to him or to Belle. Not about Enlai, not about anything. It was all too much for her. So she lay there like a child until they all could face the world again.

Eventually the three friends reluctantly moved. There was still a corpse to deal with.

————

They returned to the high road. Enlai's body lay there on the ground, stark and cold. Ice-death. Flor had come back while the others were gone. Flor had laid the morris stick by his side, and covered his face with her dancing kerchief. She sat down beside him and wept.

Fay looked on this and remembered a song. Enlai needed a song to send him on his way. She wished there had been a song for Persa. She wished she had thought of it. There were not many choices in her mind. Her brain was bit odd right now anyway. What was there was old-fashioned and safe. Like Fay herself.

She was safe. This realisation was such a relief. She was safe and all her still-living friends were safe. Her eyes wept with relief that there would be no more un-timely death.

Safe songs were English in her book, so she sang an English folk song. There was no magic in it, unless saying farewell is magic. *The Three Ravens* mourned a fighter, without regard as to whether the deeds of his violent life had been good or bad. And the fighter had a lover by his side. It seemed right somehow. She did not sing it all, because Enlai had no hounds and no hawks. And Fay did not want to tempt fate, because the song ended when the lover died alongside the knight. Enlai had caused too many deaths. But she sang enough, slowly, mournfully, to serve as a dirge for he who was gone.

Oddly, there was no relief in his going, despite all the horror and havoc of his last years.

The dirge was also for Persa, who should have been teaching children, and who had deserved, far more than Enlai, the honour of a good farewell.

Gilbert did not prevent the strange ritual. He stood beside Fay, supporting her. He said nothing.

———

*There were three ravens sat on a tree,*
*Down a down, hey down, hey down*
*There were three ravens sat on a tree,*
*There were three ravens sat on a tree,*
*And they were black as they might be,*
*With a down. Derry derry derry down down.*

*And one of them said to his mate.*
*"Where shall we our breakfast take?"*

*Down in yonder greene field,*
*Their lies a knight slain under his shield.*

*And near him lies a fallow doe*
*As great with young as she might go.*

*She lifted up his bloody head,*
*And kissed his wounds that were so red,*
*With a down. Derry derry derry down down.*
      *(Traditional)*

———

As Fay sang, Flor wept. She looked like she belonged in an eighteenth century rose garden, mourning a lost lover.

Fay's eyes were not without tears. Enlai had been wrong. He had even been evil. He had stolen from deep within her to kill other people. But he had also been her friend. It was right that his ex-lover mourned him. And it was right that Fay also wept.

It was also right that, near the end of the song, her eyes lingered on the dance stick and kerchief. She wondered if Flor had done it instinctively, or because of all her friends who had been killed. She suspected that Flor had a nasty streak, just like Enlai. She suspected that Flor genuinely mourned Enlai. And that she had known exactly what she was doing in covering his face with the kerchief and in putting the stick in his hand.

Enlai would not have liked to have been remembered, in death, as looking like a morris dancer.

# CHAPTER TWENTY-ONE

*Three gypsies stood at the castle gate they sang*
     *so high*
*they sang so low*
*a lady sat in her chamber late,*
*her heart it melted away like snow*

*They sang so sweet, they sang so shrill*
*that fast her tears began to flow*
*And she laid down her silken gown*
*her golden rings and all her show*

*She plucked off her high heeled shoes*
*a-made of Spanish leather, O*
*She would walk in the street with her bare, bare feet*
*all out in the wind and weather, oh (Traditional)*

"THAT'S IT!" FAY EXCLAIMED.

"What?" Belle looked curious.

"I'm totally sick of this."

"What?" asked Belle again.

"We need to see this prince guy. Together. So we can come to an end of the next bit of the mess."

"We do," laughed Belle. "We should have done this a long time ago, you know."

"I know," said Fay, glumly, "But I just wasn't thinking straight."

"Enlai."

"Of course Enlai. And I am not super happy now, but at least I have my brain back."

"Oh, I'm not sure about that," something about Belle was mischievous.

Fay decided she would just wait and see what it was. Belle's mischief was gentle and emerged in Belle's own sweet time, anyway. From the look in her eyes, something was going to emerge soon, anyhow. "I need a song if we are going to do this, Fay."

This was a surprise. Belle did not ask for songs. "What sort of song," asked Fay, suspiciously.

"I know exactly the song I need. You sang it a long time ago. All about plucking off high heel shoes."

"Oh," Fay was blank. Then she realised. "You want The Wraggle Taggle Gypsies. But why would you want to sleep in the wide open fields and all that?"

"I don't," said Belle. "I want you to sing just the beginning of it so I have an excuse to wander and so that the Prince will come and meet us somewhere to find out what we are doing."

"Can't we do that without magic?" asked Fay, suspiciously.

"We could, but I won't do it unless you put the magic in. I just don't want to." This was a kind of blackmail. What on earth was Belle up to? "I'll be back in a little—I just have to see the housekeeper. That gives you time to think."

Fay grumbled to herself she didn't want to think. She didn't want to do magic. She just wanted to find the prince and settle things. Belle was not there though, so the grumbling was not much use.

When Belle returned, Fay asked her straight out, "Belle, what are you up to?"

Belle just laughed and said, "Sing, Fay."

So Fay sang the first verses of the song through once. That was all that she would do. That was it. No more. Belle obliged by plucking off her high-heeled shoes. "Are they made of Spanish leather, O?" asked Fay, picking one up.

"Leave that alone, we're going wandering down the roads and fields and things. We don't need my shoes."

Fay left it alone, but said, "Better than you than me," and shuddered at the thought of being barefoot for that long.

Belle merely laughed again. "I'm going to wear walking shoes, silly," and went to a chest. She took out some shoes and put them on. She then took out a bag and handed it to Fay. "This is for you," Belle said, "I was waiting for you to be ready for it."

Fay looked at the bag curiously, and then opened it. Inside was a green velvet cloak. "You remembered my dream," Fay said, softly, letting the fabric swim over her hands. Her eyes filled with tears.

"I did," answered Belle, "And it seems to me you have found that security, so you need a special cloak to help you remember."

"Thank you," smiled Fay and swirled the cloak around her shoulders.

They marched down the street in fine style, and into the countryside. It was a bit like a two person procession, because Belle seemed to know where to go and was in no hurry. This was not hunting a stray prince who refused to be found. It was purposeful. Fay really wanted to know what Belle's purpose was, but she was silent about it.

For all the stolid pace and clear goal, they did not take the most direct route. Fay was a bit mystified by the whole thing. Belle was still planning something.

Fay finally had her green cloak, however, and she was surprisingly content, even though only part of her life had been sorted. Maybe it was knowing she was free of Enlai that did it. Maybe it was the feel of the cloak around her shoulders. Maybe it was the freedom of walking the streets in search of more solutions. Maybe. Her life was still full of maybes.

Finally they came to the road out of the town. It was the third time they had crossed the road, so Fay was surprised when Belle turned down it. In the distance was a small figure, lounging nonchalantly. As they came closer, they saw it was Gilbert.

Belle said, "Don't give him his cloak back."

"It's his?" Fay was now totally mystified. Not just partially.

"Yes," Belle smiled again. "I saw it in his things one day and asked if I could take it for you."

"So whatever happens I have his cloak. I like that," Fay said. She was not sure of anything, and there was a surprising security in knowing she had the cloak. Just not quite the same security she had associated with the green cloak when she had dreamed it.

As they came up to Gilbert, Fay noticed he was grinning, almost manically. More of Belle's little plot. At his feet were the high-heeled shoes. Fay stopped about six feet from him.

"That's it. I am not going any further. I want to know what's going on."

"But isn't it obvious," Belle's smile was sweetly triumphant. "You said you wanted to meet the prince. Fay, His Royal Highness, Your Royal Highness, here is someone who wants to consult with you."

"Bloody hell," said Fay, and sat down right there in the middle of the road.

Gilbert helped her up. His eyes were merry. "I didn't believe you didn't know."

"Well, I don't believe I didn't know," retorted Fay. "I feel very stupid. And thank you both so much for the pleasant walk. I bet you were in the castle all the time."

"I was. I have to say, from my point of view it was worth the wait of you to find out. And well worth the walk," said Gilbert.

"Why?" Fay was suspicious, and worried that things were going to change.

"Oh, Fay," it was Belle who answered, "The look on your face was just priceless."

"Damn you both," grumbled Fay. "I need to sit down again."

They went to the verge, and sat down in a row, with Fay in the middle. At first things were a bit quiet. Fay had a lot to digest.

Gilbert broke it. "I know you have a lot of questions you want to ask me, but I have to ask you one. It's very important," his eyes crinkled.

"What is it?" Belle was more curious than Fay.

"I want to know what Fay's world is like. She told me a bit once and I couldn't make enough sense from that bit. It's one reason why I have been so ineffective. And that worries me. So I want to know more about the relationship between the two worlds, and especially about Fay's world."

"Oh," was Fay's intelligent response. She thought a bit.

"Is your world special in any way?" asked Gilbert. "How is it that it has power over this one?" This was an oddly hard question. Fay sidestepped by pretending to misunderstand what Gilbert was asking.

"My world is okay, you know, but nothing special.

*This* world is special, because it's the way I think in my dreams that a world ought to be. But I can't stay here because it's imaginary."

"You still think it is imaginary, after all that has happened?" asked Gilbert.

"I just don't know," answered Fay abjectly. "It probably isn't. But what if it is? There are too many things I see even when I walk down the street here – things that come from my imagination. It is so strange, seeing things I thought up, in a dream, pretending to be real."

Belle spoke up. "Sorcery isn't a part of what you imagined, and nor HRH here," she gestured rudely at Gilbert, who grinned.

Thank goodness he was still himself, even with the lurid title. And she still felt stupid about not seeing that there was just one person and not two. All the hints had been there. At least it solved her worry about whom she had been sleeping with unawares.

Gilbert then took up the argument, "So there is an outside: does that mean there's no inside? I mean we each exist as individuals, and have power over our own lives. Even the royal family," and he grimaced—he was as unhappy with his status as Fay was—she smiled a little at him in reassurance, "only has power because it is agreed upon. If we were hated and reviled, I cannot think that the power would survive."

"A democratic royalty?" and Fay's eyes gleamed.

"We were chosen for the task because, as a family, we seemed to have the right characteristics. It keeps us modest whenever we think about it, and we all outdo each other, always, in proving that we are individuals, not, not..."

"Royal clones," suggested Fay. They other two looked her blankly. There were still some concepts this new world did not accept from her old one. "Anyway," she continued, "I am beginning to think on those sorts of lines—about power, not about royal clones. My power is a freak thing, because I come from somewhere so very different. Something went wrong, though, you can tell by all the strangeness. So how does it all operate, and how can I change things?"

Gilbert's eyes lit up and he looked enthusiastic. "I have a theory," he said.

Belle interpolated, "Oh dear, Fay, you've got to look out for his theories, they go on forever."

"I can be brief," he said, in a little huff. He looked directly at Fay. "Your magic is a heart–magic, as you have been discovering. When you're clear and know yourself, it will work out. Or when you think of it ahead, as you did with the songs."

"So when I'm unhappy, it goes wrong?" asked Fay.

"Not when you're unhappy. You could be suicidal and it would still be effective. As long as you were clear as to who you were when you were suicidal, it would work. Self-understanding and acceptance are everything."

"Is it common? And is this your theory or one from a book?" Fay was certainly curious about it, but she was still not sure how much she believed.

"Mostly mine—padded out from my reading. So I could be wrong. It fits everything I know of magic, and everything that happened. I believe that Enlai took advantage of your uncertainties. There were times when you were so certain of yourself; when we were together, for instance. And there were times you seemed determined to let yourself fade, to cease existing as an individual. "

"And now?"

Gilbert shrugged, "I don't know."

"She is clear about who she is," said Belle.

"True. Or mostly true," and Gilbert and Belle looked

across at Fay as if she was some sort of zoo specimen. Curious. Objective.

T.S. Eliot sprang to mind – something about being caught on a pin with the light. It should have been clinical and shattering. Instead Fay found herself laughing. She found herself answering the speculative gazes with a quote, "It's all about those women, who talk of Michelangelo. T.S. Eliot had it right."

"What's that?" asked Belle.

"Nothing—it was just a poem I was thinking about. We belonged in it for a fraction of a second."

"Just as well," murmured Gilbert, ominously. "Belle, would you do me a favour and take this cloak and sit a little bit further along? Over there, perhaps? We will be with you shortly."

"Certainly," Belle said, graciously, and took the cloak. In a moment she was out of earshot.

Fay wondered what strange revelation was to come. She wouldn't mind a kiss, she thought wistfully. But these days she just wasn't certain of anything. She and Gilbert had made up: he was so unpredictable though. She could not see what he did and when. He was probably going to suggest that she either go or stay or put her on a town watch to prevent sorcery. Or something. It was the something that she was unsure of.

"My God, this is difficult," he said, into the silence. Fay was pleased she had left the silence alone. At least he was saying something. Though, not, perhaps a reassuring something. "I thought this was going to be so easy. I have spoken to my parents and my siblings. But I can't seem to speak to you!"

"You want me to go home and never come back," said Fay, convinced this was the end of everything. It was the only way of seeing things. It made sense.

"You idiot," said Gilbert fondly. "I want you to marry me." Gilbert took her silence as an opportunity to kiss her soundly. Fay kissed him back, enthusiastically. "I take that as a 'yes'," said Gilbert, a bit flustered.

"No. I just like kissing you," said Fay, smiling up at him. "Actually, I need to think. I'm going to see if Belle wants a quiet walk."

Gilbert didn't push her. This was one of his strengths, Fay decided. He had asked her, and now he was trusting her to make a good decision.

"I will be back as soon as I can – but I will try to sort it out now. I don't want to keep you waiting any longer than I have to."

"What more could I ask than that?" asked Gilbert wryly.

"Well, a lot," answered Fay. "But I wouldn't give it to you. I am a mean and stingy person."

Gilbert laughed. His look sobered as Fay walked off, however. His eyes followed her. This would not be a happy wait.

As Belle and Fay returned from their supremely quiet walk, Fay burst into song. "You don't know, and I don't know, and neither does the cow—hey!" Belle looked across at her.

"I hope you have no plans for that tune?"

"What kind of plans could I have?" asked Fay. "To make a cow look stupid?"

Belle laughed. "I don't know."

"And neither does the cow. Hey."

Belle laughed again. "I can't help thinking you have mischief somewhere there though."

"Not mischief, precisely," said Fay, cautiously. "It is just that I have been thinking about what Gilbert said, just as I said I would. In fact, exactly as I said I would. I wasn't quiet for nothing, you know." Her tone took on a spurious air of aggrieved virtue.

"And?"

"And I'm going to tell him first—but if you are very

lucky then I might tell you later. If you are lucky. Very, very lucky." Fay grinned.

"He's not going to like what you are going to tell him?" Belle sounded very worried.

"Oh, I don't know. He may love it."

Belle sighed. This new, confident Fay was going to take some getting used to. She sat down on the green cloak on the verge, and watched as Fay walked back to Gilbert, a very cheeky smile adorning her visage.

Fay wasn't as confident as she looked. It had been hard thinking. She had turned her own world upside down yet again. And she wasn't sure she could handle it, whether Gilbert agreed with her suggestion amicably, or not.

It was all his own fault, she thought. Maybe it was partly her stupidity, but it was also his sense of mischief, and the fact that he would take off without talking to her. That he could ask her something so very important with no warning and not nearly enough time together.

He was a prince. That was another issue too. She was no-one's adjunct. Not now. Not ever. It was another kind of fading. Trying to fade got her into this mess in the first place. Fay was sorted. The next decision was Gilbert's.

"A song of love is a sad song," she started humming, and stopped herself quickly. There was a great deal still to do in terms of training her mind, thinking things through. And she was not going to risk making an already-difficult decision worse by singing bad things into existence.

However this next few minutes worked out, there was a great deal to do. Fay sighed.

Gilbert was there where she had left him. Minus green cloak. With Belle's shoes sitting at his feet. The shoes looked lonely. Gilbert didn't, he just looked pensive. His worried-clown look.

"Hiya" she said, and he looked up and smiled. It was such a glorious smile. The smile of someone who had just been made perfectly happy. Fay couldn't help it. She smiled back.

"Well?" he asked.

Fay laughed. "I have a proposition for you," she said.

"I make you a proposal and you come back with a proposition?" His eyes glinted.

"I always thought eyes glinted in books. How did you do that?" she asked.

"Fay," Gilbert's voice was warning.

"It *is* a proposition. Because I have to say 'no' to the proposal, but I still want to be with you."

"Please explain," asked Gilbert, totally still.

"If you had been your own lieutenant or a knight or something more junior, I would have married you in a flash. Or if we had spent more time together. Knew each other more. Because I do love you. I want to be with you. But there are too many changes for me to deal with. I can't cope with being all the things I am discovering I am, plus you being a prince. It's very complicated," Fay sighed. "The thought I keep coming back to is that I need to be me. Not your adjunct."

"You would not be my adjunct, you would be my wife."

"But I don't know what that entails. Whether I get to manage my own life if I am your wife. Hey, I rhyme!" Fay smiled, hopefully, before she got to the tough bit, "I don't know what half of *you* entails. I love you as you are. As I know you. But I don't know enough about the bits of you I haven't seen. The bits that can kill and rule and do all the big stuff. The bits that are there for other people all the time and won't be there for me much."

"So marry me and find out."

"No. Not yet. Maybe someday."

"So it is not a 'no'. It is a 'wait and see'."

"It's a proposition," answered Fay, firmly. "I'm happy to be your mistress. And an enchantress or whatever it is I am. Do all the things I meant to do in my own right, and learn about living with you at the same time."

She tried to explain it better. "I need to fill my obligations. I need to earn my keep. And I need to know what you are—as a prince." His lack of understanding exasperated her, "Can't you see? How that affects both of us." He obviously didn't, but she ploughed in regardless, "And you need to know the whole lot in inverse. When we know a bit more, when we are both ready, we can talk about marriage."

"I can't have a mistress—I need a wife."

"But you could sleep with me."

Gilbert grinned. "That was not planned."

"I bet," said Fay.

There was a silence. "You're very serious about this, aren't you?"

"Yes," said Fay. "I am. I think it would be very bad for both of us if I changed who I was deep down, and if you changed yourself in any significant way. We need to get to know each other. And we need to get to know how to remain each other with each other." Fay wondered if her sentences could get any more tangled.

"Princes don't usually marry their mistresses," Gilbert objected.

"Well, you were the one who proposed," Fay answered. "And, from memory, the one who seduced."

"So I did," and Gilbert smiled again. It was not the same smile. It was rueful, and not necessarily unhappy. "Now it is my turn to think. I might go for a walk, too."

"Think all you need to; walk as long as you have to. I will be with Belle."

"Don't sing while I am gone?" he asked, plaintively.

"For you, I will not sing. Until dinnertime. That gives you hours to think."

"You lack ethics," Gilbert complained.

"I know." Fay smiled. Gilbert laughed, kissed her lightly and walked off.

She went back to Belle and told her everything. They watched Gilbert until he was out of sight. Then Belle produced a pack of cards from her pocket.

"You took off your shoes but put cards in your pocket?" Fay quizzed.

"I didn't know *what* was going to happen. So I prepared for all eventualities."

They played cards until Gilbert came back in eyesight. It was up to Gilbert—should she stay or should she go. Should she grow or should she fade?

This was the moment of truth. If Gilbert was prepared to accept her as she was, without marriage, then Fay could safely stay in her dream world.

Life would have been much easier if she was traditional and had just married at age twenty. Fay's thoughts went round and round in a circle while she waited. She wanted to marry Gilbert, desperately. Her Happy Ending. Her Prince Ever After.

Gilbert had obligations, however. As a leader. As whatever else he was. She didn't know who he was yet —not really. It kept coming back to that. He also had prior beliefs. Things that could not be put aside for Fay's needs. Or (except when they overlapped) even Fay's own obligations. It had already been the cause of so much missed communication between them and so much loss of understanding.

Fay had to know how they fitted together with who she was before she could agree to being a part of all Gilbert's life. She was prepared to try. And Gilbert knew it. The question now was if Gilbert could live with anything other than the fairytale future?

Dear reader,

I don't know who you are or how you managed to find this. I am glad you did.

I don't know what has happened to me. I've written up what I saw happening as far as I could because I wondered—what if my imaginary world is like the drawers of that old lady I once knew—if no-one knows what is in it and if it ceased to have a context, does the memory die? And if it does, do I die too?

I don't know if I'm in a coma as you read this, or asleep, or dead, or disappeared into nothingness. Maybe I'm just living out a normal life, but with my soul and spirit elsewhere. I don't know any of the answers. All I know is I'm not coming back to the ordinary world. I am living in enchantment, with all its trials and problems.

It's real. I know it's real. I have my best friend and my lover to prove it. I have my soul-home. I like hedging my bets, though. That's why I'm writing this all up. As I saw it, as I experienced it. Not necessarily as it happened.

I still don't feel a hundred per cent sure that my fantasy world exists. Ninety-eight percent, which is enough to take a chance on, but not a hundred per cent. That was always the catch.

So read this story and treasure it, and remember it. I hope it will give you some entertainment. I hope you never forget it and that you pass it to your children, and that they give it to their children.

That way I can remain in my fantasy world forever.

Dear reader,

We hope you enjoyed reading *The Art of Effective Dreaming*. Please take a moment to leave a review, even if it's a short one. Your opinion is important to us.

Discover more books by Gillian Polack at https://www.nextchapter.pub/authors/gillian-polack

Want to know when one of our books is free or discounted? Join the newsletter at http://eepurl.com/bqqB3H

Best regards,

Gillian Polack and the Next Chapter Team

# ACKNOWLEDGMENTS

This novel has had a strange path to publication. It's often been called the cursed novel, because of the number of hurricanes, earthquakes and other events that prevented Trivium Publishing from bringing it out then the collapse of Satalyte.

I very much appreciate Next Chapter (and, earlier, Satalyte) for taking it on. Without Tamara Mazzei, however, this book would still be in my 'Unfinished Fiction' folder, rather than plaguing the world. Tamara is the editor who told me I should be publishing again and persuaded me that this novel and *Illuminations* had to be seen. She is the editor who changed my life.

Special gratitude goes to my family and folkdance friends, especially in Canberra and Melbourne. Marilla Cooper, Robyn Priddle and Ernie Gruner started me on that journey, though I'm not sure they knew it. Marilla lured me into morris dancing, for the record. Without friends such as the McCulloch-McLennans, the Formiattis, the Roses, Bev Beattie and my email friends (especially the somewhat lunatic penmanreview email list) my life at the time I wrote this novel could easily have been like Fay's, which it never was. Thank you, all.

# ABOUT THE AUTHOR

Gillian Polack is an award-winning Australian novelist, editor and historian. Her hobbies include reading, cooking and making bad jokes.

The Art Of Effective Dreaming
ISBN: 978-4-86745-625-5
Mass Market

Published by
Next Chapter
1-60-20 Minami-Otsuka
170-0005 Toshima-Ku, Tokyo
+818035793528

30th April 2021

CPSIA information can be obtained
at www.ICGtesting.com
Printed in the USA
LVHW041301130521
687330LV00007B/752